I0624914

A Tapestry of Fire

Applied Topology Book 4

Margaret Ball

Galway Publishing

ISBN Paperback: 978-1-947648-14-2
ISBN eBook: 978-1-947648-15-9

Printed in the United States of America
Cover art: Cedar Sanderson
Formatting: Polgarus Studio

1. A particular talent for seeing hidden connections

Wimberley, Sunday

The Inner Light guest house was actually two buildings: a narrow three-story frame house and a long, low and much more modern building of native stone, which was where the office was located.

Getting to the retreat at Inner Light Guest outside Wimberley this afternoon had supposedly been so urgent that nobody had time to brief me, so urgent that I couldn't take time to look the place up and get an idea of the setup, so urgent that I had to throw a few respectable clothes into a suitcase and take off with faith that the GPS in the car would find the place. But apparently it hadn't been urgent enough for one of the owners to wait in the office and give me a clue where to go.

I dropped my suitcase on the stone-flagged floor and headed for one of the squashy leather sofas under the chandelier. Doubtless not where the hired help were supposed to hang out, but I could hardly be blamed for that, could I?

I had just sat down when I heard a couple of people laughing and joking outside. The French doors opening on the deck out back were brilliant with afternoon sunlight; the couple who stepped inside paused for a moment, blinking, no doubt readjusting to the shadowy interior. My new bosses? No, they looked too young, too rich and too carefree to be the Fosters. Guests, then; some of the people I would be expected to wait on as soon as the Fosters turned up and briefed me on my duties.

"Oh, you're here already!" the girl, a lanky brunette with an incipient sunburn on her exposed shoulders and midriff, squealed as soon as she registered my presence. "*Isn't* it *marvelous*, Chet, she won't miss any of the activities!"

The young man with her looked like a Chet. Probably short for something like Chester Allandale Whitehead III. Artfully cut blond hair, horn-rimmed glasses, designer shirt, khakis: he could have posed in *GQ* over a caption like, "Weekend Chic."

The brunette closed in on me while I was making these observations. "Hi, I'm Ginny," she said, holding out her hand, "and you must be Sally. I do hope we're going to be friends."

Sally, yes. Potential friend, no. "I think there must be some mistake," I said. "I work here – that is, I hope I'm going to work here. Is Margo Foster around anywhere?"

Ginny dimpled. "Oh, don't bother with that silly cover story!"

Damn. Busted *already*? I was going to have a hell of a time getting out of this big, squashy sofa. And then there would be the problem of running in these high-heeled sandals. I hadn't exactly dressed for flight. But then, hadn't it been reasonable to expect my cover would hold up for more than fifteen seconds?

In emergency, I could always teleport, but we were discouraged from doing that in view of outsiders. Maybe I could sneak out using camouflage.

"The Fosters told us at lunch that you'd be coming," Chet said.

"But you don't really expect us to believe that you're just some extra help they've hired, do you?" asked Ginny. "Not after that story in *Whirred*?"

What story?

"We know you're here to spy on us," Ginny said. "But it's just silly for you to pretend to be some little waitress, especially after that photograph! We don't have any secrets! We all talked it over after lunch and decided the best thing was to include you in all the retreat activities. After all, the whole point of the retreat is for us all to get to know each other better and make a stronger team. And obviously you're going to be a team member – at least I hope you will."

"What photograph?" This time I said it aloud.

"Just this afternoon. Didn't you see it? I've got my phone set to alert me every time there's a new posting on *Whirred*. They have all the *best* Austin-area industry news and gossip, and usually before anybody else." Ginny's coral-painted nails tapped at the surface of her phone. "See?"

The words "Secret Love" dominated the screen. The man who was the reason for my coming here was pictured just below that, with a paragraph of dreadfully coy, gossipy innuendo about how the reclusive Austin financier Shani Chayyaputra had lost his heart to a certain young lady. Below that was a blurred picture that, okay, could have been me. Could have been almost any short girl with spiky black hair, though.

"Mr. C. probably thought it would be funny to slip you in here without telling us who you really are. Tell the truth now: didn't he want you to find out what we say about him behind his back?"

"He never suggested any such thing to me," I said with perfect truth.

"And is your name really Sally? Or is that just part of the cover?"

"For now," I said, trying to look knowledgeable and mysterious, "Sally will do just fine." And if I was slow in answering to that name, well, they'd already come up with an explanation for that, hadn't they?

"But you *are* Mr. C.'s fiancée," Ginny pushed.

I looked at my nails. "I wasn't supposed to…"

"It's all right," Ginny said, "when he gets back we'll explain to him that you tried to slip in incognito but we saw through your act. He can hardly blame you for the fact that you couldn't fool a group of brilliant, highly intuitive people with a particular talent for seeing hidden connections!"

When she put it that way, I had to admit that it seemed silly even to try.

"And I *love* your belt," Ginny added. "Did Mr. C. give it to you? Is it, like, some piece of antique Indian jewelry?"

I warmed to her. Some people thought that the belt of silver scales, finished off with an elaborate silver knot around a beaky protuberance, was a bit excessive on somebody as short as I was. "Actually," I said, "it's Mesopotamian."

Chet looked down his patrician nose. "I heard a lot of Iraqi national treasures disappeared from their museum during the war."

"Well, this isn't a museum piece," I told him. Even if part of it was three thousand years old, the rest was all modern manufacture. And I hadn't gotten the authentic part of it out of a museum; I found it in a turtle pond. Or you could say that it found me.

I wished one of the Fosters would turn up. I wanted to unpack. I wanted a shower. And most of all, I wanted to get away from ebullient Ginny and patrician Chet, and call back to find out how I was supposed to handle this.

Not that anybody I could ask was likely to have a good answer.

Like an answer to prayer, a slim middle-aged woman in leggings under an embroidered tunic glided into the room. "I'm Margo Foster," she announced. "And you must be Sally. Come along now, you've barely time to change before we start serving dinner, and you certainly can't wait tables in those heels."

"Oh, Sally isn't going to be working here as a waitress," Ginny said.

Margo Foster managed to raise one eyebrow without disturbing her makeup. "She isn't?"

Ginny produced a positive shower of dimples. "She may have fooled you and David, but *I* stay up to date with industry news!"

"Industry gossip, anyway," said Chet.

"Oh, you!" Ginny elbowed him and giggled. "Sally is Mr. C.'s mysterious fiancée. He sent her down here to find out how we talk when he's not around, but *I* saw through her at once!"

"You... did?" Margo couldn't frown; it would have cracked her makeup. The most she could manage was a slightly puzzled expression.

"She had to admit it when I asked her straight out, didn't you, Sally?"

"Oh, well, in that case..." Margo's voice trailed off.

"She needs to join the retreat with us," Ginny said. "That way we'll *really* get to know all about her."

Oh, I hoped *not*.

"And she'll know all about us."

At last, something consistent with my original plan.

"Now don't be difficult, Margo darling," Ginny urged. "You know there's plenty of space. Your brochure says you can handle groups of up to ten, and there are only six of us – well, seven, now that Sally's come."

"And how am I supposed to handle *any* groups without a waitress?" Margo snapped.

Ginny shrugged. "Put out everything buffet-style," she suggested, "and we'll serve ourselves. Nobody will mind. And now that we know who she really is, we'd be *much* more uncomfortable having Sally wait on us!"

By the time I got to the guest bedroom Margo had hurriedly assigned to me I was exhausted just from agreeing with Ginny's assertions and saying nothing that would contradict the story in her head. Well, actually that second bit wasn't too hard; what *would* have been difficult was getting a word in edgewise.

Ginny would probably have been exhausting even if I hadn't been acting a part; that woman should come with a warning sign reading CAUTION – HIGHLY INTERACTIVE. Pretty much the exact opposite of me, that way.

Once alone, I sagged down on the end of my bed and tapped the ornate flourishes of my belt buckle. The tapered silver coils unwrapped; the turtle head looked up at me with bright black eyes. Mr. M. slithered out of my belt loops and undulated across the floor to the bureau. (Mr. M. is short for Mr. Mesopotamia, which is what we called him after it became clear that our American tongues were never going to wrap around a Babylonian name that *started* with 'Niiqarquusu Adrahasis Galammta-uddua' and went on from there.) Anyway, there he was on the floor, giving the bureau the evil eye.

"Climbing this thing will be too much work," he complained. "I need coffee."

"Can't you fly?"

"That would be even more work. Coffee!"

I was *not* going to deal with a hyper-caffeinated, snake-bodied turtle mage on top of everything else. He would never be able to hold still enough to pass as an ornate belt if he got into the coffee. Worse, he'd probably want to sing.

Instead, I scooped him off the floor and set him on the top of the bureau, where he promptly arranged himself in a spiral around a ceramic candleholder.

"Mr. M., what am I going to do now?" I asked him. "I was going to be a *waitress*. A semi-invisible servant. I can't possibly pass myself off as Shani Chayyaputra's fiancée!"

"The role is, indeed, loathsome and abhorrent," Mr. M. agreed, "but since you are not required to consort with the man in person, I see no reason why you should not allow these people to believe what they will. Participating in their planned activities should give you a far better chance of penetrating SCI's secrets than merely eavesdropping on them at their meals."

"Yeah, until they see through me. Then what?"

"*If* they suspect you," Mr. M. said cheerfully, "then boot, saddle, to horse and away! Or, to be literal, *Brouwer!* and away!"

"If I have to teleport out of this mess," I said, "Chayyaputra will know *exactly* who's been spying on him." I flipped my suitcase open and stirred the scanty contents: a few solid colored T-shirts, denim and khaki skirts and shorts, sandals and running shoes. Not very *me*. Amazing that I'd been able to assemble such a bland collection; I must have too many clothes. I'd have been happier if I'd been allowed to take just one vintage rock band T-shirt. "Do these look like the holiday clothes of a mysterious international beauty who's just latched onto Austin's most eligible bachelor?"

"You packed appropriately for the part of waitress," Mr. M. said, "which is what we have claimed Shani *dev* asked you to do. You can say that it's not your fault that Ginny penetrated your disguise so easily."

"And that's another thing." His mention of Shani *dev* had reminded me. "He's not a man; he's a *god*. How do I play the part of a god's fiancée?"

"He is not a god here in America. Only in India." Mr. M.'s sniff suggested that anybody could become a god in a country as lax as India. He was inordinately proud of his own origins in Nebuchadnezzar's Babylon and his years of experience, even though he'd spent the majority of those years living as a common box turtle with a spelled ring inhibiting most of his powers.

The ring had been removed by an unethical jerk who didn't mind decapitating Mr. M. to get it. That in itself wasn't necessarily a problem; it took more than mere beheading to kill the mage. Unfortunately, the unethical jerk had been unskilled with a hatchet; instead of taking one neat whack, he'd turned Mr. M.'s body into scrap meat. Mr. M. lived briefly as a disembodied head until we found a robotics engineering student who consented to join the head with one of her spare robot snake bodies. The project had required a continuous feed of the mini-stars Mr. M. had brought with him from Babylon. It had also required a serious suspension of disbelief on the part of the engineering student, who had spent much of the subsequent weeks muttering, "Holy shit," and "If I hadn't been there I wouldn't have believed it."

Mr. M. rather liked his spiffy snake body, which was a lot faster than his turtle body and which had subsequently been augmented by Meadow, the engineering student, with Wi-Fi, GPS, retractable lasers and focused ultrasonic beam projection. She had just added something resembling retractable torpedo tubes for launching miniature flash-bangs; that was the least lethal of the enhancements he'd been demanding.

Since our first meeting with Mr. M., we'd learned more about the infinite set of little sparkling points of light he had brought with him. Mostly they could be used to augment and power the things we could already do by mentally applying various bits of topology to the real world. The Brouwer Fixed-Point Theorem, for instance, could be visualized in a way that teleported the user to a pictured location. The only catch was that my maximum distance, pre-stars, had been two feet – and that was the record in the Research Department. With stars? We hadn't yet found a maximum distance.

Mr. M. also possessed an enviable level of self-confidence. He'd never yet encountered a situation which he didn't think he could deal with. Me, I wasn't quite up there with him. This project, for instance, was beginning to seem way beyond me. They should never have sent the worst liar in the Center for Applied Topology on a mission which was shaping up to be nonstop lies. Our receptionist and official liar, Annelise, might not have a talent for achieving paranormal effects via topology, but her personality was *much* better equipped for this job. We didn't need applied topology skills here, we needed imaginative fiction skills. Why had I let Ben hustle me into this when his girlfriend would have been the ideal candidate?

Well, it was done now. After that gossip piece in *Whirred*, there was no way I could trade places with a tall, leggy blonde. I needed to talk to Jimmy DiGrazio. He was the only person at the Center with the computer skills to slip something like that into Austin's favorite news-and-gossip site for the silicon-based community. Actually, I needed to *kill* Jimmy. Why hadn't he warned me?

And just in case I didn't already feel overwhelmed, my phone rang and precipitated me into the middle of yet another mess which was definitely beyond me. And which I had foolishly thought I could escape for a few days by accepting this assignment.

"No, Mom, I haven't arranged any cake tastings with bakers. Why don't we just have baklava? Everybody will like that."

Outraged screeches. Evidently my wedding wouldn't be legal unless it was celebrated with a multi-story wedding cake equipped with white icing balconies, pergolas, gardens and a tiny bride-and-groom pair perched on the very top. And I was also supposed to ensure that this monstrosity would *taste* good? I was prepared to argue that point, but before I got my words in a row she'd moved on to the next absolutely crucial decision.

"No, I don't really care what color the tablecloths and napkins are. How about white?"

More screeches. Apparently white was *de rigueur* for cakes but absolutely unacceptable for napkins. Who knew?

It took me nearly an hour to get off the phone; now that she had me, Mom wanted to discuss wedding dresses, wedding *shoes*, florists, hair and makeup artists, photographers, music… the list was endless. Partway through, Ginny tapped on my door and opened it. "Dinner," she whispered.

"Look, I really can't talk any more now," I said, interrupting the discussion of bouzouki bands versus string quartets.

It didn't work. We had to cycle through endless other decisions. What color should the flowers be?

I wasn't sure whether flowers were have-to-be-white or cannot-be-white. "Um, red?"

That would clash with the pink napkins.

We were having pink napkins?

"Ok, how about pink, then? To go with the napkins?"

What should we do for wedding favors? At Calla's daughter's wedding they had given everybody a little model of the Parthenon, but Mom thought that was kind of strange and anyway, she didn't know where she could get a hundred and eighty Parthenons.

A hundred and eighty guests?

This thing was getting way out of hand.

"Can't we just do little bags of *koufeta*?" No Greek wedding was complete without the sugar-coated almonds.

Mom sighed. "Of course you're having *koufeta*. In bowls on the table. Don't you remember? I told you just last week. So we need something else."

"We could skip the bowls on the table, then almonds would be fine for the favors."

Another deep sigh. "If you want your father to look cheap. It's *your* wedding. Did I mention that Calla and Kosmos gave out little models of the Parthenon? How about—" Mom ran through half a dozen other ideas for wedding favors, most of them so outrageous that I finally agreed to the suggestion of miniature Greek goddess statues. Even then more decisions were required.

If we had to do goddess statues I'd actually have preferred Athena, but Mom nixed that suggestion in favor of Aphrodite. The whole thing seemed dangerously pagan for a wedding that was to be celebrated in a Greek Orthodox church, but at least we wouldn't be distributing the goddesses inside the church. I suspected she was pushing Aphrodite because of the fertility symbolism; in Mom's view, getting married was like firing a starter pistol in the grandchildren race. I was kind of counting on the Pill to defeat ancient goddesses of fertility.

"Guest list for what? The shower? I'm not having a wedding shower!"

Evidently I was now.

Mom kept going for over an hour. However, it's an ill wind and all that; by the time I got off the phone, the others had all finished eating. I made a sandwich of the leftover sliced turkey (dry, and the bread was so healthy it crunched) and took it back to my room. I wouldn't have to face the entire crew until the official beginning of the retreat, tomorrow morning.

And I even snagged a cupcake for Mr. M., who likes sugar almost as much as caffeine and doesn't get nearly as hyper on it.

2. Two truths and a lie

I woke long before breakfast, tense and nervous. To fill in the waiting time, I reviewed what we knew so far.

The Center for Applied Topology had tangled with Shani Chayyaputra before, so we knew better than to underrate him; his magic and his command of grackles were formidable, as one would expect from a sinister god whose chosen vehicle was a large black bird. After the last debacle we'd taken a few steps to improve our defenses. Mr. M. had helped us devise shields that could be locked in place – not requiring a topologist continually visualizing a mathematical construct, which was the way we achieved most of our paranormal effects - and that would prevent anybody except Center staff from teleporting into our offices and homes. Unlocking the shields was a more complicated issue, which is why we still used temporary personal shields elsewhere.

We'd hoped that he would stop attacking the Center, and so far we'd been lucky. The problem was that he was still doing things we couldn't, in good conscience, ignore. At least not after they became personal with Jimmy DiGrazio's friend Logan.

Naturally Jimmy, our resident computer nerd, hung out with similarly minded nerds outside the Center. One of them was Logan, who had recently started a company called Protect Your Privacy. Supposedly he hoped to market something called zero-knowledge proofs. Jimmy had explained the concept exhaustively to all the Center's research fellows, aka topological magicians. We still didn't understand how it worked; all we got was that it was a way to authenticate your identity – you know, that information every Web site tries to hoover up – without revealing private data. Like your email address.

The problem was that so far, every implementation of the algorithm used way too much memory and computing power to be practical for personal computers. But two of Jimmy's other friends, Will and Eli, had specialized in mathematical computing and thought they were close to a solution for that problem. Logan had optimistically started his company in the hope of being first to market a zero-knowledge product.

Then Will and Eli vanished.

Because technical types seldom think about what can go wrong, Logan hadn't bought key-person insurance.

The company crumbled, and Logan was now deep in debt and seriously depressed.

How did the Center's research fellows get involved?

To all appearance Will had simply walked out of the office one evening and never reached home. But Eli had vanished from a locked room leaving only a handful of grackle feathers on the floor. Grackle magic meant the Master of Ravens was involved (nobody has yet been able to convince grackles that they're not related to ravens). And the Master of Ravens was currently living in Austin as Shani Chayyaputra. So we started looking into Chayyaputra's most recent venture, a business called, with typical modesty, Shani Chayyaputra Investments, or SCI.

All we'd learned so far was that Chayyaputra, as you might expect, was inordinately secretive. He barely interacted with his own staff; the company didn't have a website; uninvited visitors were thrown out before they got farther than the lobby; and he never took vacations. (That last wasn't so much a problem for us as an indication that he was up to something secret.)

When he closed the company for a week to pursue urgent business in India, we found an opportunity. He was too paranoid to allow his small staff free rein in his absence, so he sent them all for a week of team-building exercises and personal growth at a retreat out in Wimberley. As soon as we heard about this plan, my colleagues had been insistent that I should go to the retreat undercover and see what I could find out from interacting with Chayyaputra's employees. The first cover we'd been able to wangle was a temporary job for me as a waitress at Inner Light Guest House.

Even as that was being organized Jimmy had kept talking about creating a better cover story for me and planting things in the media, but I'd barely had time to pack and drive down to the guest house after the job was arranged, so I hadn't paid much attention.

I was going to have to have a serious talk with Jimmy quite soon. But for now, I headed to the dining deck with other questions on my mind, the principal ones being, "How does destroying Logan's little start-up company benefit Shani Chayyaputra? And what happened to Will and Eli?"

I paused at the door to look over what I was stepping into. Six people. Great view. And nothing but granola and bluish skim milk on the serving buffet. Well, I was certainly getting some insight into how the Fosters turned a profit. Too bad that wasn't one of my questions.

While half of Shani's employees were milling around and admiring the view (and putting off facing the granola) I secured a strategic seat in the middle of a bench at the picnic table. In retrospect, a place at one end might have been a better choice: easier to get away.

Opposite me sat a guy who looked somewhat older than the others. Dark hair cut very short, narrow face, slightly squinty dark eyes. Not appealing. I was still fingering a spoon and steeling myself for granola with skim milk when he launched an attack.

"It seems odd to me that we never heard about the boss planning to marry *you*." He invested the last word with a snide intonation that seemed to convey "you, of all people."

"Shani is a very private person," I said, and took a mouthful of granola to give myself time to think. I had more time than I really needed; the stuff combined a chewy texture with the taste of recycled cardboard. I chewed carefully while gazing over my attacker's shoulder at massed greenery and the hint of a creek, dark and shiny behind the trees. It was a nice morning: cool for May but not overcast. It would probably get hotter later on, but just now it was perfect for breakfast on the deck.

"All the same," the creep continued, "one article in a notorious gossip rag hardly seems like proof to me. Do you have any idea how many scandal stories *Whirred* had to retract last year?"

I finally got that first mouthful of granola down. "No, should I?" Maybe it was time to go on the attack. "And I resent your characterizing my engagement as a scandal story." I loaded my spoon again and looked at it dubiously. It didn't seem like a good tactical plan to gag myself with more granola.

"Oh, drop it, Webster. Sally spent a solid hour on the phone last night planning her wedding. She wouldn't go through all the hassle of picking flowers and napkins and a coordinated color scheme if she weren't stuck with an actual wedding to plan." Ginny set a bowl of granola on the table and sat down next to me.

"I hope I didn't disturb you."

"Oh, don't worry. The walls *are* thin, but I took your wedding preparations as an Awful Warning. I'm planning to get married next year, and after hearing what you're going through I think I'll forget about the white wedding of my dreams. Maybe I can persuade Adrian to elope."

"So she's planning a wedding," Webster muttered, "but does Shani know about it?" But he dropped the subject when the other people started introducing themselves.

Hien, the small dark girl who'd seated herself on my other side, was tech support. She was also even shorter than me. I liked her already.

Chet and Ginny, financial analyst and office manager, I'd met on Sunday, and I felt that I already knew Webster better than I wanted to. The other two were Yung-Su Park and Alec Somebody, software analysts.

"I sneaked a peek at Margo's schedule," Ginny announced ebulliently. "First we're going to do a trust-building exercise—"

"Oh, wonderful. I hope it's not that thing where you fall backwards and hope the others catch you," murmured Hien. I hoped so too, and I liked her even better for that comment.

"And after that," Ginny continued, "we're going to play 'Two Truths and a Lie,' where each of us has to make three statements and the others have to guess which is the lie. Sally's at a disadvantage because the rest of us are already acquainted, so let's tell her about ourselves over breakfast."

Alec stared into his bowl and Yung-Su announced, "I am Korean. Not Chinese. Not Japanese. *Korean*."

"The Chinese-American community thanks you for that clarification," Hien said under her breath.

"And?" Ginny prompted Yung-Su after a lengthy pause.

"That's all."

He was awfully tall for a Korean, but apparently he didn't plan to discuss that. Or anything else.

"I don't think y'all are getting the idea," Ginny announced. "I'm Ginny, I'm going to marry Adrian next year, I hate rap music and I never met a meal I couldn't like."

That much I could have deduced from the enthusiastic way she was spooning up the granola; what I couldn't figure out was how she stayed so lanky.

"Ha," said Webster, "you should try field rations. Oh, I'm Webster and I served in the army, which is why I'm older and wiser than the rest of this crew."

"You think." Hien was an enjoyable, if barely audible, chorus.

The rest of the introductions washed over me. I was too busy trying to think of statements I could use for the next exercise, so I didn't learn much about Chet, Hien and Alec. Oh well, it wasn't like I was trying to win the stupid game. Not being exposed would be good enough for me... unless one of the crew accidentally revealed something about Chayyaputra's reason for using black (bird) magic against a small start-up company. I hoped some of them would say *something* useful. Could I think of a statement – either "true" or "false"—that would elicit a useful response?

For the 'trust-building exercise' Margo moved us to a different deck, one without tables or chairs. She told us that each of us in turn was going to have to navigate an obstacle course blindfolded while the rest of our team gave us directions. The obstacles were big upside-down cans inside a large chalked rectangle and they got rearranged every time a new person was blindfolded, so simply memorizing their initial positions wouldn't work.

We were put in two teams. I got Alec and Hien; the other team comprised Webster, Yung-Su, Chet and Ginny. Having more people, they had to start first. Webster was first up while Ginny and Chet shouted directions. They were about as accurate as you'd expect people in management and finance to be; Webster kicked all but two of the cans. *Good.* Wait, was I actually getting invested in this stupid game?

Well, I like winning. And while Alec was being blindfolded and Margo Foster was rearranging the cans, I decided to add a little of the precision that the tech people really should have thought of for themselves.

"Is there any rule that the directions have to consist of telling the blindfolded person where to step next?"

"Not necessary," Margo said, "what else could you say?"

"What about telling them where the cans are? That isn't against the rules, is it?"

"How could we do that?" Hien asked.

"First we establish a metric."

Light dawned.

"We could use one can-diameter! And the whole space is eleven cans wide by…" Hien's lips moved soundlessly.

"Alec, don't start yet!" I called. "We are going to do something different this time."

"By twenty-one cans deep," Hien finished.

We agreed on coordinates for all the cans in their current configuration.

"But Alec won't know what we're doing?"

"We'll tell him before he starts."

"Then the other team will know too."

"Doesn't matter. They couldn't copy us if they tried; they'll stay with counting steps," Hien said confidently. "Yung-Su is the only one who'll even understand the concept of x and y coordinates, and he won't be able to explain it to the others."

"All the same… Is there a rule that we can't talk to Alec before he starts?"

Margo threw up her hands. "No, there isn't. Why would there be? I've already told you what you have to do. Normally people just follow the directions."

"We're not normal," Hien and Alec said in unison, "we're tech people."

Hien darted around the obstacle course and whispered in Alec's ear for a moment. He whispered back.

"I told him the course dimensions and metric," she reported on her return, "and we're going to give him x and y coordinates in the usual style, but we're going to tack delta onto the x's and epsilon onto the y's. That was his idea. Just to foment a little more confusion on the other side."

I grinned. This was beginning to be fun.

"Alec," I called, "you can start now, and you're clear through three delta, three epsilon."

Alec took three mincing steps forward; his feet were almost as big as the cans.

"Obstacle at 3 delta, 4 epsilon," Hien called, and Alec took a small step sideways.

"Next obstacle at 4 delta, 6 epsilon," I called.

That, of course, was no obstacle from Alec's present position; he just had to be sure not to veer to his right with the next three short steps.

We took turns calling out the coordinates. Alec made it through unscathed and we cheered as he pulled off the blindfold. Margo's lips were pursed, but she didn't say anything.

For a grand finale Alec and Hien called directions to me alternating the sequence of coordinates. When Alec called a location of "5 delta, 7 epsilon" it translated to 5x, 7y. But when Hien called "12 delta, 9 epsilon" that meant a location at 9x, 12y. There really wasn't any point to that bit of mental gymnastics, except to make it more interesting for me; the non-tech team was already totally lost. But it all worked out well. Even though we had a handicap of plus three to make up for only having three players, we finished with a score of five to thirteen.

"I don't know how good that was for team building," Margo said, "but I certainly have to give you credit for innovative problem solving. Now, we're a little behind schedule thanks to *some people* taking long pauses between contestants, so let's move right along to the next exercise."

Oh, help. I'd been so involved in the obstacle game that I'd forgotten to think out my three statements. I'd have to wing it.

Once the cans were neatly stacked against a wall, Margo had us all line up in front of them. She explained that she would call one person at a time to stand in front and deliver their three statements. "Remember," she said, "you can use body language as well as your knowledge of your teammate to guide your decisions. Sally, why don't you begin?"

Silence.

"Come on," Ginny said to me after a moment when nobody moved, "don't be scared, we don't bite."

Oh, right. *I* was Sally. Oops. I stepped forward and turned around to face them – and prayed for inspiration. "Uh, I'm engaged to Shani." I'm not as bad a liar as my colleagues claim; I managed to say that without touching my cheek. I stared past the bright young staffers and tried to think of something else to say. Preferably including a lie so obvious that it would carry them right past the possibility that I'd already lied to them just now. "And, ah, I'm five feet three inches tall and… and I love tuna salad."

They conferred for a moment. Webster was loudly in favor of the first statement as a lie, but the rest of them squashed the suggestion. "*I* know," Hien said. "We can test the second one right now." She darted forward and stood eye to eye with me. "I am five feet *two* inches tall," she announced, "and unless you're counting her hair, so is Sally."

"You're wrecking my self-image," I complained.

But five of the six – Webster loudly abstained- decided that 5'3" was the lie. "Sneaky of you to put it so close to your actual height," Ginny said, "if it weren't for Hien we'd probably have accepted that one."

Dear, darling little Hien, whom I suddenly liked a lot less than earlier. I bet she was at least five feet two and a half, anyway.

For the rest of the game I generally deferred to the others' opinions, occasionally selecting a statement at random to make it look like I was really trying. To my disappointment, none of them said anything about work. I learned more than I needed to know about Alec's vacation with his girlfriend in Hawaii, Webster's army service and Ginny's social life. All useless.

Lunch was next on the program, and I sat as far as possible from Webster. It didn't help much; they were all curious about me, and this was their first chance to ask questions.

"Do they still divide people up into castes in India?" Ginny began.

Fortunately I'd read an article about that recently. "Most do," I said, "but the community of people who are fluent in English is sort of getting past that. More modern. What someone knows and can do is more important than who his parents are."

"So it doesn't matter that Shani is so much darker than you?"

"Not a bit," I said truthfully over Alec's whisper of "Ginny, that's *racist.*" He started a long, involved story about the time he had to go to Chennai on business and then asked if that was the way Indians always did business.

"Um, sorry," I apologized, "I wasn't quite listening to all you said."

Hien giggled. "Alec talks too much, doesn't he?"

A couple more questions about India and I thought of an excuse for my ignorance. "Look," I said, "I'm American-born, my family isn't at all traditional, I really don't know that much about old-fashioned Indian ways. They didn't even give me an Indian name."

They wanted to know how I met Shani and I punted on that one. "Actually it was my *father* who met Shani first. On business." And wouldn't that be a surprise to Dad if he ever heard about it! I clasped my hands in my lap, fighting the urge to touch my cheek.

They wanted to know what sort of business, and I made some vague noises about international finance.

Somehow my last name came up. "Bhatia," I said firmly, that being the only Indian surname I knew, and if Prakash Bhatia hadn't interned with us this semester I would have been really hard up for an answer.

"Ah," Chet said knowingly, "you must be one of *those* Bhatias, the industrial millionaires. No wonder Shani—"

I saw an excuse to cut off the India questions. "That's enough of that," I snapped. "How *dare* you intimate that Shani only wants to marry me for the family connection? I've had enough of this!" I threw down my napkin and stomped off the terrace. I didn't want any more of the mystery casserole Margo had served for lunch anyway, and the fresh fruit was all gone. I wished I'd thought to pack some candy bars.

3. Something fishy

Meanwhile, back in Austin – though I didn't know this at the time – Jimmy-the-computer-geek and my fellow topologist Ben were doing their own investigation of SCI. It wasn't their first such experience.

Dr. Verrick had started the Center for Applied Topology for the benefit of three of his topology students – first me, then Ben, and finally Ingrid. A year later Colton had found his way to us from one of Dr. Verrick's introductory classes. We had discovered that we shared his secret and slightly unnerving ability to affect real-world objects by visualizing certain topological ideas – a power of which he'd thought himself the sole possessor or, as he preferred to say, sufferer. When the Center was set up we'd all envisioned a life of stress-free pure research. However, he'd accepted funding for the Center from a secretive three-letter agency which liked us to do useful snooping for them, and there went our purity.

To be fair, snooping was a lot more fun than writing papers which, by the terms of our non-disclosure agreements, we would not be allowed to publish in this millennium. So we got along pretty well with the agency rep, Brad Lensky, who'd been assigned here to convey requests and, if possible, to prevent us from getting killed.

Actually, I got along better than "pretty well" with Lensky. At least when we weren't shouting and throwing things at each other.

Ben had already been in the lobby of the SCI building on a first, more casual attempt to learn something about the business. The main thing he'd learned was that Chayyaputra was serious about security; he'd never made it past the lobby. But he had also discovered that a huge, showy aquarium was the focal feature of the lobby – a lighted tank at least six feet long by three feet deep, placed on a three-foot stone plinth. That should make just about a perfect focus for teleportation now that the office was closed, allowing them to bypass the locked outer doors of the building. There was just one potential catch. Had Chayyaputra shielded the offices against unauthorized teleportation, the way the Center for Applied Topology was now shielded?

He had not. Ben and Jimmy arrived without incident in the middle of SCI's lobby. They took a moment to admire the display of coral and artificial rocks with brightly colored tropical fish flitting around the upper waters of the tank. Actually Jimmy had more than a moment to gawk at the aquarium, because getting past the inner doors was a little trickier; Ben had never been inside the office space beyond the lobby, so he couldn't just teleport them in there.

Fortunately, the one aspect of small object manipulation that Ben had mastered had to do with moving tumblers, gears, and latches. His collection of topological tricks was a virtual lockpicking toolkit and a work still in progress. He had even disassembled various locks to help him visualize their inner workings. He still hadn't found all the tiny parts that hit the floor and rolled into crevices when he dropped the outside lock for the office, but that wasn't a big problem; as I've said, the Center was shielded against teleportation by anybody except us, and none of us had anything expensive and portable to be stolen from our personal offices anyway. Not on the pittance Dr. Verrick, our director, paid research fellows.

Jimmy had little to do while Ben worked on the lock between the lobby and the rest of the office, so he whiled away the time watching the brightly colored little fish darting around the aquarium. Well, most of them were tiny and colorful. There were a few unattractive fish, mud-colored and lumpy and considerably bigger than the decorative ones, lurking at the bottom of the tank. He supposed they served some practical purpose. Then Ben opened the double doors between the lobby and the rest of the office, and he had more important matters than fish to think about.

Evidently Chayyaputra believed in the abomination known as an open-plan office. The inside of the first floor was just one large room with a small maze of cubicle partitions like an island in the center of the room. Beyond the cubicles, at the back of the room, Jimmy could see a flight of stairs. Ben had stopped at the cubicles, though. He was squinting at the arrangement as though trying to memorize it.

Jimmy coughed; he'd learned not to walk up to research topologists at work and tap them on the shoulder.

"*What?*" Ben said crossly. "I'm trying to memorize the layout in case we have to teleport again."

"Thought that was what you were doing," said Jimmy. "Didn't you notice that the cubicle walls are easy to move?"

"I'm trying to get a fix on this room so if I have to teleport here again, at least I can land in here and save the trouble of picking a lock."

Jimmy patiently repeated that the cubicle walls could easily be moved. "I don't know what would happen if they rearranged them and you visualized the wrong configuration."

"Oh. Yeah. Probably nothing. I mean, Brouwer teleportation just wouldn't happen. We wouldn't arrive in the middle of a wall, if that's what you're worrying about." Brouwer teleportation obeyed some of the laws of classical physics, like not allowing a research fellow and a wall to occupy the same space. "Not likely to be a problem this week, with everybody out of town, is it?"

"No, but we might need to come back after this week."

"OK, what in this room *isn't* movable? I know – the stairs!"

Ben wandered off in the general direction of the stairs, working his way through the cubicles with a few false starts and muttered curses. Jimmy looked after him, shaking his head slightly. Sometimes he felt that only half his job involved hacking into databases and doing other covert computing tasks; the other half consisted of gently redirecting topologists from hopeless or dangerous tasks. He wondered if the topologists outside the Center, the ones with no paranormal abilities, were equally prone to doing the equivalent of walking into walls and off the edges of cliffs. Probably not, since he'd never heard about the math building on campus exploding or disappearing or catching fire. But he wouldn't have taken any bets on it.

Fortunately, computers made more sense. Jimmy settled down happily to infiltrate SCI's system.

In his experience, computer users either had long, complicated passwords that they had to write down somewhere, or simple and obvious ones that they could remember without strain. Though few were idiot enough to use "password" for their password, apart from that one – oh well, most people in politics weren't terribly computer-savvy, that guy was just at the far end of the bell curve.

There wasn't a piece of paper with a string of nonsense letters and numbers on the desk, or in the top drawer, or stuck to the monitor on a Post-It note. That covered most of the places people put their passwords; after all, they had to be easy to reach. Nobody wanted to fish out their keys and dig through a locked filing cabinet every time they logged in. And that fact alone destroyed ninety percent of the effectiveness of complex passwords. Maybe more.

If he'd known last week that this opportunity would arise, Jimmy could have had some fun inventing identities and phishing the staff members for their passwords. Now he briefly considered checking out the other cubicles for a written password. Oh, well, he could always do that if necessary – but if whoever sat at this desk didn't need a written reminder, he'd be willing to bet he could guess the password. He grinned and flexed his fingers over the keyboard. Naïve users were *so* predictable. What would these particular users think was a good idea?

"Chayyaputra" was his first guess. *They'll think nobody could spell it. Forgetting that anyone who tries to get into the system is already showing interest in the business.*

That didn't work, and his second guess, "Shani" was kicked back for being too short. Jimmy frowned and, after a moment, remembered what the Indian intern had called Shani. Oh. Shani *dev.* "Dev" probably meant "god".

Not that it mattered. "Shanidev" without spaces opened up the entire intranet of SCI's computers to him.

"I'm in!" he called across the room to Ben.

"In what?" asked a voice behind him. Jimmy whirled and saw a young woman who definitely did not fit into his impression of office staff for a financial company. She looked like a theater arts student who'd somehow wandered out of her proper context. Or maybe music? Performance art? Something along those lines, would be his guess. He catalogued blue jeans, some kind of floaty and semi-translucent top, huge black-framed glasses covering most of her face; bangs down to her eyebrows, freckles where her face was actually visible, mousy brown hair down to her shoulders.

"Um, I'm with Comtech Computer Services," he improvised. "Mr. Chayyaputra asked us to come in and optimize the system while everybody's out this week." He hoped that rolling the name off his tongue without hesitation would impress her.

"Oh! Thank goodness! When I saw the parking lot empty, and then the office was so quiet, I thought they'd gone out of business since last Monday. But where is everyone?"

That, at least, he knew. "Mr. Chayyaputra's away on business, and since he couldn't be here, he took the opportunity to send the staff to a team-building retreat. In Wimberley," he added. "At Inner Light Guest House. Paid for by the company."

The girl smiled. "Oh, Inner Light? I've always wanted to do one of their yoga retreats, but I never could afford it. Mr. C. certainly is generous to his staff!"

More likely, he's afraid to let them work here while he's away, for fear one of them will stumble on something that makes them suspicious. Jimmy squelched that thought and agreed that Mr. C. was generous indeed.

The girl put something on the floor – *a bucket? What's she doing with a bucket? Cleaning lady? She doesn't* look *like a cleaning lady* – and extended a hand. "Well, nice to meet you. I'm Harper, and I come in every Monday to take care of the aquarium. But the folks here are always too busy to talk to me," she said, sounding regretful. "That's why I didn't know about the retreat. In case you were wondering."

Now *she* seemed to be trying to convince *him* that she was a legitimate visitor. He guessed that meant she didn't suspect them... yet.

"Not at all," Jimmy said. "I was surprised, that's all. Mr. Chayyaputra didn't happen to mention you, that's all. Well, I guess I'd better get back to work. He's not paying me to stand around and chat with pretty girls."

Harper flushed and bent her head slightly forward so that her long hair fell to cover even more of her face. "Yes, well, I suppose I'd better get to work too. This aquarium setup needs a *lot* of maintenance." She retreated to the lobby and set up a stepladder. With relief, Jimmy got back to work. He stuck a USB stick in the machine he'd accessed and started downloading files. Then he frowned at the screen and tapped random keys so that he'd look as if he was actually doing something, just in case Harper came back while he was waiting for the download to finish.

Ben materialized at his elbow and startled him. "Aren't you done yet?"

"Where did *you* disappear to?"

"Upstairs. About half of the second floor is *very* securely locked up. Beyond my skills, actually; I've never seen locks quite like those. Why do you suppose that area gets special protection? I'd like to know what's in there. Are you done yet?"

"Not quite. I'm still collecting data. After that I want to leave a little present on their hard drives."

"What kind of present?"

Jimmy was gratified to see that Ben jumped just as much as he had on hearing the girl's voice.

"A, um, a protection against malware," Jimmy improvised. "Oh, Harper, this is my colleague." And they were lucky she hadn't wandered in here a couple of minutes earlier, to see Ben carelessly stepping out of the air. The topologists really weren't careful enough about this stuff. He turned to Ben. "Harper comes in every Monday to do the aquarium maintenance. I was just explaining to her how Mr. Chayyaputra asked Comtech Computer Services to come in and optimize the system while everybody's away this week. Only I've detected a virus infecting some of the files, so our first job will be cleaning that up." He faked a sigh. "I can't believe how naïve some users are about cyber protection."

"Never mind," Ben said cheerfully, "think of them as potential customers for our special services. Are you done yet?"

Jimmy wondered what Ben's hurry was, but he didn't want to ask in front of Harper. Fortunately the computer beeped at him just then. "That takes care of the data download," he said, pocketing the data stick. "We, ah, we can analyze the data remotely, then come back to do the actual optimization. It's less expensive for Mr. Chayyaputra that way." He didn't want to install his own virus while Harper was wandering around and asking questions. Getting the virus to hide itself on the hard drive and resist cleanup attempts required a bit of poking around, and she might wonder why it took so long to install a simple anti-malware program. Too bad he hadn't had time to automate the installation process. But they'd been in a hurry, and he'd expected to have plenty of time here. Undisturbed time. *Harper*-free time. Didn't the woman have any other aquariums to clean?

Ben must have been thinking along the same lines. "Don't you have any other aquariums to clean today?" he asked Harper.

She flushed and looked at her shoes. Potential mathematician? Jimmy wondered. "I'm sorry, I didn't mean to interfere with your work. It was just nice having someone to talk to... and I was wondering if you could tell Mr. C. about the fish."

"About the fish? What's the problem? Not that I know anything about aquarium maintenance," Jimmy added hastily.

Harper pushed a little hair away from her face. "I'll show you. If you don't mind? You see, it keeps getting worse, and everybody here is so busy, I haven't had a chance to talk to Mr. C. about it." She headed back to the lobby and he and Ben followed her.

"It's the machalees," she said, gesturing towards the bottom of the tank.

"Those big mud-colored ones?" Well, comparatively big, at around eight inches.

"Yes. I didn't know what they were at first," Harper confessed, "but Mr. C. told me. He said they're from India and they make him think of home. Although," she added, frowning slightly, "he doesn't spend a lot of time looking at them."

Jimmy thought that was quite understandable. They were easily the least attractive fish in the tank. Why Chayyaputra had wanted them at all was a mystery to him.

"And the problem is…" he prompted Harper.

"I looked them up," she said, "and they're supposed to be *pink*. I think the dull color is a sign of illness. The first one was pink enough when I spotted it."

"The first one?"

"Yes. There was only one to begin with. Then there were two, then three, and a few weeks ago there were five."

Jimmy squinted at the tank. "I can only see four. Is one of them hiding, or what?"

"No, it's not hiding," Harper said, sounding tearful. "A couple of weeks after the last two appeared, I came in and there were only four of them left. Mr. C. said he'd had the janitor scoop the dead one out of the tank because he didn't want to upset me."

"Considerate of him."

"Yes, but…" Harper swallowed hard. "I think the other machalees are dying too. They look worse every time I come here. And there's more."

"There is?"

"Yes! Look at that one's dorsal fin… oh, darn, he's swimming away… that one, then!" She pointed and Jimmy bent down for a closer look.

"What's that lump on its back?"

"I don't know," Harper said. "The pictures I saw don't show anything like that. With the first one I thought it was some kind of deformity, but they all have it. So maybe a contagious growth of some kind? And whatever it is, the machalees don't like it. They're all the time rubbing up against the decorative coral, as if they itch right there, and the coral is ripping up the webbing between the spines. See how ragged they all look? So I was thinking, you have to talk to Mr. C. about your work, and maybe you could just mention that I'm afraid the machalees are dying?"

Jimmy and Ben looked at each other. Then Ben fished out his glasses and stared at the tank. Coward! He was leaving Jimmy the task of letting the girl down.

"I don't think…"

Jimmy stopped at the stricken look in Harper's eyes and started over.

"We're probably not the best people to approach the boss about this. I mean, we don't know anything about fish."

"Yes, but if—"

"It's not a natural deformity," Ben interrupted her, straightening up. "Not a tumor, either. It's been *put* on them." He glared at Harper as though it was her fault. "What kind of an idiot clamps a huge heavy metal tag on fish? Oh, I guess there are places where you could do that without harming them, but *not* in the webbing of a fin!"

"All right, then," Jimmy said briskly, "we know what the problem is, Harper. All you have to do is explain to Mr. Chayyaputra that the tags are harming them…" He trailed off at the look of betrayal on Harper's face.

"I told you, he's always too busy to talk to me."

"You'll just have to be firm."

Harper's brown eyes filled with tears, and Jimmy realized it was no use telling her to be firm, any more than you could tell a kid to be mature.

"And besides," Ben said, "she'd have to wait a week to talk to him, and who knows how many of the fish will be left then? Tell you what, Jimmy. Let's scoop one of them out and see if we can't remove the tag ourselves."

"Oh, *would* you?" Harper looked up at Ben as if he was her hero. The lank brown hair fell back from her face and this time she didn't brush it forwards. She had a *lot* of freckles.

"Sure," Ben said, "no trouble." He looked at Jimmy. "We won't charge Mr. Chayyaputra for the time this takes, will we?"

"Certainly not," Jimmy said. It wasn't as if they were going to charge him for any of their time here.

4. Practical demonology

Collecting one of the machalees proved to be a tricky job. Ben had to climb to the fourth step of Harper's stepladder in order to reach down to the bottom of the tank with her long-handled net. He rolled up his sleeve but still had to reach down so far that it got wet, and his groping fingers found nothing but the sharp edges of decorative coral.

"You need to get the net a couple of inches lower," Jimmy told him, and Ben stretched to obey.

"A little bit over that way!" Harper called. "No, *that* way!"

"I can't see…"

"What? I can't understand you!"

"When I'm diving into the damned tank," Ben said, righting himself temporarily, "I can't see where you're pointing, so saying '*that* way' is no help whatsoever. And exactly how much is 'a little bit' when it's at home?"

Finally he felt the rim of the net brushing against something soft. He leaned even farther over, dipped and scooped, and was rewarded with a machalee flopping desperately inside the net. Standing, he decanted it with a plop! into the shallow plastic tub which Harper had already filled with water from the aquarium.

"Look at that!" Ben said indignantly as they bent over the fish. "That thing is *iron*. It's *rusting*. And whoever put it on punched a *huge* hole in the fin. I tell you what, Jimmy, this isn't so much a tag as a fish torture device."

Jimmy remembered, tardily, that Ben had double-majored. If mathematics was his first love, marine and freshwater biology was a close second. No wonder he was bonding with Harper over the mistreated fish. Jimmy wasn't at all sure that a fish's nervous system was capable of saying more than "Yes" and "No," but he was pretty sure that this fish's system was saying "No no no no no!" It arched and writhed away from Ben's hand when he reached into the water to touch the tag.

"You know, Ben," he said uneasily, "maybe we should wait and let Chayyaputra handle this. Harper could get in trouble if we kill one of his fish." Not to mention that if she told the truth about what happened, Chayyaputra would know that somebody had infiltrated his offices and his computer system.

"I don't care about that!" Harper exclaimed. "Do you really think I could be so, so mean and selfish? The poor thing is hurting now, and that horrible tag is going to kill it. We *have* to get that thing off of it! And we'd better do it fast," she added, "because there isn't enough water in the tub to let it breathe comfortably for long."

The fish flopped and writhed, breaking the surface of the water. "Oh, hold still, stupid!" Harper said. "He's not going to hurt you. He's going to *help* you." And the fish actually did stop thrashing, almost as if it understood her words. More likely, Jimmy thought, it was just exhausted. This time, it let Ben touch the iron tag without flinching away from his hand.

"I can't find any kind of a clasp," Ben said in frustration after a few minutes of feeling around the tag and fin. "I mean, there's bound to be some way to remove it, but I can't tell what from just touching it and I can't get a good look because the fish goes crazy if I try to bring it up to the surface. I don't suppose you have bolt cutters in your car, Harper?"

"I'm sorry," she said. "I've never needed anything like that, and I didn't think— I'm *sorry*," she apologized again.

"You could hardly be expected to carry a complete tool shop for emergencies," Jimmy said. "Ben, can't you open it some other way?"

"I can hardly do it with my bare hands!" Ben snapped.

"I know. But you've got *other ways* to do things," Jimmy said. He knew that all of the Center's research fellows could teleport, move small objects, and light fires – that last had been sort of an accident, an unexpected consequence of Ben's attempt to make light, but it had turned out to be surprisingly useful. They had other paranormal abilities too, though he couldn't offhand think of any that would serve to slice through an iron fish tag. Why iron? he wondered. Didn't whoever tagged the fish realize that an iron tag would rust and eventually fall off?

"Ben. Let me check something, okay?" He knelt beside Ben and reached one hand into the tub.

After a moment's fumbling, "I meant, move your *han*d so I can feel the tag."

Both flat sides of the tag were rough with rust, but nowhere near rusting away. But the bar that passed through the dorsal fin to connect them, that was a different story. The corrosion had gone deep here. Ha! Who said they couldn't do this with bare hands? Jimmy put his other hand in the water, grabbed the back side of the tag, took a firm hold of the front piece and twisted. The oddly shaped front and back pieces didn't give, but he thought he could feel a slight motion. He twisted the pieces, moved them, twisted the opposite way. He could definitely feel some motion now. Another couple of twists of the rusted bar—

The lights dimmed, and the fish was writhing and struggling under his hands, and the water was growing colder so fast that his hands ached with the cold. But the tag had snapped loose, leaving him with a piece in each hand. He didn't look at the pieces, though, because like Ben and Harper he couldn't look away from the thrashing body in the water. The water itself was roiled as if a storm was raging inside the plastic tub; there was ice around the rim of the tub; the thing inside it no longer looked like a fish.

It was pink, though.

The lights dimmed even more and the shadowy air around him became icy. His dripping hands were no longer dripping; the water on them had become a thin film of ice.

"What's happening?" Harper whispered.

Jimmy shook his head. Had Chayyaputra embedded a curse inside the tag? It seemed likely, but that was a theory that wouldn't reassure Harper. It didn't reassure him all that much either. Neither he nor Harper was equipped to fight back; they'd be dependent on Ben to save them. And Ben was somewhat flaky at the best of times.

The mini-storm in the plastic tub reached a howling peak as if actual winds were lashing it, and something pink and much larger than the machalee fish rose from the water, filling the tub. What was it, some kind of demon? Had it been bound by the iron tag? He was still holding the two halves of the tag; in desperation, he threw them at the pink shape.

"Ow!" said a very human-sounding voice. The thing rose higher and higher yet, its shape swelling and rippling as it grew, and the cold in the room chilled him to his bones. But he hardly noticed in his astonishment as the thing, now more than five feet tall, took shape as a naked human.

A naked *woman*.

A *screaming* naked woman.

"You son of a bitch, I'll sue you for everything you've got!"

It didn't exactly sound like a typical demonic utterance. Jimmy wrenched his eyes from the woman and looked at Ben. He seemed equally nonplussed. Bad sign, that. *Bad* sign. Jimmy's role at the Center for Applied Topology was wrangling computers; the research fellows like Ben were supposed to deal with the paranormal.

Harper jumped to her feet and ran outside. A wise move, Jimmy thought.

But in a moment she was back with some kind of rug, or something, which she threw over the figure as if she thought blinding it would slow it down.

The screaming stopped abruptly; the very human-looking hands grasped two edges of what Jimmy could now see was a stained and tattered blanket and wrapped the fabric tightly around its body, just under the armpits. A well-padded, middle-aged woman with short frosted hair glared at them. She no longer reminded Jimmy of anything demonic – until she opened her mouth. "I'm glad to see that *somebody* here has some sense of decency! You two jokers can quit staring now, the show's over. And give me back my clothes!"

"And shoes," she added, stepping out of the tub. She left wet footprints on the polished tile of the lobby floor. "The floor is *freezing*. And why were you making me stand in a tub of ice water? Is this supposed to be some kind of torture? Because it's not working!"

Jimmy recovered his wits. "Uh, ma'am, we weren't trying to make you stand in the tub. We were actually trying to get you *out* of the water." Not that they'd exactly known it at the time.

"Then who took my clothes away and made me stand here?" she demanded.

"We were hoping you could tell us that."

"Well, I can't. The last thing *I* remember is telling that cyber-pirate Shani Chayyaputra that he couldn't buy my company."

"Ah. As it happens, we have a problem with Chayyaputra ourselves." Jimmy glanced apologetically at Harper, but she wasn't looking at him.

"Then what the hell are you doing in the lobby of his building? And where's everybody else? And why—"

"Lady, that's a *long* story and I'm not sure I want to trust you with it."

Harper had busied herself with putting away her tools and mopping up the puddles of water on the floor. Now she intervened.

"I expect this lady—"

"Renata," the woman snapped. "Renata Rivera, CEO and owner of Rivera Cybersecurity. As you people perfectly well know."

"Renata. Wouldn't you like to go somewhere more comfortable to talk this over?"

Renata twitched the edge of her blanket. "What, dressed like *this*? I'm not going anywhere until you give my clothes back!"

They wound up back in the main office, scrounging chairs from four cubicles so that everybody could sit down. This room wasn't quite as cold as the lobby, and in any case the whole building was slowly getting back to normal.

Renata told them that her fledgling computer security company had suffered several accidents in the past months, culminating in a planted virus that sneakily introduced subtle errors into the code of the program they were developing for sale.

"If those hadn't been caught," she said, "our product would have been dead in the water. Fortunately, my best developer guy has a fantastic memory. When he spotted lines of code that hadn't been there the day before, it took him and the rest of the tech team about five minutes to verify that none of them had done it, ten minutes to disable the code while leaving it in place, and fifteen minutes to notify me."

Jimmy wasn't surprised to hear that it had taken the programmers longer to decide to notify Renata than to fix the code. The CEO was a formidable lady; he too would much rather interact with a computer.

"The next day – *the next day*," Renata said, "your Mr. Chayyaputra—"

"Not ours," Ben interjected. "Jimmy told you, we have a problem with him too."

This time Harper looked upset, but not nearly as unhappy as Jimmy had expected. Perhaps discovering this one of Chayyaputra's dirty tricks had changed her feelings about the man. Or – more likely, he thought – she was just saving her breath for a really good fit of hysterics, and who could blame her?

"Oh? Well, it can hardly be as bad as what he did to *me*." Renata forged ahead, eager now to recount the rest of her story. "The bastard called and said he wanted to do me a service. He felt I should be warned that CodeSense – that's our proprietary software – contained fatal errors and would likely damage any computer that it ran on. He said that his people thought they could fix the software and that he'd buy it from us—at about the price we'd planned to charge for *one license*. I hung up on him and then I came right over here to tell him in person what I thought of his mob-style 'offer.' I told him my guys had already identified and disabled his code and that we now had a copy of CodeSense stored on a computer with no Internet connections.

"He laughed at me! He said he didn't need the Internet to wreck our software, that we were going to continue having problems until I gave up, that the software wasn't very good anyway and I'd be much better off accepting his offer than trying to market it myself. That Rivera Cybersecurity was a tiny company that no one had heard of and that no one would pay us to handle their security.

"I told him that we got one of SINET's awards for innovative security technology last year, when we were running a much less powerful version of CodeSense than we had now." She dusted her hands together. "So much for being unknown! And then I told him that he couldn't buy me *or* my company, and…" She frowned. "I was going to threaten to sue him, but I suddenly had trouble breathing. And then everything went weird. I fell down – I was choking – and then I had the damnedest hallucinations. Thought I was flying through the air, then imagined I could swim underwater for hours and hours without suffocating. It seemed to go on forever. He must have drugged me somehow, and now it's worn off." She shivered in the cool room, and pulled Harper's blanket up over her bare shoulders.

"I'm afraid it's worse than that," Jimmy said. He looked at Harper, who was sitting bolt upright and twisting her fingers together, and then turned back to Renata Rivera. "Ah – when did you visit SCI, Ms. Rivera?"

"Today!" She frowned. "Yesterday? It was cloudy then."

"What day of the month was it?"

"Is this some kind of a joke? The fourteenth, of course."

Jimmy and Ben looked at each other. It was the last day of April. At a minimum, Renata Rivera had been a fish for two weeks.

"April?"

"March! Do you think I don't know what month it is?"

"Harper, what's today's date?"

Harper stared at him. "Don't you know?"

"I just want Ms. Rivera to hear it from somebody she doesn't already distrust."

"Oh, all right." At least she was still speaking to them. And not screaming. Jimmy was in a mood to count even the tiniest of blessings. "It's April 30."

The blood drained from Renata Rivera's face. "That's not possible!"

"Step outside for a moment," Jimmy suggested. "And then tell me when it's ever been ninety degrees and sunny in March."

"I'm not going anywhere until I get something better to wear than a filthy blanket that smells like it's been on somebody's car floor forever," Renata said firmly, "and anyway, Austin always has occasional freakish hot spells. Weather doesn't prove anything."

"Ben," Jimmy said, "Can you get Ms. Rivera here some clothes and a copy of today's *Austin-American Statesman*?"

Ben frowned at him. "Not without, ah…, *you* know. I mean, oh well, I guess I could go out to the lobby…"

"You might as well do it from here," Jimmy said tiredly. "Harper hasn't run away screaming yet, and I think Ms. Rivera here might be able to understand the situation better if she sees a practical demonstration."

Ben shrugged and stood up. "Okay, but you better catch her if she faints." He turned sideways and disappeared.

Jimmy had an extremely difficult half hour while they waited for Ben's return. Renata Rivera took Ben's disappearance into thin air as proof that she had been drugged and that the hallucinogens were not completely out of her system. She announced that she needed to go to the emergency room to be screened for drugs as soon as she was decently dressed. Harper, on the other hand, took Ben's disappearance as proof that her two new acquaintances were magicians with unlimited powers.

"What's taking him so long?" she asked after only a few minutes had passed.

"It may take a while for him to find clothes. I don't think any of Annelise's will work." Ben's live-in girlfriend, the receptionist at the Center for Applied Topology, probably weighed as much as Renata Rivera, but she was significantly taller.

"Can't he just magic them into something suitable?"

"No."

"Anyway, shouldn't he be right back? I mean, even if it takes him an hour to find the clothes, can't he just travel back to the time when he left here?"

"Are you kidding? That would be *time travel*." Jimmy couldn't help thinking of his previous experience with time travel, and he could feel his face heating up and his ears turning as red as his hair. "In my next life I want to be tall, dark and handsome," he muttered.

"Well, you've got the *tall* part down, anyway," Renata said.

"*I* don't think he's all that bad looking," Harper said.

"For a computer geek," Renata qualified.

"How did you know that's what I do?"

Renata sighed. "You look *exactly* like one of my software developers. Bad haircut, glasses, ink-stained shirt…"

"Nice smile," Harper said.

Harper, Jimmy thought, was a nice girl, but he sort of wished she wouldn't keep trying to make him feel better. It was the kind of thing Ingrid would not be understanding about.

"Ben should be back soon," he said.

"I'd like to know how you two work that little trick," said Renata.

So much for breaking the news to her gently.

"Why don't you do it too? I'll watch more closely this time," she suggested.

Jimmy sighed. "I'm not the one who can teleport. That would be Ben."

"You can't, but your friend can?" Renata scoffed. "Oldest con game in the book! 'There really is magic, only *I* can't show you, but my *friend* could demonstrate if he were here.'"

"They don't call it magic," Jimmy said. "They prefer to say 'applied topology.' It's based on mathematics."

"How do you do magic with topography?" Harper asked.

"*Topology.*" The mathematicians were extremely picky about that word, though not so good at explaining exactly what it meant.

"Okay, you yourself can't teleport, what *can* you do?" Renata demanded.

Jimmy took a deep breath. "Just about anything to do with computer software. In Java, C-sharp, C plus plus, Python or R. And without applying any topology. I'm just that good."

Renata's eyes narrowed. "What a coincidence. CodeSense is written in R. You wouldn't be the bastard who messed with our code, would you?"

"No," Jimmy said, telling himself to stay cool, "that would be someone who actually works for Shani Chayyaputra."

The air behind Harper thinned, showing a colorless chaos that made Jimmy's head hurt, and then Ben stepped through to them and the opening disappeared.

"Skirt, blouse, um… other stuff," Ben said, proffering a double armload of colorful fabric. "I'm sorry, the skirt might be a bit long on you." Jimmy recognized the long cream and maroon skirt. It had been a midi-skirt on Annelise, and she was considerably taller than the irate CEO. He thought that Ms. Rivera would probably trip over the trailing hem and break her neck. He wasn't sure he cared.

"Newspaper?" she demanded.

It was tucked under Ben's arm; now he flourished it.

"Give me that!" Renata's improvised blanket-sarong slipped a bit as she reached for the newspaper. She looked at the header on the front page and her eyes widened; then they rolled back in her head and she slipped from the chair to the carpet, unconscious.

"Oh, shit! Harper, get her some water."

"Why?" Jimmy asked.

"I don't know. That's what they always do on TV. Come on, Harper, can't you wake her up? I draw the line at wrestling clothes onto an unconscious naked lady."

While Harper knelt over the unconscious woman, trying to revive her, Ben looked at Jimmy. "And you'd better brace for another fight."

"How come?"

"Lensky's back." Ben paused for effect. "And he's *not happy.*"

5. The ice princess and the floozy

Ben persuaded Lensky to wait in his office until the present emergency was sorted out. "You'll be happier," he pointed out, "if you don't know exactly how many non-disclosure rules we're breaking."

"Oh, are there some you aren't breaking?" Lensky asked. "Oh, okay, get on with it, and what I don't see or hear, at least I won't have to report to the Agency. But make it snappy. We've got to do something about Thalia."

Snappy? Ben was already tired and spacy after teleporting everyone back to the Center for Applied Topology. But as he'd told Jimmy, he felt it was past time to get out of there; all the time they'd been in Shani Chayyaputra's offices he'd been antsy, fearing that someone would come in unexpectedly. The fact that Harper had done just that hardly added to his peace of mind. In fact, he teleported them out of the building so fast that Renata was still trying to get into her borrowed clothes when they materialized on the top floor of Allandale House.

"Where's Annelise?" Jimmy asked. He'd been the last to be teleported back, and he'd expected to see Ben's girlfriend at the reception desk. In fact, he'd been rather counting on her to calm Ms. Rivera down.

"Obviously, we had to go home to get the spare clothes for Renata," Ben said. "I asked her to drive herself back here; I'd already figured out that I was going to have to do too much teleporting this afternoon." He took a long swallow from the Coke that Harper had helpfully brought him from the second-floor vending machine. "Even using the stars, dragging the ladies and then *your* great heavy body through the in-between was enough to affect my blood sugar." Although teleporting had definitely been the way to go; it spared him having to escort a partially clad Renata up two flights of stairs before an interested audience. The Center for Applied Technology had the third floor of the Victorian mansion known as Allandale House, but the first two floors were occupied by special collections curated by librarians. The librarians frequently mentioned that they wondered just what the mathematicians up on the third floor *did* that involved fires, things crashing off the roof, strange singing noises and other odd phenomena. Ben had no desire to add a half-naked, cursing woman to their list of interesting anomalies.

"You should have let me drive us all over in my van," Harper said. "You didn't mention that... what just happened... was going to exhaust you. I'll have to go back to get it now."

"I didn't think of that," Ben confessed. He finished the Coke and sank down into Annelise's desk chair. He wondered if he should ask Harper to go back downstairs, not talk to any librarians, and get him another soda from the vending machine on the second floor. He really felt as if he still needed sugar therapy.

"Do you have a safety pin?" Renata asked, ignoring the discussion about something that she refused to think about and that probably hadn't happened anyway. She appeared to be wrestling with Annelise's midi-skirt. So far, the skirt was winning.

"It'll take more than one to raise the hem," Harper said helpfully.

"Never mind the hem," Renata snapped, "I need something to close the waist. I can't exactly button a waistband that's six inches smaller around than I am!"

"Probably not more than three inches," Ben said while rummaging through Annelise's desk. "Annelise isn't all that slender."

"It. Is. Still. A. Problem." Renata said through her teeth, "and I can't get back to my own office until I'm decent."

Jimmy put his hands in the air around her waist to estimate just how many safety pins would be needed.

It was, perhaps, unfortunate that at just that moment Ingrid Thorn, hearing unfamiliar voices in the open office, walked a Möbius strip through the doorless wall partitioning off the Research Division offices to see what was going on.

"James," she said as soon as she was clear of the wall, raising her eyebrows, "aren't you going to introduce me to your *new friend*? Or would you rather wait until she gets her clothes back on?"

"She's practically dressed," said Jimmy. "We just need a couple of safety pins. Well, maybe more than a couple. Depends on whether she can button the blouse, once she gets it on."

"They're Annelise's clothes," Ben contributed. "Would you get me a root beer or something from the vending machines, Ingrid? I'm feeling sugar-shocky."

"Of course they are. That makes everything perfectly clear," said Ingrid, ignoring Ben's request. Her voice dropped several degrees, from cold to frosty. Jimmy shivered. He'd had enough cold in the lobby of Chayyaputra's offices to last him for some time. And he was fairly sure that Ingrid could duplicate the feat of lowering the ambient air to freezing if sufficiently displeased. That was the kind of thing you just had to deal with when your girlfriend was a tall, pale ice princess with applied topology skills.

"Ingrid, I can explain everything," he said, and immediately realized that had been the wrong thing to say. *A* wrong thing. There were probably plenty of others available.

"Oh, that hardly seems necessary," Ingrid said, sweeping across the room to look down at Renata where she perched on a corner of Annelise's desk. The blond braids wrapped around her head seemed to be crackling with energy and trying to escape the hairpins that kept them in place. "The situation explains itself, does it not? All I want to know is why you brought your floozy into the office. If you were going to run around on me, couldn't you at least keep it private?"

Three of the four people facing her spoke simultaneously.

"Why couldn't she be *my* floozy?" asked Ben, as though logic was going to be any help in this situation.

"Ingrid, why are you immediately assuming the worst?" Jimmy asked, as though even more logic would do the trick.

"*Who are you calling a floozy, you Anglo beanpole?*" Renata screeched.

Ingrid looked down her patrician nose. "Very well. Cougar," she amended. "Aren't you ashamed to go after young men? At your age?"

Renata pulled one arm back to swing at Ingrid. Jimmy caught her just in time.

"If you're still my fiancé," Ingrid announced, "you'll quit manhandling your bimbo."

"He's just trying to keep it from getting worse," Ben said.

"Ms. Rivera, sit down and let me handle this," Jimmy said, pushing the indignant woman towards a chair and putting Annelise's blouse in her hands. If they could just get the woman covered up maybe Ingrid would calm down.

He turned back to Ingrid, grateful as never before that his height allowed him to look her in the eye. "And *you*, if you're really *my* fiancée, how dare you jump to the conclusion that I'm cheating on you? Didn't you learn anything from that mix-up last fall? You've got a hell of a lot less excuse for your suspicions than Annelise and Lensky had then – and they, *if* you remember, were dead wrong."

"Do you have the gall to pretend this is the same kind of situation?"

"Damned right I do," Jimmy said between his teeth, "except this is much less misleading, and you're incredibly dumb, Brainy Math Girl, for making such stupid assumptions."

Ingrid gasped. But before she could say anything, Jimmy had grabbed her shoulders and shut her up with a kiss. He'd started out as furious as Ingrid, but as she stopped trying to hit him, and slowly began to return his kiss, he began to have trouble remembering to be angry.

Eventually they had to come up for air.

"You've got a hell of a nerve, Computer Geek," Ingrid said, but she didn't sound cold and detached any more.

"Let's go into my office," Jimmy said, "and discuss why a beautiful woman like you is so insecure that she assumes I'm cheating on her based on the flimsiest of evidence."

"A reasonable question," Ben said judiciously. He was exploring the back of Annelise's top desk drawer as he spoke.

Ingrid turned on Ben. "And you've got a nerve too, opining on something that's none of your business, you idiot!"

"I," Ben said, "am the hero of the hour. Behold, safety pins!" He held up a shiny chain of linked safety pins and Renata snatched them out of his hand.

"All I want," she said, pinning furiously, "is to get away from *all* of you maniacs and find out what's happened to Rivera Cybersecurity."

"I can't teleport you," Ben apologized, "I've never seen your offices."

"And *Dios mediante*, you never will! Just call me a car, I have an account with Uber. I'll wait downstairs." In a flurry of long trailing skirts, she headed down the stairs.

"An impressive woman," Ben said to Harper. "She didn't even trip over Annelise's—"

There was a thud in the stairwell, followed by more footsteps and enough Spanish curses to turn the air blue.

"I guess she's all right?" Harper said tentatively.

"Let's hope so, because I'm tired of her." Ben sighed. "Some people aren't very grateful for being rescued from the life of a fish, are they? Come on, let's get some bolt cutters and go back to free the rest of the prisoners."

"I thought you were tired of... doing whatever you just did," Harper said.

"Yeah," Ben sighed. "If Colton – my other colleague – is here, maybe he can take over the transportation. Or we could just wait until Annelise brings my car over, and maybe she'll bring some doughnuts. I really am getting shocky from applying all that topology."

"And I thought you were afraid of being caught there," Harper said.

"I was. I am. But I'm not coward enough to weigh that against the rescue of prisoners who are already in sad shape. In fact, I'm not tired enough to keep them waiting, now that I think about them." He placed his open hands on the top of the desk and levered himself upright. "Let's go!"

"Wait!" Harper caught hold of his sleeve. "You can't free the others now."

"Why not? I may be feeling a little shaky, but I *can* do this, Harper."

"Because if you try to do it all at once you'll kill everybody who's still in the aquarium. Didn't you notice how cold it got when Ms. Rivera transformed?"

"Yes. Hmm." Ben took off his glasses, polished them with the cuff of his shirt, replaced them. "Mass. Energy. The transformation sucked energy out of the air to replace mass? I wouldn't have thought that would have been nearly enough energy, though."

Harper shrugged. "I'm not so hot at math and physics and all that sciency stuff. All I know is, when everything else got cold, so did the water in the aquarium. My fish just got lucky that it was a big tank and the water temperature didn't drop enough to kill them. But another blast of cold before the tank warms up again probably *will* kill them."

"Okay," Ben said, "so we take three of those big plastic tubs and put one of the fish-prisoners in each one. Then we don't have to worry about one of them freezing in the tank. If I can cut the tags off fast enough—"

"That beautiful blonde of Jimmy's was right," Harper interrupted him. "You *are* an idiot. What do you think will happen to all the other fish if you freeze the aquarium?"

Ben shrugged. "The little colorful ones? I didn't see any tags on them. Ergo, they're not people, just fish."

"*Just* fish," Harper repeated scornfully. "And that makes it all right to kill them?" She pushed the hair off her face, the better to argue. Her cheeks were getting red and her eyes sparkled behind those heavy glasses and she looked, Ben thought, better than she ever had up to now. Not that it mattered to him – nobody who had a girl like Annelise would go shopping around for somebody else—but it was interesting to see this drippy Harper looking like somebody who might actually be attractive if she put a little effort into it.

"Okay, okay, I do see your point," Ben said. In fact, now that he got it, he was totally with her. When he'd met Mr. M. as a disembodied turtle head, he'd refused to kill another turtle just to provide the Mesopotamian mage with a new body, hadn't he? Fish were just as entitled to live their lives as turtles, weren't they? "So, we have to wait until the aquarium water gets back to a normal temperature. How long do you think that'll take? Let's see, if the aquarium contains n cubic feet of water and it lost, say, twenty degrees…"

"I may not be an expert in math and physics," Harper said, "but I do know aquariums. It won't be back in balance until tomorrow."

"Couldn't we, I mean, doesn't it have some kind of heater?"

"That's allowing for the fact that I turned the heater on before we left."

"Really? I mean, that's *slow*. What if we added a stronger heater?"

"You want to *cook* the fish?"

Ben threw up his hands. "All right! All right! Let's see, if we do one fish a day… well, that should work out okay. Tuesday, Wednesday, Thursday, and I assume Chayyaputra won't be back before the weekend."

Assumptions are dangerous things.

***

What was left of Monday was taken up with plans and explanations. First Ben had to explain the situation to Harper, who pointedly said that she'd taken a *lot* on faith already and she needed to know what was really going on. It was fortunate that she'd had some time to absorb the idea that "that nice Mr. Chayyaputra," was, to say the least, not at all "nice." That seemed to trouble her more than Ben's discussion of applied topology, paranormal abilities, and their reasons for going up against Shani Chayyaputra – at least the most recent reasons; he didn't have the energy to give her the full story of the Center's conflict with the Master of Ravens.

"Are you allowed to tell her that?" Jimmy asked when he and Ingrid emerged from his office to hear Ben skating lightly over the topic of teleportation.

"I asked Lensky not to listen," Ben said.

"And I haven't decided how much I believe anyway," Harper added.

Once they'd thrashed things out to Harper's satisfaction and taken her back to her van, there remained Brad Lensky to deal with. The time spent sitting in his office so as not to hear rules being broken had not made him any happier.

"What were you thinking to send Thalia by herself into a nest of enemies?"

he demanded as soon as they entered.

"I was thinking of keeping her well away from Chayyaputra's office," Ben defended himself.

"You know if she were here, she'd be searching his office with us," Jimmy said.

"The only way to keep her safe was to make sure she didn't know about it," Ben finished.

Lensky actually laughed. "Fair enough. She's tried to do the same thing to me more than once; serves her right to have her own trick played on her. But I still can't think that being surrounded by Chayyaputra's employees is exactly a safe situation. I'm going to pull her out tonight."

"What, and waste the superb cover I created for her?" Jimmy was indignant.

"Create covers for your own girlfriend," Lensky snapped, "keep your hands off mine!"

But he had to admit that planting a story on the *Whirred* website about Thalia's engagement to Shani Chayyaputra had been a brilliant idea. "And from all my research," Jimmy added, "it really looks as though Chayyaputra's employees aren't in on whatever his scheme is. They're all recent graduates – young, naïve – well, except for the security guy, and from all accounts he's dumb as a box of rocks. This is the first time Chayyaputra's been away from the office since he started operating in Austin again, and he made sure that the entire office staff would also be away at the same time, going to this retreat. That looks to me like –"

"Somebody who doesn't dare leave the office for fear that an inquisitive employee – or even just an overzealous one – will discover exactly what he's up to," Lensky finished, and nodded. "Yes. Looks like that to me too. All the same—"

"You still want to pull Thalia out?"

"I do. But if you're going to continue sneaking around the SCI office—"

"We have to. At least for the next few days." Ben explained about the transformed fish prisoners. Lensky was momentarily distracted from worrying about Thalia.

"That angry woman I heard screeching in the outer office was an ex-fish? What kind, a sting ray?"

"No, she couldn't have been that, rays are marine fish. This is a freshwater aquarium. They're more stable than saltwater tanks, you see, because…"

"It was a joke," Lensky said, interrupting him. "I forgot you had a second major in Reptiles and Amphibians."

"Freshwater and Marine Biology," Ben said stiffly.

"Whatever. So… you've got three more fish-people to rescue, and your aquarium girl says you have to wait twenty-four hours after each transformation because turning fish back into people sucks energy out of the air and chills water."

"Conservation of mass and energy," Ben said. "But there's something wrong. I haven't had time to work out the numbers, and anyway I don't have before and after temperature records, but I'm intuitively sure the transformation isn't draining anywhere near as much energy as it should to create a person-sized mass."

"Fine, after you figure it out you can write a paper about the relationship of classical physics to magic."

"*Applied topology*, not magic." Why did people have so much trouble grasping the distinction?

"Whatever! Anyway, I agree that if you're going to be in and out of SCI all week, there's something to be said for keeping Thalia out of the loop. All right, she can stay at the retreat for now. On one condition."

"What?"

Lensky leaned forward over his desk and stared at the two of them intensely.

"Jimmy, you need to figure out a cover for me to join that retreat as well. I want to keep an eye on Thalia and be in a position to get her out myself if she's burned."

6. The imminent prospect of being unmasked

Wimberley, Tuesday

Tuesday at Inner Light opened with a bombshell I could well have done without. Margo Foster announced over breakfast (granola and yogurt, today, as a change from granola and skim milk) that a close friend of Shani's, an American named Brian Lester, would be joining us at the retreat sometime today. It seemed he had come to town on an impulse to surprise Shani with a visit, and had decided he might as well spend the waiting time getting to know his friend's employees better. Margo said she was happy to invite him as his presence would get them back to even numbers, and a lot of activities were planned for couples.

From the cheerfulness with which Margo made this announcement, I suspected that the "close friend" was paying extra for the privilege of muscling in on the retreat. That may have done a lot for her mood, but it did nothing whatsoever for mine. This was not the kind of news that I felt able to face over granola and low-fat vanilla yogurt. I wondered if Wimberley had a doughnut shop, and if I could possibly sneak off and fortify myself with something involving chocolate and carbs. Then I wondered if I wouldn't be wiser to just sneak off and never come back.

I wasn't going do that immediately, though. This morning they were actually talking over breakfast about how SCI worked, and I thought I was making some interesting connections.

Chet and Yung-Su had started it, gloating over their stock options. It took only a couple of innocent questions to get them going on how they expected SCI to make them all rich.

"It works like this," Yung-Su explained. "Austin's a fantastic place for start-up tech companies. In fact, there's probably more innovation happening here now than in Silicon Valley. Venture capitalists want to get in on the action, but it's hard for them to judge which companies are good bets. That's where SCI comes in."

"Telling the venture capitalists which company is going to be the next Google?"

Alec laughed. "I wish! We're not quite operating at that level. Yung-Su and I track new start-ups and evaluate them in technical terms: how useful is their idea, are they actually going to be able to produce, are their key people well thought of in the business, and who's their competition. At the same time, Chet looks to see if their finances are sound. When we all agree on which companies are likely to be the major players in a new field, Hien takes all of our data and packages it into an interim presentation for Mr. C."

"Why interim? It sounds pretty complete to me."

"Ah, but that's where Mr. C. works his magic. He's got an incredible intuition for which one of the start-ups is going to pull ahead and dominate the field. Why, just a couple of months ago we evaluated two small companies that were both pushing zero-knowledge identification programs. Neither one had an algorithm ready for market, but Mr. C. put his finger on one of the firms and said, 'This one,' and steered his investors to it."

"We shouldn't bore Sally with all the dreary details," Yung-Su said with a smile. "Especially over breakfast."

"Oh, no! It's fascinating to learn how this actually works," I said. No lie there. "How did Shani know which company would succeed?"

Yung-Su spread his hands. "That's why he's the boss and we're the underlings, Sally. He has a gift for this sort of thing."

"The important part," Chet said, "is that when he makes his recommendation, he gets part of his remuneration in stock options, and so do we. So we all stand to profit if his choice is right."

"And it always is!" Alec burst in. "Take those two companies I was talking about—"

"Alec, didn't you want to make some calls before the morning activities start?" Chet asked.

He shook his head. "*I* couldn't tell which one was going to have the breakthrough first," he told me. "On paper, they looked exactly even. But then the damnedest thing happened, just two weeks after PriPro got a massive cash infusion from Mr. C.'s venture capitalists. The—"

"Alec, I hate to drag you away, but I need your advice on something," Yung-Su said, putting one hand on Alec's shoulder.

Before they came back, Margo was already nipping at our heels, figuratively speaking. She was eager to line us up for the first activity on the day's program, something called "Helium Stick." So I didn't get a chance to ask Alec what he had been going to say.

"This exercise," Margo said, "is a demonstration of the power of coordinated group activity. You're going to accomplish something that people working alone could never do."

She herded us into two lines facing one another, standing closer together than I really wanted to stand to my opposite number – Webster. Naturally. We followed Margo's instructions and put our hands out at waist height, then adjusted to get them all at the same level; Hien and I had to reach up, naturally, while Chet and Ginny and Yung-Su had to reach down a little. Some day I'd like to play a game that's normalized for short people.

"Palms down, backs up," Margo instructed us. "Now close your hands and leave only one finger out."

"I know which finger *I'd* like to stick out," Webster muttered. Okay, he was still a creep, but I gave him a few non-creep points for hating what looked like another touchy-feely activity. However, I noticed that he, like everybody else, used his index finger. Delete the points for not having the courage to follow through.

After a long spiel about the magic of cooperation and group effort, Margo brought out a long cardboard tube mostly covered in holographic silver wrapping paper. A couple of rips showed the underlying brown cardboard.

"This," she announced, "is a magic stick. I'm going to lay it across your fingers, and then you are to lower it to the deck while keeping all your index fingers in contact under it. No grabbing the stick, no talking; you'll have to develop a unified strategy based on body language."

Didn't seem like it was going to need a whole lot of strategy; all we had to do was lower our hands to the ground without dropping the "magic stick." That would be a lot easier for Hien and me than for beanpoles like Ginny and Yung-Su. OK, not such a bad game after all.

Except that the stick, after she laid it on our outstretched fingers and stepped away, *rose*. And our hands rose with it, naturally, because we weren't supposed to lose contact.

"What the *hell*?" Webster muttered.

"Actual helium?" Yung-Su bent and tried to peer through the hole in the tube at his end.

"Watch it!" Chet snapped. "You're about to lose finger contact!"

Chagrined, Yung-Su straightened up and watched the blasted stick rise another quarter of an inch.

"What did I say about talking?" Margo trilled in the dulcet tones of a kindergarten teacher.

I blinked and concentrated on the silver-wrapped tube. Pictured an identical tube lying flat on the deck. Simultaneously, I pictured two glowing parallel line segments. A simple geometric function would map the top line onto the bottom one... In a non-metric space, they were identical...

There was more weight on my fingers. I bent my knees, then knelt. Yung-Su, at the other end of the line, was having more trouble contorting his rangy limbs to get to deck level while keeping his own index fingers under the stick. It tilted slightly, then leveled off as Yung-Su and Ginny got themselves low enough. We flattened our hands on the smooth wooden planks of the deck, pulled them out from under the stick and stood up.

"Done!" Chet announced, beaming.

Margo wasn't beaming. In fact, she looked distinctly sour. "That," she said, "was not supposed to happen."

"Huh?"

"It's what you *told* us to do," Ginny said reproachfully.

"Every other team that has done this exercise," Margo said, "has seen the stick *rise*, and felt like it was floating, because the collective force used to keep your fingers in contact with the stick is greater than its weight. It's *supposed* to be an illustration of the unexpected benefits of team cooperation."

"I guess," Ginny said brightly, "we just happen to be the most cooperative team *ever*, because without knowing that we all lowered our hands at exactly the same rate."

"I… suppose so," Margo said, sounding less than totally convinced. She took the silver-wrapped tube back.

"What's next?"

What indeed. The stick game had actually distracted me for a while from the disaster heading towards me from Austin. While Margo explained the rules for the next activity, I tried out lines to explain why Shani's close friend had never seen or heard of me.

None of them were terribly convincing. I would have done better to be thinking up questions for the next activity. Margo made it sound like a combination of Musical Chairs and impromptu interrogation. Six people sitting on chairs in a circle, one person – "It" – standing in the middle. You ask a question of the form "Have you ever…" – it's supposed to be something that you yourself have done – and everybody who answers "yes" has to stand up and move to another seat while you try to nab one of their chairs.

Good enough. We started with Ginny being "It." I hoped she'd give me a chance to lose my chair and become the interrogator; I wouldn't be in any hurry to "win." For me, "winning" would be the opportunity to ask as many questions as I liked. Sure, they were supposed to be questions that I myself would answer "yes" to, but as you may have noticed, I don't mind cheating under these circumstances. The only problem would be remembering what I'd asked.

I got lucky; Ginny started with, "Have you ever planned your own wedding?" Naturally I had to stand up for that one. They'd all heard my interminable telephone discussion with Mom last night. So, to my surprise, did Hien. I headed in the wrong direction for Hien's chair; she grabbed mine and Ginny took hers.

Showtime!

I turned in a slow circle, surveying all their faces. Ginny looked brightly interested; Webster looked as if he'd found a cockroach in his morning coffee. The others were somewhere on a scale between Bored Silly and Cheerfully Cooperative. I wondered if anything ever dented Ginny's good cheer. Ah well, not the issue at hand. Where to begin?

"Have you ever worked on a project you had to keep secret?"

All three of the tech people stood up. I was, carefully, too slow to get any of their chairs.

"Have you ever identified key technical personnel for a small business?"

Only Yung-Su and Chet stood for that one, and they switched chairs so quickly that nobody could reasonably have expected me to grab one.

Hm, finance paired with tech. That could involve Logan's company, Protect Your Privacy. Had that been the company competing with PriPro, the one Alec had identified as Shani's choice? What could I ask that might shed some light on the real question?

"Have you ever been involved with a company that unexpectedly lost key personnel?"

No takers. Either they hadn't been in on the assault on Protect Your Privacy, or they were lying. Well, I'd lie too, if somebody asked me if I knew anything about a murder I'd committed. *Subtle*, Thalia, *subtle*. And I needed to ask something that the non-tech staff could relate to, or they'd start grumbling.

"Have you ever gone dancing at the Broken Spoke?"

Everybody stood up, and they milled around so long that I had to take one of the empty seats; even I couldn't be clumsy and slow enough to plausibly miss this opportunity. Oh well, I could sit for a while and think up better questions.

Webster became the new "it." He'd angled for it, just as I had; I'd seen him dawdling, changing direction, trying to look confused. That would have worked better if he hadn't, now, looked so smugly satisfied.

I braced for an attack, and here it came.

"Have you ever lied to your friends and associates?"

Nobody moved. Well *I* certainly wasn't guilty here. These people were not friends or associates of mine.

"Have you ever pretended to be someone you are not?"

I may be a lousy liar, but even I could figure out that I had to sit tight for that one. Alec raised his hand. "Ah, does acting in a school play count?"

When Webster nodded, both Alec and Yung-Su stood up.

"Who were you playing?" Ginny demanded.

"That's *not* the question format, and it's not your turn." Webster glared at her.

"Oh, relax, Webby," Hien, beside me, said. "We want to know!"

"C-Threepio," Alec said, grinning, "in a *Star Wars* parody. I had a costume made of gold-painted aluminum foil."

"Yung-Su?"

"I will go to my grave," said the tall Korean, "bearing the ghastly secret concealed in my bosom." But his lips twitched; he wasn't as serious as he was pretending to be.

Ginny pouted. "I'm going to ask Margo if we can play Truth or Consequences. *Then* we'll be able to grill you."

Webster cleared his throat and launched into a long, boring question about entering restricted areas without a security badge.

"*Webby?*" I whispered to Hien.

"He resembles a swamp creature," she whispered back. "With webbed fingers. Don't you think?"

I did indeed.

Webster, getting no response to his security badge question, moved on. "Have you ever been to India?" Maybe he'd been there during his military service? Or maybe, like me, he didn't mind cheating.

Alec stood up. Oh, right, he'd had that business trip to Chennai.

Hien poked me. "Wake up, Sally!"

Oh. Had I ever actually claimed to have been to India? I knew I'd told them I was American-born and my parents weren't all that traditional. I couldn't remember what else. But it was plausible that Sally Bhatia, Shani's fiancée, would have been to India at some time, if only to meet his family.

Did a god have family? Irrelevant, for now. Playing it safe, I stood up.

Alec zipped into my chair and Webster and I competed for how slowly we could get to Alec's empty seat. I won, naturally; I yield to no one in my talent for heading the wrong direction, walking into walls, and tripping over my own feet. And now I had some really good questions prepared.

Unfortunately, I only got to ask one of them.

"Have you ever profited from someone else's disaster?"

Yung-Su stared past my head. Chet twitched slightly, but no one had actually moved when Margo interrupted us.

"Time's up!" she said cheerfully, clapping her hands. "I hope we all know each other a little better now. But we need to move right along to your scheduled hour of being in Nature before lunch."

Huh? We were sitting on an outdoor deck. No air conditioning. Blue sky overhead. Trees, and the glimmer of a creek, visible beyond the deck. What about this didn't count as 'being in Nature?'

Turned out Margo was thinking about something a little more intense. She planned to space us out all around the guest house property so we could sit on the ground, work on awareness of our surroundings, and meditate on our relationship to Nature.

It didn't seem to have much to do with the stated purpose of this retreat. I suspected Margo was recycling certain elements of her more mystical programs. Not that I had any objection. I could do with an hour of not having to answer questions and juggle lies.

I didn't get it.

Mom called again just as Margo was finishing her spiel and preparing to lead us off into the woods, or up the creek, or whatever she had in mind.

"Sorry, Margo," I apologized, "I have to take this."

I ducked into the cool, shady interior of the guest house. Outside, I heard Margo saying sourly, "Evidently I failed to emphasize this aspect of the retreat, but would the rest of you please turn off your phones now?"

I would've been willing to eavesdrop for longer, but the others moved off with Margo. Anyway, Mom was claiming all my attention. She wanted me to come back to town to pick the invitation cards. And settle the wording. And choose *fonts*. No, I couldn't just pick one font for the whole card, different types of information should have different styles.

"Times New Roman," I said at random. "Verdana. Calibri. Uh… Arial. OK?"

Not OK; four types of fonts was too many.

"Tell you what," I said, "why don't you design the invite and send me a picture, and then I'll tell you if there's anything I need to change?" Which, I was resolved, there would not be.

Mom could not do that. She absolutely could not even begin to think of how to do that. Didn't I know that she didn't know anything about computers? And we were already late sending out the invitations; they should have gone out two weeks ago.

She had no clue about computers, but she could harass me about fonts? No use arguing. She was invoking Mom Privilege, the sacred and universal law that your mother is an expert on whatever she wants to be an expert on but knows nothing whatsoever about things she prefers not to deal with.

"Get Andros to do it." I might wind up with a logo for DeathVikings 3.3 on the top of the wedding invitation if my video-gaming kid brother was in charge, but at the moment that was a price I was willing to pay.

That did not, of course, get me off the phone, but at least Mom moved on to the next major issue on her list: did I want to save money by using pink votive candles in the floral arrangements?

"How does that save money?"

"Well, the florist won't need as many actual flowers."

"Fine, do it, I'm happy. Let's have pink candles."

"Well… all right; it's your wedding." Mom's voice practically screamed "You're making a terrible mistake!"

It cost me a full ten minutes to elicit that even though she'd *said* pink candles, she didn't literally *mean* pink candles, because the flowers were going to be pink so she really thought ivory was a better color for the candles, but of course if I really wanted pink candles she'd just have to work around that…

What I really wanted, at this point, was to elope and get married in some place without extradition. But I couldn't hurt Mom that way. The real point of this over-the-top Greek-American wedding was for Mom to enjoy a triumph over all the friends whose daughters hadn't yet achieved a good marriage. What would really make her day would be if I came marching up the aisle with a visible baby bump: chastity might be desirable in theory, but grandchildren were better for bragging rights.

Of course I might well be back in Austin tonight anyway, though I didn't mention that to her. I still didn't know what I was going to do when Shani Chayyaputra's dear old friend Brian Lester showed up and said, "Who the hell are *you*?" or words to that effect. If I had any sense I wouldn't be here for the confrontation. But I still hadn't gotten back to Alec about those two companies, and I really wanted to find out if the other one had been Logan's firm.

I brooded about that over lunch. Which consisted of tuna salad and canned peaches in sugar-free syrup. In case you haven't experienced the second, let me tell you that sugar-free "syrup" isn't. As for the canned fish – something I had hated ever since Mom used to put it in my sandwiches for elementary school lunch—Ginny announced brightly that she'd told Margo that tuna salad was one of my favorite foods and Margo had agreed to put it on the menu as often as possible.

Oh, *thanks*, Ginny.

Nice, thoughtful, considerate people can be such a drag.

Over lunch, to distract myself from the disgusting taste of canned tuna, I brooded some more over this Brian Lester who'd been sprung on me out of nowhere. His name had never come up in any of our previous dealings with the Master of Ravens, so maybe he wasn't such a close friend as all that. Maybe I could get away with reiterating that Shani was a very private person. In her babbling yesterday, Ginny had mentioned that she found that statement of mine easy to believe given that he spent most of his time incommunicado in his office on the second floor and mostly communicated with them by email. She thought Shani must be one of those introverts. (Clearly a foreign species to her.)

She was wrong about that, but I didn't correct her impression.

I was one of those introverts; another reason I was the wrong person for this assignment.

When Margo clapped her hands for attention I thought that lunch was over and she wanted us to move on to another activity. Hallelujah! I had an excuse for abandoning the rest of the tuna salad that Margo had so generously piled on my plate.

Wrong. "I have an announcement to make. As I told you this morning, an old friend of your boss is joining the retreat, which is *wonderful* news as it will make our numbers even again, so much better for the couples activities. I want you all to welcome Brian Lester."

I cringed in my seat.

A broad, blond man with very dark blue eyes walked out on the deck to stand beside Margo.

I stopped cringing. I even got up and went around the table to hug him. "Brian! Lovely to see you again. I hadn't expected to have the pleasure so *soon*."

"Good to see you too…ah…

"Sally," I murmured, very low.

"Sally." He turned to Margo while I returned to my seat. "Sorry to be so late. It took a little while to arrange transportation. The car I normally use in Austin was… *not available* today."

He gave me a hard stare. I kept my head down and concentrated on choking down the rest of my tuna salad. The task wasn't made easier by the way the new arrival kept looking at me with barely-concealed amusement, as though he knew exactly how I felt about the meal.

After lunch Margo ran us through activities, activities, activities. They were all physical in nature, giving me no chance to pry. An egg relay race. A 'teamwork' challenge involving cardboard tubes, strings and rubber balls. Balancing on one leg. Balancing on one leg and *hopping*. Balloon volleyball.

I was lousy at most of these; coordination isn't exactly my strong suit. Oh well, I might as well admit it: physical activity isn't my strong suit. I spend most of my life sitting at a desk and thinking about topology, or for excitement, drawing diagrams on a whiteboard and thinking about topology. This lifestyle is perfectly fine with me, but it doesn't exactly prepare you for balloon volleyball.

The guy who'd been introduced as Shani's friend was on the opposing team, and he was insanely good at just about all the activities. As one might expect of a man who'd taken off his sport coat to reveal a toned, athletic body. When I wasn't thinking about how to approach him, I thought about the unfairness of expecting me to compete in physical contests with someone like that.

Okay, I'm a little bit competitive. (Ben and my other colleagues would probably say, a *lot* competitive.) Even though I wasn't here to shine at these stupid activities, I still vastly preferred winning.

Not much of that came my way on Tuesday afternoon.

We had a pre-dinner break to shower, which had become increasingly important to me over the course of the afternoon, and which effectively isolated me from any chat before dinner with Shani's dear old friend Brian Lester.

Dinner consisted of tuna noodle casserole and Ginny's nonstop chatter about the activities, which prevented the rest of us from getting a word in edgewise. Or saved us from thinking up anything to say, depending on how you looked at it. I was growing increasingly frustrated with the difficulty of questioning Alec in this crowd. I picked at the tuna casserole, considered the likelihood of fainting from hunger, and zipped off early with a cup of coffee and the excuse that my mother was leaning on me to finalize the wedding invitations.

"You haven't sent those out yet?" Hien exclaimed. "When's the wedding?"

"Third week of June."

"Oh-oh. Only a tad over six weeks to go. Yes, you definitely need to get those done!" I guess she did have experience planning her own wedding. I'm sure everything was done perfectly and right on time.

This thing was coming at me way too fast. I'd rooted for an August or better, September wedding, on the excuse that Ingrid and Jimmy were planning to get married in June and I didn't want to step on their parade. Mom had countered that the first two weeks of August were off limits, being devoted to the Virgin Mary – and besides, August and September were much too hot for the outdoor reception we were planning. (This was the first I'd heard of the outdoor reception. I suspected she'd made it up to force me back to June, which I didn't like because (a) it was considered an auspicious month for fertility and (b) I wasn't exactly ready to get married. An extra two months would have given me a little more time to accustom myself to the idea.)

Then Jimmy, the traitor, announced that Ingrid's mother wanted them to wait until fall so she'd have plenty of time to organize their wedding, and there went my excuse.

Anyway, when I sat down on the bed and checked my phone I discovered that Andros had already formatted the wedding invitations and sent them to me. If I could send them back today that would be one less thing for Mom to nag me about. Hmm, make some editing changes so she'd think I had given this the appropriate amount of attention… ask Andros to change this font, put this bit in italics. And for God's sake get rid of the bit about "their beautiful and brilliant daughter Thalia." Maybe it *was* a good thing that Mom had made me look at the invitations. This cut down by one the number of ways she could embarrass me.

Unfortunately, N-1 was probably still an unacceptably large number.

I was contemplating that fact when my phone rang. And this time it wasn't Mom.

"We need to talk."

"So?" I wasn't in the mood to cut him any slack.

"My room. Third floor."

Talk about bossy!

Once I got there, though, I understood his point. The four guys from SCI filled the first floor, so Margo had put him on the third floor instead of with us women on the second floor, and he had no neighbors. Given the thinness of the walls, this was a better rendezvous than my room, which was sandwiched between Ginny's and Hien's.

"You *rat*," I said as soon as the door closed.

He raised one eyebrow. "Is that any way to greet someone who's come all the way from Austin to offer you moral support?"

"It's how I greet someone who caused me a morning's intense terror. After Margo announced that an old and dear friend of Shani's was coming I wasn't able to think about anything besides how the *hell* I was going to greet Shani's BFF and how I was going to explain why he had no idea who I was." I sat down on his bed. "You could have warned me!"

"Yes," he admitted, "but that wouldn't have been nearly as much fun as seeing your face when Margo introduced me. Besides, I owed you something for taking off like that when I wasn't around to discuss it with you."

"You mean, when you weren't around to *stop* me."

"Yes. Probably. I don't know. Yes. On balance, I think you're taking an unacceptable risk."

"Not nearly as much as we thought it might be. I'm pretty sure now that Chayyaputra plays his cards so close to his chest that even his staff doesn't know much more than we've surmised about what he's up to." I thought that over. Was it really true of them all? "Chet and the Korean guy *might* have a clue. This morning Alec – the other software analyst – was trying to tell me a story that might have been about Logan's company, and those two kept interrupting him and trying to change the subject. They succeeded, too, and with everybody milling around and playing these stupid games I haven't been able to corner Alec to find out exactly what he was talking about. But I think that apart from Chet and Yung-Su, they're just nice young people enjoying what they think is a really good starter job."

All but one, anyway. "Except Webster. He's not nice. He's also suspicious of me."

"Isn't it handy that you've got me here now? To corroborate your story?" He started unbuttoning his shirt.

"Hey! What are you thinking?"

"That it's high time I reminded you whose fiancée you really are." The shirt went flying and barely landed on the back of a chair.

"We can't do *that*," I said from the narrow bed. "Not here."

"You have access to a better room? No? Then this will have to do."

Sculpted shoulders and arms rippling with muscle; tanned, toned, solid torso; sprinkling of gold body hair arrowing down into his pants; he *knew* what taking his shirt off did to me.

"Here at the retreat," I said, staring at the hands on his belt buckle, "I'm

supposed to be Shani's fiancée, and you're supposed to be his best friend."
But I didn't get off the bed while I still could.

"Maybe he shares generously with his friends."

"Eeew."

He dropped his pants and sat on the end of the bed. "Oh, I wouldn't share
if you were mine," he said. "Oh, wait. You are mine. Aren't you?" He snaked
an exploring hand up under my shirt. I suppose I could have stopped him
then, but he was unfairly overwhelming me with pheromones.

There really wasn't room for two people on that narrow bed, especially if
one of them was as enthusiastic and energetic as Brad Lensky. We managed
to overcome that little problem.

(Lensky says that in fairness, it should be mentioned that I too displayed
a certain enthusiasm. I believe the words "mink in heat" were used. Naturally,
I would never include a phrase like that in a report, even an informal one.
And he's not the boss of me, even if he does try to stealth-edit my work.)

I was still catching my breath, and reflecting that there were definite pluses
to having Lensky sneak into the retreat, when a tapping on the window
startled me.

"Get your pants on," I whispered. "There's somebody at the window."

"Thalia, this is the *third floor*. Do you think there's a Peeping Tom on a
ladder out there?" But he started getting dressed anyway. I was slightly better
off; he hadn't given me time to take my skirt off. I yanked my T-shirt on,
then caught sight of my bra on the floor – good thing it was bright red and
easy to spot – and stuffed it into a skirt pocket.

When I peeked out the window, I saw a long, shiny silver-scaled shape
dangling down from the gutter. Its pointed end was tapping irritably on the
glass.

"Mr. M!" Thank goodness the guest house was an old building with
windows that actually opened. I pushed the bottom half up, leaned out, felt
dizzy, caught hold of the snake body and hauled him inside without banging
his head more than once or twice. Not hard, fortunately, because the head
was the one irreplaceable part of him. "What are you doing here?"

"Protecting you," he said with an offended sniff.

"You don't need to protect me from Lensky!" The two of them had had their differences in the past, but this was a serious overreaction.

"No. In the larger scheme of the universe, he is negligible." Another sniff. "The one you refer to as 'Webster' is lurking in the hall outside this door. I surmise that he hopes to catch you *in flagrante* with Lensky."

"Oh *shit*."

"Inelegantly phrased, but my sentiments exactly."

"Oh, well. Not really a problem, Mr. M." It turned out to be a good thing that Lensky had insisted on meeting here; it would have been much more difficult for him to leave my room unnoticed. For me, disappearing was a piece of cake. "We can just teleport back to my room." I wrapped him around my waist, pecked Lensky on the cheek, turned sideways and vanished.

7. A rajah's palace

On Tuesday morning, Harper picked Ben up at the apartment he shared with Annelise and they drove to the SCI office building. The parking lot was as empty as it had been on Monday; good. And having Harper let them in with her key was easier than teleporting the two of them inside. After all that had happened on Monday, Ben was okay with not taking any topological short cuts today until he absolutely had to.

They were better prepared than they had been yesterday. Ben brought in Harper's stepladder; she carried the fishing net, bolt cutters, and a large terrycloth robe. They had no way of predicting whom they'd free this time. Ben was hoping for either Will or Eli, but to be on the safe side they'd acquired this unisex, one-size-fits-all garment from Walmart.

"Although," Ben mused, "we do have almost a 67 percent chance that the next rescuee will be a guy, since Will and Eli have to be two of the three remaining fish."

"Don't you mean a two-thirds chance?"

Ben shot a glance at Harper. She appeared to be serious. She must have meant it when she said she didn't do math.

This time Harper had also brought a significantly larger plastic tub and a dipper for scooping water out of the aquarium tank. They hoped that the increased amount of water would keep the captive in fish form comfortable

65

while they lugged the tub into the cubicle area and closed the doors to the lobby, and Harper hoped that the slight added distance would mean that less heat got sucked out of the water left in the aquarium.

They hadn't thought enough about the fact that the large tub would be a lot heavier when it was filled with water. After they netted and transferred a machalee fish, it took both of them to drag the tub and its furiously thrashing prisoner into the office space beyond the lobby doors. Water splashed on the lobby tiles and soaked into the office carpets, and the tub hung up on something every few inches.

"Next time," Ben groused, "let's bring something on wheels so we can just roll the thing in here. My back!"

"You should do yoga," Harper said. "*My* back is fine."

"You," Ben pointed out, "did not have to bend nearly double to accommodate your *much shorter* partner." Actually it wasn't Harper's fault that he was nearly breaking his back to grasp the low edge of the tub; the two of them couldn't begin to lift it off the floor once it was full of water, so that was that. But he felt like blaming somebody.

"Oh, quit complaining and give me the bolt cutters!" Harper snapped.

"Nope. This tag is still pretty solid, just beginning to rust; it'll take a man's strength to cut through the bar."

Ben stood a moment, frowning down at the mud-colored fish in the tub, while Harper knelt and got a grip on it.

"What are you waiting for?" she demanded once the fish was trapped in her hands.

"I don't know. Seems like we ought to have some kind of ceremony. This is deep magic; much stronger than we've ever done with applied topology, even using the stars. Well, apart from the time-travel incident, and I wasn't in on that one."

"I thought you couldn't do time travel."

"Oh. Well. It might be more accurate to say, we're never doing it again. We nearly lost four people last time." After which it had been agreed that time travel was not going to be part of the Center's research. "And maybe we should have brought the other research fellows."

"Jimmy?"

"No, he's only support staff, can't do applied topology to save his life. I mean the other topologists in the office this week – Ingrid and Colton. Even Prakash, if he's around. What if whoever we liberate isn't any more our friend than Chayyaputra's? We don't know who else he transformed – or why."

"If you'll get on with it, we can find out. Come on! I can't hold this guy forever, you know."

Ben fitted the bolt cutter blades around the iron bar that joined the two flat tags and squeezed.

"A little harder, Mr. Masculine Strength?"

"I liked you better when you were this shy, mousy little thing who kept apologizing. What did you do, take assertiveness training overnight?" Ben exhaled hard while pushing the handles of the bolt cutter together.

There was an audible *click* as the cutter blades met; the two halves of the tag fell back into the tub and the machalee fish writhed under Harper's hands. She let go and jumped back, and the eerie sequence of the previous day repeated; lights dimming, a film of ice on top of the water in the tub, something growing and swelling and taking form before them.

Something relatively short and slight, compared to Renata Rivera.

Well, mostly slight, anyway. Some parts were… impressive.

Her long, wet hair clung like seaweed, partially obscuring her most impressive assets. There wasn't quite enough of it for a full Lady Godiva effect, though.

And she too was screaming.

"You let me out of here *this minute*, you ugly little creep!"

Maybe this one would calm down once she had some clothes on. Ben stepped behind the girl and threw the terry-cloth robe over her. She thrashed like the fish she'd been a moment earlier, landed an elbow on Ben's nose and knocked his glasses off.

"Cut that out," Ben panted, "we're friends!"

"Get your hands off me!"

Harper reached out to take one of the girl's hands. "We really are your friends," she said in a soft, unthreatening voice. "Whoever was just attacking you, it wasn't Ben. Turn around and see. Does he *look* like the guy you were screaming at?"

The girl turned her head, gasped and relaxed at the innocuous sight of Ben on his knees, feeling for his glasses. "No," she said. "He doesn't look like somebody who'd attack *anybody*. But if he's a friend of that son of a bitch…"

"I am not," Ben said stiffly, rising with glasses in hand, "in any way friendly with, or associated with, or helping Shani Chayyaputra. I assume that's who you mean?"

"I don't know his name."

"Dark guy, kind of short, uses scented hair oil?"

The girl nodded slowly. "Then you'll let me go?"

"If you want to go," Ben said, "you're free to do that."

"But you might want to let us give you some better clothes first," Harper suggested. "And shoes."

"Oh. Yes." The girl looked down at the edges of the bathrobe and pulled it around her. "Shoes… My feet are freezing! Why am I standing in a tub of ice water?"

"It's a long story," said Ben, offering her a hand to help her step over the side of the tub, "and better discussed elsewhere than in the middle of Chayyaputra's office building." He was beginning to think that he should have written a little explanatory pamphlet that could be handed to rescued victims of the fish transformation. Oh well, after this explanation he'd only have to repeat himself two more times.

"You want to drive? Or go… the other way?" Harper asked. "Or you could take her now and I'll drive over."

The girl dropped Ben's hand. "Excuse *me*, but after what that creep just tried to pull on me I'm not going anywhere alone with a man. Not even this guy. No matter how nerdy and harmless he may *look*."

Harper looked at Ben's indignant face and snorted. He definitely preferred her mousy, apologetic incarnation.

"Okay, we'll drive." Harper made Ben put away her aquarium tools in a corner of the lobby while she pulled the van around so that the girl wouldn't have to cross the parking lot barefoot.

It did occur to Ben that some people would consider getting into a van with people you didn't know even more risky than going somewhere alone with him, but he didn't mention that. *He* knew the girl was safer with them than inside the SCI office building, and he didn't want to spook her.

On the way back to Allandale House they learned the girl's name, or at least what she was currently using for a name. She claimed to go by Faelyn, and spelled it for them. It was probably only a mark of Ben's suspicious nature that he thought "Faelyn" might be an extra-creative rendering of "Fay Lynn." A Texas accent and a body like that didn't seem to go with faery names.

She told them that she'd been working a face-painting gig at Eeyore's Birthday Party when some creepy old guy started trying to pick her up. She laughed him off and the next thing she knew she was in a bedroom with him and the door was locked. He made a move on her, she swatted him, and then…

"He must have drugged me," she said with a shiver. "But how? I wasn't stupid enough to take the cup of beer he offered me in the park… but I still don't know how he got me into that room… and right after I hit him, everything got *real* strange."

"You were on the floor?" Ben suggested.

"You couldn't breathe?" added Harper, turning to look at her.

"For pity's sake, look where you're going, Harper! You thought you were swimming?" Ben said, returning to Faelyn's story.

"How did you know? Are you *sure* you aren't working for that guy?"

"He's done something similar to other people," Ben said. "Friends of ours. We're trying to stop him. At least…" Would Faelyn have described Shani Chayyaputra as an 'old guy?' He prodded her for a description. Darkish skin, check. Slicked-back black hair, check. Wearing too many rings. And yes, she said emphatically, he was old, definitely over thirty!

"Um… how old are *you*, Faelyn?"

She was eighteen.

"When we get back to the Center," Ben grumbled, "I'm going to check for grey hairs." He had just turned twenty-five and suddenly that felt like the beginnings of middle age. What with that and Faelyn's characterization of his appearance as 'harmless and nerdy,' he felt his ego shriveling by the minute.

"I can drop you off and take Faelyn back to my place to get her something to wear," Harper offered.

"Uh, no. I, she, it would be more efficient if we debrief her while you're going for clothes." Ben had just managed to push his injured ego aside long enough to realize that Faelyn could offer the Center researchers something that might be extremely useful.

Once they got to the office, Ben's first step was to demand Ingrid come out of her nice quiet office on the private side to help him explain what was going on to Faelyn. She definitely relaxed more when there was another woman in the room.

He and Ingrid managed to "explain" what was going on to Faelyn without actually mentioning teleportation, transformation or anything else they weren't supposed to talk about. They kept it on an abstract-ish level of "This man hurt our friends and we're trying to help other people he may have hurt," and Faelyn accepted that without too many questions. She didn't want to talk about her experiences as a fish, brushing them off as some kind of hallucinations caused by "the old creep." Her main concern was learning that several days had passed since Eeyore's Birthday Party; she had a second face-painting gig for one of the upcoming Cinco de Mayo parties and since she hadn't been paid for the previous job, she really needed to do this one.

"Cinco de Mayo isn't until Saturday," Ben reassured her. "This is only Tuesday, you'll have plenty of time to prepare. And meanwhile, *you* could do *us* a big, big favor... if you would."

On the previous day, he'd told Jimmy that the security on the second floor of the SCI building was beyond his lock-picking skills. That was still true... but if his guess as to the location of the room Faelyn had found herself in was correct, they now had a second way to get there. Using applied topology.

But suggesting that she return there with him would be... tricky. The girl was understandably nervous. Ben drew Ingrid aside and suggested that she try and talk Faelyn into helping her teleport into that room.

It wasn't easy, but by the time Harper came back with jeans and a lacy blouse more or less in Faelyn's size Ingrid had persuaded Faelyn that she owed the people who'd rescued her this favor.

"I'm only asking you to show me the way," she said. "I can't do it by myself because I've never seen the place. But if you can close your eyes and try to remember *exactly* what Shani's bedroom looked like, I can take us both there… and then I'll take you right back here. I promise."

Annelise came back from lunch just in time to see Ingrid and Faelyn step out of the air and back into the third floor of Allandale House.

"Who's *she?*"

"Another of Shani Chayyaputra's victims," Ben said.

Annelise sniffed. "Well, I can certainly see the appeal of *that* one!" She looked down at Faelyn, who was filling out Harper's blouse and jeans with considerably more exuberance than Harper would have displayed. Seams stretched, buttons strained, fabric pulled taut over curves, and all in all the clothes only emphasized Faelyn's dramatic figure. Just to make matters worse, her long blond hair was still wet, and now the blouse was wet as well.

"Now, now, let's not start that again," Ben said nervously. "Yesterday Ingrid jumped to conclusions, don't you do it today."

"We're just wondering," Ingrid said, "why all the people you've rescued from Shani just happen to be short, busty blondes."

"Um… they're his type? And it's not like we can pick, Ingrid. All the fish look alike."

"What have fish got to do with anything?" Faelyn demanded. She seemed to have completely repressed any watery memories by now.

"Uh, not important. Ingrid, did you get a fix on the room? Good! Harper, can you take Faelyn home?" Ben wiped his forehead as the two girls left. Conventionally. By the staircase. Even given Faelyn's demonstrated ability to not notice anything paranormal, Ben felt happier knowing that she wouldn't have to ignore any more odd events. "Believe me, Annelise," he said, "I would rather *not* have to deal with any more rescued females." He brightened. "But then, I won't have to. There are only two machalee fish left, and they have to be Will and Eli. It'll be a nice change, rescuing somebody rational. I can hardly wait."

"Unless there are more prisoners in his private apartment," Ingrid pointed out.

"What, has he got an aquarium there too?"

"I didn't see one," she admitted, "but then, I was barely there long enough to memorize one view of the bedroom. Faelyn was in a hurry to get out of there, and I don't blame her."

"By contrast," Ben said, "I'm in a hurry to get in there. We can't spring another fish until tomorrow, might as well spend the time searching Shani's private quarters. You up for a return trip?"

"The sooner the better. I really need to take more time and get a better fix on the place. You know what, we should take Colton too," Ingrid suggested. "The more of us know how to get into Shani's rooms, the better. Is Prakash here?"

"Of course not." Ben called to Colton and he joined them. The three of them linked hands, funneled stars into the teleportation, and let Ingrid define their final location.

"A round bed?" Colton shook his head. "Never saw one of *those* outside the movies."

"I wonder how you make it?" Naturally that would be Ingrid's first question.

"This one might be in some movies." Ben had spotted a discreetly placed lens. He opened a pair of intricately carved cabinet doors and revealed a state-of-the-art digital video recording system.

Ingrid picked up the black remote that was lying on a bedside table. "Remote-controlled video? I wonder if all his playmates knew they were being filmed."

"The more we learn about this 'god,' Colton said, "the less he resembles a god. To me. I guess I don't understand Hindu theology."

"Ok, his bedroom arrangements are sleazy, and we already know from Faelyn that he's not particular about how he gets girls in here, and I could have predicted all of that from the way he tried to treat Annelise last winter," Ben summed up briskly. "How about looking for something we *don't* already know about?"

They looked, but kept getting distracted by the over-the-top décor and furnishings. The furniture was upholstered with red and purple velvet, with gold-stamped designs and gold braid trim. Anything that could be made of wood was carved into exotic shapes and painted in brilliant primary colors. Drawers opened out of strange places – they found one underneath a chair, two shallow ones in a door, and a whole set of tiny drawers spiraling up a carved post in the living room. Hanging fabrics rich with embroidery released clouds of musky scent when they were pushed aside. Stained glass windows shed rainbows of light on the rooms, creating confusing shadows.

"This apartment reminds me of a rajah's palace," Ingrid said.

Ben blinked and Colton stared. "Exactly when did you ever tour a rajah's palace?"

"Prakash talked me into going to *Jodhaa Akbar.*"

"Jimmy didn't mind?"

"He went too." Ingrid saw their expressions and flushed. "Look, it was right after that business in January, okay? Prakash was depressed because he'd finally understood that Thalia was never going to go out with him, and Dr. Verrick asked me to try and cheer him up. But after Thalia's experiences, I wasn't about to go to the movies with him unless Jimmy sat between us."

"The things we never guess about our colleagues," Ben said. "Fascinating insight – well, at least we know what Shani's decorator's inspiration was. Isn't there anything useful in here?"

There didn't seem to be. The spiral of miniature drawers housed some unfaceted stones that might have been sapphires, which was interesting in a way but didn't give them any insight into Shani's latest dirty tricks. Neither did the stack of frozen curries in the freezer in the kitchen nook, the decorative wrought-iron grille that partitioned off the dining area, or the iron trident hung high over the velvet couch in the living room.

"That thing makes me nervous," Colton complained of the trident.

"It's just a decoration."

"Yeah, but why'd he hang it with the points facing down? Would *you* like to sit under something sharp like that?"

"I wouldn't like to sit down in this place at all," Ingrid sniffed, "unless I were wearing a Hazmat suit. One more tacky decoration doesn't make that much difference. Why do you suppose anybody thought it a good idea to embed blue crystals into an iron trident? It looks like some piece of junk to sell to tourists."

"The whole place looks like that," Ben said gloomily. "If we ever dispose of Shani, his employees could make money offering guided tours of the apartment." He thought of a bright side. "At least he's not keeping any prisoners in here. So those last two tagged fish have to be Will and Eli."

8. Headstrong, reckless and irritating

Wimberley, Wednesday

For once, I was first on the deck for breakfast the next morning. The crunchy granola wasn't the attraction; it was the coffee urn. I hadn't been getting my minimum daily requirement of coffee since coming to Wimberley, and I'd finally made a connection between that and the persistent headache that had been bothering me. I was there before Margo had even finished setting out the day's ration of cardboard and raisins. On this cloudy morning I had hopes of being able to caffeinate myself adequately before, say, Webster showed up to intensify the headache.

Unfortunately, pouring myself a cup of the Inner Light Guest House's coffee awakened another persistent headache – the one threaded through my belt loops. Mr. M. had insisted on accompanying me today, saying that after last night's near-disaster we needed renewed and redoubled vigilance. Once he smelled the coffee, of course, he changed that to "renewed and redoubled coffee."

This was a problem of some delicacy. I did want Mr. M. to be happy enough to resume his masquerade as a belt before any of SCI's employees turned up; they would probably not take well to the sight of my elaborate belt buckle unwinding itself and complaining. But coffee has a way of making Mr. M. a bit *too* happy. He starts doing things like whizzing around the ceiling. And singing. And getting distracted from whatever he had been planning to

75

do. That last would make him useless as a guard, but it hardly mattered since the first two symptoms would probably empty the guest house at high speed. He was currently in a classic rock phase: specifically, this week, in a Doors phase. By the time he got through "Riders on the Storm," there'd probably be nobody left but me and Lensky – ah, I mean 'Brian Lester.'

"Coffee later," I promised him.

"*You* are indulging now."

"I," I said as sternly as I could, "do not react to caffeine by dancing on the tabletops and singing."

"What a pity," said 'Brian Lester' behind me.

At the first sound of his voice Mr. M. had whipped back into his disguise shape, an intricate knot of silver scales surrounding his beak. Now he loosened the knot enough to say, "I will not sing."

"*Promise?*"

"I swear by the Lights of the Medes, no music shall pass my beak... as long as the nectar of the gods does pass through my beak."

Blackmail or promise? It was hard to tell. I held the coffee cup just below his head for long enough for him to slurp up about a quarter of a cup. Any more, and he might start forgetting his promises, the fragility of my position here, and the entire concept of covert action. So far, the day was peaceful. It would be nice if it could stay that way.

"If I promise not to sing," Lensky said, "will you be extra nice to me too?"

"Oh, maybe…. if you play your cards right…"

"How about if I return your property?" He dangled a bit of red silk in front of me.

"Stop waving those around!" I grabbed my panties and tucked them into a pocket. Fortunately, they weren't bulky. "What are you trying to do, blow my cover?"

"I might ask you the same thing," said Lensky. "You *are* aware that you left your panties under my bed last night?"

"Oh, is that where they got to?"

"I had to stand on them for fifteen minutes," he said, "when your buddy Webster came in to 'talk' to me. I thought he was never going away."

"Oh, that explains the huge muddy footprints. Well, it's not *my* fault. I'm not the one who threw them under the bed."

"Threw what under the bed?"

I was really a terrible spy. I had not, for instance, learned to keep one eye on the door at all times. Now here was Ginny, looking bright and bouncy and curious. "Ah, my sandals," I improvised. "I had to fish under the bed with a coat hanger to retrieve them this morning."

"And I was just mentioning that despite Sally's protestations of innocence, it can hardly be coincidental that all sorts of things wind up under her bed," Lensky said.

"Oh." Ginny looked confused, as well she might be. "I guess you've known Sally for a long time, then?"

"Not nearly long enough," said Lensky, "but I'm hoping to get to know her much better soon." Behind Ginny's back, he winked at me.

Ginny had been only the leading edge of the breakfast invasion; the other employees were close behind her, and conversation died down in favor of the determined chewing required to get through Margo's granola. I filled a bowl and moved to the other side of the deck, away from Lensky and his double-entendres.

That was peaceful, but it also left me isolated when Webster strolled through the door. "*Sally*," he purred. "I've been hearing so much about you."

"What, already? Isn't it kind of early to start gossiping?" I hadn't even started on my second cup of coffee. It was still relatively cool on the deck. Too bad Webster had such a gift for poisoning the atmosphere.

"I sent your picture to some acquaintances. They recognized you."

"How depressing," I drawled, "to think we have mutual acquaintances." I started visualizing an instance of the Brouwer Fixed-Point Theorem, just in case I was going to need to teleport out of here in the next few minutes.

"They said you aren't Shani's fiancée, you're just some girl who graduated from UT a couple of years ago. Math major."

Well, nothing damning in that. Damning would be somebody saying, 'That's Thalia Kostis, not Sally Bhatia,' and wouldn't he have led with that card if he had it? I raised one eyebrow. "Webster – *Webby*," I corrected myself, "are you claiming that being a brilliant and talented mathematics student is incompatible with planning to marry Shani? I've got news for you: some men *like* bright women."

"That is low, Webby, even for you," said Hien.

"He's probably judging Shani by himself," Ginny said. "*You* don't like bright women, do you, Webby? We scare you."

Webster scoffed. "Don't overrate yourself. Being an office manager isn't exactly rocket science, Gin." He looked around, trying to bring the guys into the conversation. "Seriously, don't any of you find it strange that I could find plenty of people who recognize Sally as a math major, but none who know her as Shani's fiancée?"

"Clearly," I said, "your friends don't know me very well." If they did, they would have spilled my real name. "That is quite a relief. I'm reassured to know that my *real* friends don't have anything in common with your crowd... Webby."

Margo interrupted the nasty little showdown then and hustled us off to the other, larger deck for more Activities. Having team members verbally eviscerate each other on the dining deck probably wasn't good for the guest house's reviews.

"That little worm is seriously out to get you," Lensky murmured to me when we were paired off for a personality analysis game. "What did you do to him?" And aloud, "My three adjectives for Sally are headstrong, reckless and irritating."

"Nothing!" I leaned back on the bench and put my elbows on the picnic table behind me, prepared to defend myself. "Look, *I* don't know what his problem is. And my adjectives for Br... *Brian* are stubborn, patronizing and overprotective."

"Guys, you're supposed to do one negative, one neutral and one positive," Margo corrected us. "Like Hien and Chet."

"Chet is conceited, blond and clever," Hien said on cue.

"And Hien is sarcastic, fluent, and quick-witted."

"Sally and Brian, why don't you try again?"

What with all the instructions, shuffling people into and out of teams, and quick changes of activities, it was really hard to find ways to snoop on the others. What I really wanted was to get Alec alone and learn what he'd been going to say the previous day when Yung-Su interrupted him. Why couldn't I have been paired with him for this personality game? Or for the next activity, or the next? A suspicious person might think Margo had been bribed to keep the two of us apart.

Lensky ditched the last activity before lunch with some excuse about having business phone calls to make, and he wasn't back when we gathered on the dining deck. I looked at the buffet table with foreboding. Possibly Lensky had disappeared because he'd been warned: today's lunch was open-faced tuna melts with tomato and red pepper slices. Margo said that he'd had to go into town on some errand. If I'd known, I would have asked him to get me something to eat. Something that had no connection with canned fish.

He was late getting back, too; we had to do the first two activities with an odd number of players. He slid into place after the second afternoon activity (Team Building Treasure Hunt; don't ask), looking remarkably smug for a man who'd shown up just in time to be trapped in a "game" called Fear in a Hat.

"What canary did you consume over lunch?" I asked him while Ginny and Alec were arguing about whether "girls with multiple piercings" was a valid fear or something Alec had made up to avoid digging deep into his psyche.

"There are ways and ways to learn things," Lensky said, and he refused to go into detail.

"It doesn't matter," I told him. "I will probably expire from starvation before you have a chance to reveal your nefarious schemes."

"Ah. Come to my room before dinner?"

"If I have the strength to climb the stairs."

"Use your other abilities?"

"I don't have the strength to do that either." Teleporting was hell on the blood sugar, and mine was already dangerously low.

"I brought mini bacon quiches. And cheese Danish. And grapes. Oh, and chocolate."

I decided that I could forgive a lot of secrecy and games-playing in a man who had such excellent grasp of the important things in life.

In the brief spell between activities and dinner, Lensky forked over enough mini quiches to save my life and told me what he'd been up to. He'd gone in to Wimberley to meet Meadow Melendez, who had bought the technical equipment he needed in Austin. Then, while the rest of us were making fools of ourselves after lunch, he'd bugged all the other rooms.

"Voice-activated recordings," he said, "digital, of course. I don't even have to retrieve the devices; I can remote-download them to my phone."

"Very nice," I said.

Lensky smiled. "Those of us who can't apply topology do have a few real-world skills. Who knows, sometimes the classical solutions are still the best."

"And you're going to be unbearably smug if your little bugs glean more information than I can get by applying all the topology I know."

"Do you think that's likely?"

"You could hardly get much less. The problem with being around all of them at once is that it's almost impossible to get one of them alone and lead the conversation where I want it to go." Yung-Su, for instance, had been hovering over Alec like a watchful mother ever since he'd interrupted whatever Alec had been about to tell me. That was suspicious behavior, sure, but it wasn't information. I broke off a piece of dark chocolate and put it in my mouth. Chocolate, at least, always delivered. That was more than you could say for me, this week.

"Oh well, just think of this as a vacation. Enjoy the resort amenities."

"Tuna salad, a very narrow bed, and sharing a shower with Hien and Ginny? It's more like summer camp."

He slipped an arm around me and hugged me close. "Okay, I'll enjoy it for both of us."

"Actually, I never went to summer camp," I confessed.

"Oh? Well, you didn't miss much. It was never this good. There was a phalanx of nuns with rulers between the boys' cabins and the girls.'"

I leaned against his broad, solid shoulder. "We still have to sneak around to be together. Not so different from camp, then."

He slid a hand down to my waist. "I could show you some differences... Where's Mr. M.?"

"Napping. When the caffeine wore off, he decided to sleep rather than observe more team-building exercises. But it's almost time for dinner."

Lensky indicated the remaining food stash. "We could skip dinner."

I was tempted. But – "Both of us? Webster would hot-foot it up here in the hope of catching us *in flagrante*."

As it turned out, I did miss most of dinner, but not because I was doing anything as much fun as playing summer camp with Lensky. I'd only begun to push this night's offering around the plate with my fork when Mom called and I excused myself to deal with another list of instructions, demands, and urgent questions. Having indulged freely in Lensky's quiche, pastries and chocolate, I was just as happy not to have to pretend an interest in Mexican Macaroni and Cheese. The one bite I'd taken suggested that the "Mexican" part was based on somebody having dumped a jar of mild salsa in with the yellow powdered cheese. This is the kind of provocation that could lead to another war with Mexico if they ever found out about it.

I would have bet money that even my mother hadn't had time to think of yet another thing I had to do immediately. Clearly, I would have lost that money.

"No, Mom, I haven't thought about a wedding program."

Squawk. Squawk. What was wrong with me that I hadn't thought of that?

"Well, I hadn't thought about it because we don't really need one, do we? We're getting married at Saint Elias. In the Greek Orthodox rite." The only kind of wedding my family would ever consider. Lucky for me that Lensky, having been baptized Catholic, was eligible for marriage in our church. "That means the sequence of events is already cast in concrete." I'd been dragged to enough weddings for classmates and children of Mom's friends that I could recite it in my sleep. "Rings, candle lighting, wedding crowns, readings, wine, procession around the altar, proclamation, blessings. Who needs a program?"

Evidently we needed a program in order to tell everybody that what had happened at every single Greek Orthodox wedding since the dawn of time was going to happen at this one too.

Perhaps she felt that an official program would head off possible unscheduled events such as The Bride Passes Out From Terror or The Bride

Spills the Wine All Over Her Beautiful Dress or The Bride Trips Over Her Own Feet. The possibilities for disaster, once I thought about the details, dialed up my panic from eleven to twelve. Fortunately, I could slide out from under this one the same way I'd done with the invitations. "Get Andros to format it and send it to me, I'll look over it… um… later."

Now that I'd been in Lensky's room twice, I could easily teleport to it. That was much safer than taking the stairs. It would have been safer still if I'd waited until everybody was asleep, but after yet another excursion into the Land of Brides I wasn't willing to wait. I needed him to tell me that we were both going to get through this ordeal. Also, I had remembered that along with the munchies, he'd bought a bottle of wine that we hadn't yet opened.

There are lots of advantages to being with somebody who already knows you well. For one thing, he didn't shriek and point when I stepped out of the air into his room. For another, he had already stolen an extra glass and deployed the corkscrew.

"When I heard you talking to your mother," he said, offering me a tumbler that was not nearly full enough of white wine, "I figured you'd remember where you could get a drink."

I tossed about half my wine back before thanking him. "Weddings," I said, glowering, "are *extremely unfair*. I have to go crazy dealing with flowers and programs and cake tastings, and all you have to do is show up at the church."

Lensky shrugged. "Hey, I didn't make the rules. Anyway, I'm perfectly willing to taste any cake you want to bring me."

"Just remember," I said, holding out a tumbler that had somehow become completely empty, "that part of your job is keeping me supplied with enough booze to silence that little voice."

"Little voice?"

"The one screaming, 'Run! Run now!'"

Lensky poured me a generous second serving. "I certainly don't want you to run away, so I guess I'll have to humor your alcoholic tendencies for the time being." But he held the glass just out of reach. "No more sitting on the only chair while you drink," he told me. "When I ply a girl with liquor, I like to have her close at hand." He sat on the bed and pulled me down onto his lap. I took the glass back and leaned my head on his shoulder. It was the best part of the whole day.

"If I'd thought summer camp would be anything like this," I told him, "I'd have pestered my parents to send me. But I have a feeling it would have been lacking in some vital features."

"No booze?"

"And no incredibly hot guys."

I needed my hands free; the obvious solution was to finish my wine and put the glass down. His shirt was partly unbuttoned already. I slipped a hand inside and ran it over his chest, enjoying his indrawn breath.

"I'm pretty sure Our Lady of Good Counsel Camp was sadly lacking in gorgeous girls of easy virtue," he said.

"Hey, watch who you're calling easy, or tomorrow night I'll make out behind the cafeteria with somebody else."

"I retract it. I retract everything. It's not that you're easy, it's just that you can't withstand my combination of sexy looks and incredible animal magnetism, right?" He reached both hands up behind me, under my shirt, and unfastened my bra.

"Not to mention your smooth moves. When are you going to learn how to do that with one hand?"

It wasn't trivially simple, but this time I did keep track of my underwear and made sure to retrieve everything before teleporting back to my own room.

9. What is your good name?

By Wednesday Ben felt he had the revised version of their secret mission at SCI down to a formula. Drive over to the SCI building with Harper, help her lug her stepladder and tools inside, scoop out a tagged fish, remove the tag, offer clothing and reassurance to the freaked-out human being who had no idea what had just happened to them. Then they'd take the rescuee back to Allandale House, Harper would rush off to take care of the clients she'd been neglecting due to the demands of fish rescues, and they'd try to find out if the new rescuee could shed any light on Shani Chayyaputra's plans.

"Faelyn wasn't much use," he groused, "except that now we know he doesn't limit his fish curse to business opponents. He's perfectly willing to attack people based on pure spite. Which is not a great surprise. I wish we'd got Will out instead of Faelyn, he may have some idea what Chayyaputra's up to."

"*Everybody* deserves rescuing," Harper said.

Ben backed up. "Right, sure, I'm not regretting saving Faelyn. I'm just saying I would have been okay with leaving her for last. At least today we're bound to get some useful information, whether it's Will or Eli we transform."

This time he'd added a flatbed dolly to the equipment they had to bring inside. The thing was heavy and its wheelbase had no discernible relationship to the spacing of the stairs in front of the building. After he wrestled it onto the lowest stairs, Harper put down her stepladder and came to help him. Even for the two of them, it was a job and a half wrestling the thing up another couple of stairs.

"I don't know if it's worth it," Harper panted.

"Yes, but it'll be easy once we get it inside..." Ben stopped grappling with the dolly, stood up and slapped his forehead. "I'm an idiot. Harper, let go." He grasped the handle of the dolly firmly and took a deep breath. "*Brouwer.*"

He and the dolly disappeared from the steps.

"Harper, unlock the doors," he called to her from inside the lobby.

"How did you *do* that?" she asked when she found him sitting on the dolly and breathing hard.

"Usual way," he said between gasps. "You've – seen me – do things like that – before."

"Have I? I've been carefully not thinking about it," Harper semi-explained. "That's hard to do when you make yourself and a dolly disappear right in front of me."

"Didn't disappear," Ben said, "just... moved the thing really, really fast, okay?"

"And through locked doors." Harper was pale; her freckles were unbecomingly dark against her white face.

Ben took another deep breath. "Slight miscalculation... takes way too much energy to move a big inanimate object that I can barely pick up. I should've used my stars."

"You do this stuff with a*strology?* I never realized it was actually good for anything!"

Ben figured he'd already allowed Harper to see enough to justify giving him several lifetime sentences if the Agency decided to take nondisclosure agreements seriously. He could hardly be in worse trouble for telling her just a little more. He reached into his pocket and pulled out a glittering cloud of tiny points of light swirling and dancing on his palm, fizzing with joyful energy. "Not astrology. *Stars.*"

She shook her head. "Ben, holding your hand out like that doesn't explain *anything.*"

Oh. Right. Only Mr. M. – the original source – and the Center's research fellows could see the tiny lights that amplified their topological applications. To anybody else, he was holding a handful of nothing. "Can't explain it. Sorry. Probably just as well. If I tell you too much the Agency might want to lock you up."

Harper shook her head again. "I swear, I'd stay well away from you people if it weren't for the fish torture." She thought it over. "And I'd think you were delusional if I hadn't *seen* the transformations. Oh, well. Just two more fish and then I can go back to pretending that none of this actually happened. Have you caught your breath yet?"

Ben nodded and put their largest plastic tub on the dolly. From the stepladder, Harper scooped aquarium water into the tub until it was nearly full – stopping once or twice to replace tropical fish that had swum into the dipper unnoticed. "Blasted tetras," she grumbled. "They're so little and fast and they get into anything, and they're too dumb to notice when they're in trouble."

"I don't think any fish are noted for a high I.Q." Ben commented, handing her the small net with a couple of attempted escapee tetras. "I wonder... the people we've brought back seem to have fully functioning brains. Ergo, the transformation isn't destructive. I wonder if they *thought* at all while they were in fish form?"

"From what Faelyn said, it doesn't sound likely. Gimme the big net." Harper gave Ben her dipper and took the long-handled fish net from him.

Ben snorted. "I don't believe Faelyn thinks a whole lot when she's in girl form. No, I'll have to ask Will or Eli. Whichever one we get today."

Harper leaned perilously over the aquarium and jabbed her fishing net towards the bottom. "If you ask me, your friends aren't that smart in fish form either. They're hiding under that big lump of coral where I can't get at them."

"That's not necessarily stupid of them," Ben said. "Think of it from their point of view. They've seen us take two of their kind out of the tank and we never brought them back. For all they know, we're thinking of them as *lunch*. Hey, hey, don't lean that far over!" He made a grab for Harper's ankles and barely saved her from plummeting into the tank.

"Thank you," she said breathlessly when her balance was restored. "Having a hundred-and-twenty-pound foreign body plunge into the tank would have been a terrible shock for the fish. Not to mention shedding hair and skin cells and… well, it could have been *bad*."

"Not much fun for you either."

"Oh, well, I don't melt," Harper said absently. "I'd just drip-dry, no harm done. The fish are much more important."

"Okay, to avoid accidentally poisoning the fish tank, why don't you let me handle the net? I'm taller; I won't have to practically hang off the top of the tank by my toes to sweep the bottom. And you can go and coax one of those machalee fish to come out from behind the coral."

"How?"

"You're the fish expert. Think of something!"

By the time Ben had positioned the net again, one of the machalees had come out into the more open area of the tank and was swimming back and forth in its usual monotonous loop. He scooped it up, brought the net out of the tank and dipped it into the plastic tub of water. Harper took hold of the fish, very gently, and extricated it from the folds of the net.

It took two of them to wheel the tub out of the lobby and into the office space, one to push and one to guide a dolly which was bent on turning in a circle clockwise. But that was still a great deal easier than trying to move the tub on its own.

"*Now* we'll get to talk to someone sensible who's been through the transformation," Ben said, feeling for the connecting bar on the fish tag while Harper held the fish still. "Here—ah! Got it!" He positioned the bolt cutter blades, stood up and pushed them together with all his strength. There was a sharp click as the blades met, and then the increasingly familiar sense of energy being drained from air and water. The lights dimmed, the temperature dropped towards freezing, a film of ice kept trying to form on the surface of the water. And something that was no longer quite a fish thrashed, rose out of the water, took shape.

"Ben?" Harper said hesitantly as the shape became solid flesh.

"Mm?"

"Is – one of Jimmy's friends – very short, and very brown, and kind of *old?*"

Ben shook his head, staring at the naked man standing in the tub.

"I'm pretty sure that's not Will. Or Eli."

Harper picked up the bathrobe and offered it to the strange man. He pressed his palms together and bowed to her, then wrapped the bathrobe around himself.

"Give him a hand," Harper said, "I don't think he can climb out on his own."

Ben reached out a hand, then moved closer to the tub so that their new companion could lean on his arm. It was true that while the dolly had made it easier to move a large tub of water, it had also aggravated the difficulties faced by a rescuee. Now, in addition to stepping over the foot-high edge of the tub, they'd also have to step down an extra six inches from the bed of the dolly to reach the floor. And for someone as short as this guy, that would be quite the stretch. Ben had to practically lift him out of the tub.

When he had both feet safely on the carpet, the little old man bowed again, repeating that peculiar gesture of pressing his hands together.

"I am giving many thanks for preserving of my life and restoration of freedom," he said in a heavily accented voice.

"Who are you?" Ben demanded. *Only one fish left, and we're still missing two people.*

"Pandit Navinchandra Balakrishnan, of Hindu Temple Austin, your most devoted servant," said the man, bowing yet again. "Pandit is my title, Navinchandra Balakrishnan is my name. And may I inquire, sir, what is your good name?"

He seemed a lot calmer than Renata or Faelyn had been, though his experience had been much the same as theirs. Perhaps being a Hindu priest, Ben thought, had accustomed him to volatile gods working their will on hapless humans.

But when he voiced that thought, the Pandit rejected it almost violently. "No, and no, and no! This being is taking the name of the god, but he is *not* the god."

"What is he, then?"

"He is partial avatar of Shani *dev*," the Pandit said. "It is common misunderstanding among ordinary people that Shani is god of suffering, cruelty and despair. But this is error!"

"So… what is the real Shani *dev* god of?"

"Something much more frightening," the Pandit said dramatically. "He is god of karma! Or you might say, of justice."

"There seems to be damned little justice about the way this, ah, avatar is behaving," Ben said.

"Yes, yes. He understands only dark side of Shani." The little man launched on a detailed description of the true god Shani, waving his hands so vigorously that the robe threatened to fall open. "He is associated with Saturn, thus his gravity is more than this planet's. What we plan or do, both good and bad, the weight of Shani's power lies upon us and we receive the consequences of our actions. To man who thinks and does good, Shani *dev* is friend. But for man who does bad deeds, he is Sade Saathi, disaster and an enemy. This avatar is not properly understanding whole truth of Shani *dev*."

Ben was beginning to feel overwhelmed with theology. Better to concentrate on what had actually happened.

"Is that why Shani *avatar* turned you into a fish? A theological argument?"

"I was here to represent his errors to this avatar," the Pandit agreed. "I was also attempting to banish him, to send him back into the true god so that he would know the completeness of Shani. But he is more powerful than I realized."

"Clearly. He turned you into a fish. Why a fish? Prakash – a colleague told us that Shani's vehicle is a black bird, and up to now he has worked all his magic using black birds. If he was collecting shape-changed prisoners, I would have expected him to make a flock of ravens. Or maybe grackles, considering this is Austin."

The Pandit nodded, shook his head, nodded again. "Birds are not so easy as fish to keep as prisoners," he said. "Also, some wise men are saying that Shani *dev* is favored by Lord Vishnu, whose first avatar was Matsya, divine fish. Perhaps Shani *avatar* is also drawing upon powers of Lord Vishnu. This is trouble to the maximum! I must return to temple where we will work to weaken this avatar."

"How?"

"We shall make offerings to please Shani *dev*: iron objects, black cloths, black sesame seed. Also, I will recite Shani mantra one hundred plus eight times. This is very powerful mantra for averting wrath of Shani." He took a deep breath and began chanting in a reverberating voice, "Neelanjana Samabhasam Raviputhram Yamagrajam Chaya Marthanda Sambhootham Tham Namamy Shanaishyaram."

"Also," he said, reverting to a normal speaking voice. "will be saying Hanuman *chalisa* on Tuesday and Saturday. As well as many other prayers, and offerings of oil."

Ben thought he wouldn't hold his breath waiting for help from the Hindu temple. "Ah, yes, I see. Great. Would you like us to take you to the temple so you can get right on it?"

Harper drove.

10. I have no fiancée

Wimberley, Thursday

Webster didn't show up on the dining deck for lunch on Thursday, which suggested either that he was up to something (my theory) or that he'd been forewarned about the menu (Lensky's theory). I didn't think the latter was probable. "He already ate tuna salad, tuna noodle casserole, and 'Mexican' mac and cheese. Broccoli lasagna isn't any worse than those." I'd been careful not to serve myself a large portion. I took a cautious bite. "And at least there isn't any tuna in it." Maybe I could hide the rest of mine under the wilted lettuce salad.

"Only you would consider that a positive feature," Lensky murmured. "Tuna would add some protein."

And we had thoughtlessly consumed the rest of Lensky's food stash the night before, after he assured me that midnight feasts were an absolutely necessary part of the summer camp experience. "Want to go in to town tonight and get barbecue?" A body like Lensky's required regular fuel, lots of it, and plenty of protein. Cardboard granola for breakfast and broccoli lasagna for lunch weren't going to sustain him for long.

"Is there a barbecue place in Wimberley?"

"It's Texas. There'll be barbecue." I tried to remember what other options were reasonably close. "Or... if you don't mind a slightly longer drive... we *could* go to the Salt Lick." I hadn't been there for a while and wasn't sure I could teleport there accurately. Prudence suggested we use an actual car to get to the restaurant.

"Salt Lick! You do know how to make a man happy," Lensky said. "Can we park somewhere after dinner?"

"Oh, maybe…" I singsonged, "if you play your cards right…"

"This week is like a tour of the best moments of my adolescence," Lensky said happily. He thought that statement over. "The anticipated ones, anyway. The *actual* moments never quite lived up to my hopes."

Our plans were interrupted by Webster's arrival on the deck. For a smallish guy, he certainly had a heavy step; his boots crashed down on the planks and momentarily halted all conversation. Everybody put down the forks they'd been rather languidly plying and looked up at him.

"Guess what," he announced into the lull, "Mr. C.'s back already. And we just had a *very interesting* little chat."

"Does he want us to come back to the office tomorrow? Or today?" Even Ginny, who claimed that she'd never met a meal she didn't like, appeared to be perfectly willing to miss out on Inner Light's last day and a half of catering.

"We didn't talk about that," Webster said with an ugly smirk. "I *just happened* to mention how much we'd enjoyed meeting his fiancée. And you'll never guess what he said!"

Looking at his satisfied smirk, I had an extremely good guess. Margo Foster was hovering in the doorway behind Webster, looking unhappy; had he already shared his bombshell with her? My mind started whirring. I could teleport myself and Lensky out of here, and then Shani Chayyaputra would know exactly who'd been spying on him. I could endure a very unpleasant conversation and then leave by normal means, possibly keeping at least some of my secrets. Or – was it possible I could talk my way out of this? An idea was beginning to dawn on me. The best part was that I wouldn't even have to lie. For some values of "lie." Our Director, Dr. Verrick, holds that it's not lying to be selective with the truth. Our Indian intern, Prakash, had talked about a marriage arranged by his family…

"He said," Webster announced loudly, "'I have no fiancée!'"

Into the stunned silence that followed, I said, "Of course he did."

"*What?*"

"Haven't you ever heard of an arranged marriage? We haven't been negotiating personally; where there's money on both sides, the complications are daunting. It's best to leave that to one's family. The actual agreement is quite recent. I myself found out only about the same time that squib appeared in *Whirred.*" Shortly afterwards, to be precise – thanks to Ginny. "Shani's been out of town on business; he probably hasn't got the memo yet."

"Oh… Is that why you sounded sort of tentative on Sunday, when I showed you the article?" Ginny asked.

"It sometimes takes a little while for one to fully take in good news." That statement was true enough, and it wasn't my fault if she applied the generality to my present situation.

"This week must have been quite disorienting for you," Hien observed. "Imagine getting the news of your engagement and immediately being thrown together with all of your fiancé's employees!"

"I don't have to imagine it."

"Oh. Right."

Webster broke into this feast of agreement. "Didn't any of you hear me? Sally is *not* Mr. C.'s fiancée. She's an impostor!"

Ginny waved a dismissive hand at him. Her engagement ring looked bigger than ever. Oh-oh, something else to explain. "Oh, dry up, Webby. We heard you, and then we heard Sally, and her explanation makes perfect sense. Is that why you don't have an engagement ring, Sally? I was wondering, but I didn't like to ask."

"That, and the fact that I don't want one. I lose stuff. Frankly, I don't want the responsibility of walking around with a huge expensive rock on my finger." True enough; I'd already been over that with Lensky. "And you can imagine the kind of ring Shani would think appropriate!" Every sentence was true, even if the last one didn't have any connection with the first two.

Fortunately, Alec chose that moment to make a crack that diverted the inquisitors.

"So what's he going to get you, a nose ring? You wouldn't lose *that.*"

"Alec, that's racist!" Ginny hissed.

"*I* don't think she's even Indian," Webster said. "She's not dark enough."

"Webster, *that's* racist!" Hien said.

"I can personally assure you," Lensky said loudly, "that Sally has been planning her wedding for quite some time."

My mother had, anyway.

His interruption broke up the question-and-answer session long enough for me to excuse myself without looking like I was running away. I shamelessly abandoned the broccoli lasagna. God never intended lasagna to be *green*.

"You're just lucky Webster didn't think to ask Shani about 'Brian Lester,' I murmured after we escaped the dining deck.

"He seems to dislike you so much that he can't think about anything else. You must have done *something* to piss him off."

"Not a blessed thing, I swear by the sacred knucklebone of Saint Elias. I think he came out of his mother's womb squint-eyed and suspicious. Assuming he even had a mother. You ready for the afternoon games?"

"I have to make some calls," said Lensky, retreating.

He looked desperately worried. Why? I thought I'd slithered out of Webster's latest trap very neatly. And having given up on extracting any meaningful information out of all these nice young people with their average brains and super-sized egos, I intended to indulge myself this afternoon by *winning*.

First up was something involving tossing eggs from one person to another; I think the object was for all of us to end up spattered with egg and agreeing that we weren't perfect. Well, I may throw like a girl, but I have finely-honed skills in small object manipulation. I wouldn't say 'perfect,' but certainly good enough for government work.

I was basking in my egg-free status, and Margo was handing out cue cards for the next game, when Lensky burst out of the residence building and came galloping over to the big deck. "Can I borrow Sally for a minute?" He didn't wait for permission, grabbing my hand and drawing me away from the group. "We have to get back to Austin," he announced, "sorry to miss the rest of this wonderful retreat, but it's urgent."

"What is it, Mr. C. can't wait to see Sally?"

"Something like that. Come on, Sally, pack your bag." He hustled me into the residence building and up the stairs.

That little job didn't take me long. It's always easier to pack for going home than it was to pack for the outward journey; all you have to do is look around the room and fill your bag with everything that isn't guest house property. Given the apparent rush, after packing I even slung Mr. M. around my neck rather than taking the time to thread him through my belt loops. But Lensky was even faster; he was waiting for me at the door downstairs.

"If it's an emergency, shouldn't I teleport us?" I asked under my breath.

"It's an emergency," Lensky agreed, "but not one that will be improved by hurrying once we're out of here. I need to get my car back to Austin. And I can fill you in on the way."

But once he'd shaken the dust of Inner Light Guest House off his tires, he seemed reluctant to start talking. When we reached Dripping Springs I decided it was on me to break the silence.

"So what kind of emergency demands that we leave immediately, but it doesn't matter when we get to Austin?"

He sighed. "I should think that would be obvious. Remember what Webster said? Chayyaputra's back."

"So?"

"So what happens if he decides to go to Wimberley and have a look at his so-called fiancée? He knows he's not engaged. He also knows what you look like. I don't see a good outcome for that scenario. I wanted to pull you out of there before you got caught."

"Oh."

He was right; I should have thought of that for myself. I had been too wrapped up in the clever way I'd danced around Webster's attack and re-established my credibility.

I watched swathes of Texas sweeping by. The brooding silence resumed, and I felt it was heavier than before. Mr. M. was the only occupant of the car who wasn't on edge; he was snoring gently. Eventually I asked, "What are you not telling me?"

"What makes you think there's something I'm not telling you?"

"The quality of your silence." I'm not a telepath, but I do know Brad Lensky. What filled this car was *not* a restful silence between two people who know each other well enough to feel no need for conversation.

"Wait till we get to Allandale House, okay? You'll want to hear it from Jimmy, and there's no point in going through it twice."

I thought there might be some point in relieving my anxiety, but it wasn't worth starting a fight with Lensky. Probably. We were already on Mopac; in a few minutes I'd know whatever was wrong.

But what did Jimmy have to do with it? If Chayyaputra's return had caused a crisis, wouldn't it affect the other topologists, rather than the support staff?

Indeed it had affected us, as I learned when we got to the office. Since it was the middle of the afternoon and there were people around, we took the conventional route: climbing the stairs.

The double doors at the top of the stairs opened on a scene of confusion and despair. Jimmy was slumped over Annelise's desk, head in his hands. Ingrid was tentatively patting him on the shoulder, in the manner one would expect from somebody brought up in a family that eschewed casual touching. Standing in one corner, looking bemused, was a short stocky guy with wet hair, wearing clothes clearly designed for a much taller person.

"Where's Annelise?" was my first, probably irrelevant question.

Jimmy jerked his head towards Meadow Melendez' office. The door was closed. "She's in there with Meadow, having hysterics."

Okay, maybe it had been a relevant question, because Annelise had never become hysterical before. She had handled everything from topologists flying around the office to being magically whisked to India with admirable aplomb. And if she was upset, why wasn't Ben taking care of her? Where *was* Ben, anyway? Come to think of it, it was also out of character for Meadow, our resident robotics engineer, to put up with Annelise being hysterical. I'd have expected her to tell Annelise to stop making that (expletive) noise and get a (profanity plus obscenity) hold of herself.

I looked at Lensky. "Is this the emergency you wouldn't tell me about?"

"More like the results of it."

"Will somebody *please* tell me what's been going on here? Brad?"

He gestured at Jimmy. "Ask *him*."

"It's a long story," said Jimmy, raising his head. His eyes looked haunted. "It all started Monday, when Ben teleported me into SCI's lobby."

Of course. I should have known somebody was up to something when they insisted it was vitally important I spend the week in Wimberley, spying on a bunch of clueless employees. If I'd been here—But I hadn't. And was it something we were allowed to talk about in front of outsiders? I tilted my head towards the stocky stranger. "Ah, should we…"

"He's already been transformed into a fish and back again," Jimmy said wearily. "It's a little late to worry about non-disclosure agreements."

"A… fish?"

Lensky nodded. If he confirmed this story, it must be true.

"Wait a minute." I pulled an empty chair up to the desk and dropped into it. This had the definite feel of a story that you didn't want to hear without a place to sit down. "I didn't realize any of us knew how to transform someone into a fish." If I'd had that ability, I might have turned our reluctant intern into a fish last January when he was making a nuisance of himself. Anybody as free with his hands as Prakash could only be improved by having to live without hands for a while.

"We don't," Jimmy said. "Chayyaputra does."

I began to grasp the nature of the emergency. "He's back in town, by the way."

"I know *that*," Jimmy said with a groan. "Now." He looked at Lensky. "Your call to warn me was a bit late."

Tardily I realized that we were missing a couple of people who really should be in on this, if it was a question of – once again – opposing Shani Chayyaputra's black magic of black birds with applied topology. "Where's Colton?"

Jimmy nodded towards the partition that sealed off the Research Department offices. "Studying transformation algorithms. Not that it'll do us much good."

"And I assume Ben is doing the same?" Although I couldn't see Ben diving into abstruse topological theory while Annelise was so upset.

"Uh, no. Ben is… not here right now. That's kind of the problem."

Oh.

And it must be a very bad value of 'not here' to have sent Annelise into hysterics.

"Tell me everything. From the beginning," I suggested for the second time.

11. Two thousand pounds of water

Before they started the story, I had to wake up Mr. M. and give him some coffee, because I wanted him to hear everything too. He didn't get very much coffee, though; I believe I've mentioned the deleterious effects of a caffeine high on his behavior.

Jimmy started with their Monday intrusion into the lobby of SCI. He summarized as best he could, given how much there was to tell. I had lots of questions, but managed to refrain from interrupting as he recounted the surprise of Harper's arrival, Ben's determination to remove a painful and crippling tag from one of the unfortunate fish in the aquarium, and the subsequent appearance of a naked, screaming woman standing in the plastic tub where they'd isolated the first fish to work on it.

"She was a little happier after Ben borrowed some clothes from Annelise for her," Jimmy finished, "but I got the impression she never wanted to see or hear from us again." Ingrid flushed, and it was clear Jimmy had left out some parts of the story. But I could find out the good stuff later.

Jimmy seemed to have run down. "So then you rescued all of the other fish that had these iron tags on them," I prompted.

"Yes, but we couldn't do that on Monday."

"How come?"

He explained how transforming just one fish had sucked so much energy out of its surroundings that the lobby was freezing cold and even the water in the aquarium was dangerously cold for the tropical fish in it. "And Harper threw a fit when we even suggested that if we just saved the ones that were people, the other fish were expendable. There were only three other tagged fish, and we figured we could do them one a day – Tuesday, Wednesday, Thursday – and still be out of there with no risk of encountering Shani Chayyaputra. Why did he have to come back a day and a half early?" he all but wailed.

With deep regret, I put aside the question of who the other "fish" had turned into until later. We needed to get to the emergency.

"Okay. I gather he caught you today. What happened to that last fish?"

"Oh, we'd already freed him and brought him back here." Jimmy nodded at the stranger. "That's Will, one of the guys who disappeared from Logan's company. No, we didn't get caught then. We wouldn't have got caught at all if I hadn't wanted to go back and install an improved version of the virus. But we should have had plenty of time!"

He stopped again.

"Okay. You and Ben were in SCI's offices; you to work on the program you sneaked into their system and Ben, presumably, to teleport you in. Chayyaputra surprised you. And— ?"

Jimmy stared at the desk. "He threw this, like, lightning bolt at Ben. Blue lightning. It transformed Ben into a fish," he said in a defeated monotone. "Shani grabbed him and clamped one of those iron tags on his back fin and threw him into the aquarium. I was waiting for him to do the same thing to me, but he didn't. He let me go. He told me to come back to the Center and tell my colleagues what had happened."

He glanced up. "I would have done that anyway. I wasn't following his orders."

"Of course you weren't," said Ingrid, patting his shoulder some more. "And it's not your fault."

"Oh, yes, it is! If I hadn't wanted to do a little last-minute tinkering with the virus... if I'd borrowed Harper's key to get into the office, instead of asking Ben to teleport me..."

"Then he would have transformed you," Ingrid said, "and we'd never have known what happened to you. I think that would have been worse."

For once, I had nothing to say. The horror of Ben's fate was choking me. A *fish*, and Chayyaputra's prisoner. What tortures would he inflict on Ben in retaliation for the invasion of SCI? An image of a fish in those beringed hands, thrashing and choking and slowly dying, tormented me.

"*Thalia.*" Large, warm hands cupped my face, then rested on my shoulders as though Lensky could impart his own strength and sanity by touch. "Thalia, I know what you're doing. You're imagining the worst that can happen."

Well, that was my habit at moments of crisis: picture the worst and then tell myself that I could deal with it.

This, I wasn't so sure I could deal with. I started shaking. *Ben.*

"Cut it out!" Lensky said roughly. His hands tightened on my shoulders and he shook me slightly. "You can't afford to go into a trance now, or let yourself be paralyzed by all the awful things that *might* happen. We need your brains and talents. *Ben* needs you."

But what could I do for him? What could anybody do, now?

I looked at the stranger. "*He* was a fish?"

"We only freed him a few hours ago," Jimmy said.

"Was he damaged in any way?"

"He seems just the same to me, but then I didn't know him all that well before. Will?" Jimmy looked at him.

"I don't feel damaged," said Will. "Confused, yes. Disoriented, yes. Mostly it's as if I went to sleep, had a *really bad* nightmare, and woke up to discover ten weeks had passed while I was dreaming. And apparently I was a fish for those ten weeks. A few hours shouldn't hurt Ben."

"You know him?"

"Ah, we met after he cut the tag off and I became human again. Seemed like a real nice guy. I hope we can get him back."

So did I. Indeed, I tried to follow Lensky's advice and not even think of any other outcome. Get him back. We needed a plan. I tried to think.

"That aquarium – how big is it?"

Jimmy pulled himself together and concentrated. "Um, six feet long.

Three feet high, but it's not on the floor, it's on a kind of a ledge that's three feet tall."

"Oh. I guess stealing the whole thing will be kind of difficult."

"Borrow a calculator?" The stocky man called Will took the one that Ingrid handed to him and started tapping the keys. "How deep is it, Jimmy?"

"Oh, about eighteen inches. I think."

"Thirty-two and a half cubic feet," Will said. "Conversion factor, hmm, I think it's about seven and a half gallons per cubic foot…" More key punching as he muttered to himself. "Approximately two hundred and forty gallons. One gallon weighs, damn, I know it in metric. Converting to liters, about nine hundred liters, one liter weighs one kilogram, so nine hundred kilos times two point two…" He raised his head. "It'll weigh just about two thousand pounds. One ton. And that's just the water."

There was no way the four of us – me, Ingrid, Colton and Prakash – could teleport something that heavy. And that was assuming Prakash would help. His semester of internship was ending and his head was already back in the math department, working on his dissertation. Most days, like today, his body was over there too.

"Okay, then we'll have to scoop him out of the tank. I don't like spending that much time there, but I guess we can go in after Chayyaputra's left for the night."

"He doesn't leave. He has an apartment on the second floor. Decorated," Ingrid said, "in a not-so-tasteful mixture of Indian Rajah and Parisian Brothel."

"How do you know what a Parisian brothel looks like?" Jimmy asked.

"I saw *Souvenirs de la Maison Close*. That's *House of Pleasures* in English," she translated. I have to admit the translation was useful; neither two years of college French nor my crazy Aunt Alesia's French conversation had taught me what you call *that* kind of house in French. University language courses never teach you anything useful, and my aunt was too much of a lady to discuss such subjects. *Maison close*, huh? Never would have guessed it.

Chayyaputra lived right there in the SCI building, right above the offices. And I bet he had the lobby alarmed. No, Ben and Jimmy had been coming and going all week. Well, he'd want to have an alarm now. Possibly he wouldn't have had time to arrange it yet. Our best chance would be to go in as soon as possible. Ingrid and Jimmy agreed with me.

When we reached that point in the discussion Lensky interrupted us. "No! You can't go there. Not this afternoon, not tonight, not any other time."

"Sure we can," I said. "Jimmy must have the location imprinted on his brain by now, and Ingrid and I can teleport with him. We can get Colton to help too.

"*I forbid it.*"

"You're not our boss," Ingrid pointed out. And Dr. Verrick, who had somewhat more clout when it came to forbidding us to do things, was out of the office as so often these days.

"And Harper has everything we need." Jimmy, looking better than he had since I'd come in, started ticking off the required items on his fingers. "Small stepladder, butterfly net, plastic tub, dipper to scoop out water for the tub. Oh, and bolt cutters. We may need to buy those; I don't know where Ben put the ones he bought."

"Everybody shut up, you're not thinking!" Lensky said, somewhat louder. "It's a trap. It's *obviously* a trap. Why do you think he spared Jimmy? So he could tell us what happened to Ben, so we could try to mount a rescue, so he could collect even more of you for his blasted aquarium!" His voice got louder with every clause; he was almost shouting at the end. Since he was standing behind me, I couldn't see him, but I felt sure that vein on his left temple was twitching again.

What he said seemed depressingly probable, but I couldn't think what we could do about it. "We have to rescue Ben. And if that means disabling some of Shani Chayyaputra's traps, we'll just have to do that too."

"Count me in," said Will, unexpectedly. "I can't do any magic tricks—"

"*Applied topology,*" Ingrid corrected him.

"Whatever you call it, *I* can't do it! But if you could use some muscle… well, Ben rescued *me*. I'd like a chance to return the favor."

"Don't you people *listen?*" Lensky demanded. "You. Cannot. Go. Into. That. Building. It's too dangerous. This kind of thing is *precisely* what I was stationed here to prevent. It's my job to stop you! It's my job to preserve the Center for use by my agency, and part of that is keeping you – you suicidal lemmings from going over the first cliff you find!"

"That old nature movie was faked," Will said.

"Lemmings don't actually do that," Ingrid explained kindly.

"Great, they're smarter than topologists. It's still as much as my job's worth to let you go off like this."

We politely refrained from telling him exactly how much we cared about his job and his agency, even if they did supply our funding. If we abandoned Ben now, we'd be too ashamed to apply any topology ever again.

"Look, I don't want to go in," said Ingrid. None of us do. But I don't see that we have any choice. The aquarium is in the lobby. Ben is in the aquarium. And we can't move something that literally weighs a ton, no matter how many stars we apply along with our topology. It's just not that powerful. Right, Mr. M?"

"I am sorry to say that you are correct." Mr. M. hated to admit that he had any limitations. "When Nabû-kudurrī-usur desired me to move the pillars of the Great Temple of Marutuk in Babylon…"

"You see?" I interrupted to cut off what promised to be an extended reminiscence of Mr. M.'s life as a mage of Babylon. "Even Mr. M. agrees that we can't move the whole aquarium."

"Can't you magic him out of it? Thalia got papers out of hotel room safes for me last fall. *Closed and locked* safes. It can't be any harder getting a fish out of a tank!"

"Fish," I pointed out, "move. Constantly. And it's not like we can get a message to Ben telling him to hold still and be rescued." What I'd done in October involved an adaptation of the fixed-point theorem that we used for teleportation together with a couple of mappings to identify the space inside another guest's room safe with the space inside our safe. I couldn't do that with a moving target.

"And even if we could get around that, a fish plus the water around him is going to be a lot heavier to move than a few papers," Ingrid said. "How much weight can you move that way, Thalia? I top out at a couple of pounds, even with stars. That time I forgot to take the turkey out of the freezer…"

Another reminiscence we didn't need right now. "I don't know. I'd need to run some experiments first. But I expect I'm in the same range as you. Water is *heavy*. Even working together – and that's assuming we could synchronize – we probably wouldn't be able to move as much water as Ben will need until we can cut the tag off him." An unwelcome thought forced itself on me. "And there's another experiment we really ought to try first."

"What?"

"We've never moved a *living being* that way." She knew that, she just wasn't thinking of everything that could go wrong. That seemed to be my specialty. "It's not just teleporting," I reminded her. There's this funny kind of sideways mapping we do with the 3-space coordinates. What if the mapping transformation kills him?"

"Better that," Will interrupted, "than leaving him to Chayyaputra's mercies. You haven't heard what happened to Eli."

I blinked. "Didn't Ben and Jimmy rescue him too?"

Jimmy shook his head. "There were exactly four tagged fish in the tank. We got the CEO of a startup cybersecurity company, a remarkably stupid girl who had made the mistake of laughing at Chayyaputra when he made a pass at her, a Hindu priest, and Will. Eli… was no longer in the tank. Harper *told* us one fish had disappeared; we just managed not to think about that until the end."

"Chayyaputra killed him," Will said bitterly. "He came in one weekend in a foul mood because Logan wasn't going out of business fast enough to please him, so he took Eli out of the tank and just – left him on the floor to die! Watched him suffering! It –" He choked. "It seemed to take forever."

"Did you understand what was going on?"

"Not everything. I couldn't seem to think clearly, or remember times before the tank. But I did know that Eli was my friend. And I knew that he was dying for the whim of that bastard – I didn't know his name then, of course – and I couldn't do anything to help him." Will's voice shook on the last words and he clamped his jaw shut, looking much older and tougher than the mild-mannered young man he'd seemed to be at first.

"It won't do any good for all of you to jump into Chayyaputra's trap," Lensky said.

That was sort of true. We should leave at least one topologist here. Trouble was, nobody was likely to volunteer. I'd always been able to trick Ben into being the one to stay behind by pretending to toss a coin... *Ben*. The friend who'd stood by me when applied topology had upended my life, when even my rat of a boyfriend bailed out. My best friend *ever*. Something hurt deep in my chest.

"I need to think about it all," I said, standing up.

"You have to *think* about rescuing your best friend?" Annelise burst out of Meadow's office with blood in her eyes.

"Annelise, it's complicated." I caught Ingrid's eye and mouthed, "Meet me on the other side?"

"It's quite straightforward!" Annelise said. "You're cowards. All of you!"

I pictured a Möbius strip lying perpendicular to the doorless wall that closed off the Research Division offices, and walked along it while Annelise's voice slowly faded. Ingrid was on my heels.

"You're not seriously going to give in to Lensky's orders?" she asked as soon as I closed my office door. I supposed it was a reasonable question; I'd just been vague about my plans, and she knew about Brad and me. Everybody at the Center knew we were getting married in a few weeks. She might think I wasn't willing to put our relationship at risk. I wasn't too happy about that myself, but I didn't see any alternative; not if I wanted to preserve any self-respect whatsoever.

"Keep your voice down, you know how thin the walls are." The conversion of the third floor of this solid Victorian mansion into office space had been done as cheaply as possible; the original walls were sturdy enough, but the new ones were about as substantial as tissue paper. Well, maybe cardboard – the thin, recycled kind they use for cereal boxes. I sank down into my desk chair and looked longingly at the whiteboard with diagrams scrawled on it, and then at the reference books on my desk. Even the crumpled sheets of paper in the wastebasket had a certain nostalgic appeal. Last week, the theorem I'd been trying to prove had seemed like the most important thing in the world. Now I was in a world where applied topology wouldn't solve our problems. Not by itself. "No, of course I'm not going to let Brad stop us from rescuing Ben, but I had to get us away from him so we could make a plan, didn't I?"

We invited Colton to join our strategy session. Our nominal intern, Prakash, was –as usual— visiting the math department, which he planned to rejoin approximately ten seconds after the end of this semester-long sabbatical that Dr. Verrick had forced on him. A pity, that; he was actually very talented at applying topology for paranormal effects.

The first problem became clear as soon as we started talking. No, not the problem that we were talking about teleporting ourselves into a trap; we all knew and accepted that. We'd just have to play it by ear. Mr. M. volunteered that he might be able to help protect us, but it depended on what Chayyaputra did. Even a three-thousand-year-old turtle-snake mage was somewhat daunted at the prospect of going up against a minor god. Not that he put it that way, of course.

That first problem was - how did we think we were going to get into the lobby, where the aquarium was? You'd think that was a solved problem, given that Ben and Jimmy had been teleporting there and back for nearly a week. The trouble was, Jimmy couldn't teleport; Ben was, obviously, out of the action; and although Ingrid and Colton had been in the building, they'd only been in Chayyaputra's living quarters on the second floor. At first I'd thought it was simple, we could let Jimmy establish the destination space while the three of us did the heavy lifting. But the experience of seeing Ben turned into a fish had been traumatic for Jimmy; he'd turned pale green when I suggested he take us back there. Did we want to risk that his trauma would result in a side-slip to some other destination – maybe one that existed only in a non-metric space? That left us with only Shani's apartment as a potential destination.

At first, teleporting into his personal space seemed like a very, very bad idea.

"We *would* have the advantage of surprise," Colton said. "He'll be expecting us to attack the lobby, where Ben is."

"Even if we do surprise him," Ingrid said gloomily, "he thinks fast and he's more powerful than any of us."

"What if we didn't try to use applied topology, just attacked him physically? It worked for Annelise." She and Ben had had a nasty encounter with the Master of Ravens last January, partially resolved when she discovered that the moves taught her by her self-defense instructor actually worked in real life. It had probably helped that the instructor was an ex-Mossad agent whose concept of self-defense included inflicting serious damage on the other person.

Colton brightened. "We could take Lensky with us. Tell him to shoot the bastard immediately, while he's surprised and before he has time to shield."

"You didn't hear the argument out in the public side?" I was surprised; emotions had been hot and voices raised.

"I was concentrating. Trying to find some topology that could be applied to transform Ben back."

"We don't necessarily have to do it that way," Ingrid said. "All the previous fish reverted to their human form as soon as Ben took that iron tag off them."

"I don't think Lensky will come with us," I said with regret. "Most of that argument you didn't hear was him trying to order us around and forbidding anyone to even think of teleporting into the lobby of SCI. He thinks it's a trap."

"It probably is," Colton agreed. "That's another point in favor of hitting Shani's private quarters. He won't be expecting us in there." He looked at me. "Any chance you could steal Lensky's gun?"

"None." When the Glock wasn't on his person, it was in a gun safe that Mr. M. had specifically warded against paranormal tampering, with specific attention to my safe-space trick. I hadn't objected at the time because I thought it was just an example of Lensky's innate paranoia; when would I ever want his gun?

Ingrid raised another point.

"We can't just pull Ben out of the tank with our bare hands. Didn't you hear the measurements Jimmy estimated? It's much too deep. For every rescue the guys took along a bunch of Harper's supplies – all that stuff Jimmy mentioned. We won't be able to attack Chayyaputra physically if our hands are full of junk."

"Bash him with the stepladder?" Colton offered.

"Better yet, take Annelise. She's already taken him out once."

"Ben will kill us if we take her into danger."

"Yes, well, he can't do much to us as a fish. Maybe we can make a deal that we won't help him transform back unless he promises not to kill us."

But first, we had to get Annelise on this side of the wall. And we had to get equipment. And, obviously, we had to do both those things without alerting Lensky. Who, I reflected, probably would kill us if we returned alive, so there was really no point in worrying about whatever Ben might do to us after that.

Ingrid crossed the wall and came back with Annelise and Jimmy. "Lensky's in his office with the door closed," she reported. "Talking to Will, I think."

Probably enjoying the illusion that he'd won the argument, and avoiding us so that we couldn't start it again.

Annelise looked determined; Jimmy looked slightly green, and this time I don't think it was entirely fear of Chayyaputra. Being walked along an invisible Möbius strip makes a lot of normal people feel seasick, and Jimmy was one of the worst sufferers we'd known.

Annelise declared that she was more than willing to tackle Chayyaputra again, and added some grisly details of what she'd done to him last time that had Jimmy and Colton crossing their legs and wincing. Jimmy volunteered to drive down to Harper's and borrow her aquarium equipment. "If she'll lend us her key," he said optimistically, "we can wait until the office is closed and then walk right into the lobby."

There was nothing to do, then, but wait and plan. We decided that Annelise and Colton would be the front line, physical troops. Ingrid and I would carry the equipment, and we would be ready to raise our super-augmented shields around all four of us if Chayyaputra seemed to be winning. And Mr. M. volunteered to ride around Annelise's neck and deploy his ultrasonic beam to disorient Chayyaputra.

After half an hour Ingrid went out to see if Jimmy was back yet. She came back with a cup of coffee.

Twenty minutes later Colton checked the front room. He came back with coffee but no Jimmy.

Ten minutes later I ran the same check. I came back with a cup of stale coffee.

Did I mention that none of us are particularly good at waiting?

By the time Jimmy finally returned, we were all awash in coffee and seriously jittery, not necessarily from the caffeine. "What took you so long?" Ingrid demanded.

"Did you get the key? And where are the tools?" I wanted to know. He wasn't exactly festooned with aquarium equipment.

He answered the last question first. "In my car, stupid. Don't you think Lensky would figure out what we're planning if I showed up in the office with a stepladder and a fish net?"

He turned to Ingrid and said, "It took so long because I had to go to Home Depot to buy everything we needed."

"Harper wasn't willing to lend us her stuff?"

"Harper," said Jimmy, "isn't there."

I assumed she was out servicing other aquariums. "When she gets home..."

"I don't think she's coming back. The room she'd been renting was empty. I know because the landlady tried to rent it to me when I asked to see it – I had hoped that she'd left her equipment, but no such luck. And she'd left a note asking somebody she knew to take over her aquarium clients."

So, no key. We'd have to do this the topological way.

"You think Chayyaputra got her too?"

"He wouldn't have given her time to write a note. No, I think she got spooked and left town. I *thought* she was being awfully calm about having all this magic and applied topology dumped into her lap without warning, but I guess she was just trying to keep us on the job until all the fish were rescued. She must have packed last night and taken off right after we freed Will today."

"Speaking of whom—"

"We can't add him to the rescue group unless you want to wait. He's still talking to Lensky."

None of us wanted to wait, and we could hardly risk interrupting Brad to ask if Will could come out and play, so we'd have to do without his muscle. Given that we were going into Chayyaputra's living space, there wasn't anything to be gained by waiting; the later it got, the more likely it was that he'd be there.

We teleported ourselves straight out of the private side of the offices to where Jimmy's car was parked, so that Lensky wouldn't notice us leaving. I took Annelise and Ingrid held onto Jimmy. After we collected the equipment, Jimmy argued that he should go with us.

"No," Ingrid said.

"There's a good reason," I added. "You're the only person here who has actually been in the lobby. If this doesn't work, we're going to need you to guide us there."

The nearest semi-private place to teleport from was the women's room on the first floor of the Student Union. Which was actually convenient, since three of us had consumed a lot of coffee while waiting for Jimmy to get back. Ingrid went in first. We were lucky; she reported that it was empty. The rest of us trooped in, festooned with stepladder and plastic tub and other bits and pieces.

"I hope they think we're the janitors," Colton muttered.

"Relax. If anybody complains, just tell them you identify as a woman and screech, 'How dare you assume my gender!'"

But I noticed a plastic sign saying "Closed for Cleaning" on one side and something about "Limpieza" on the other side, presumably the Spanish version. I opened the door a crack and placed it on the floor in the hall, right in front of the door. That should give us time to redistribute the equipment and form up for a group teleporting effort. With all three remaining topologists working together, carrying Annelise wouldn't be a problem.

"*Brouwer!*" I said when we were all ready.

12. Loaded for grackle

We were swept into a darkness shot through with jewel-tone colors: glowing lines, surfaces, points of light. We had time – the three of us who were topologists, anyway – for a good long look at the in-between. Too much time, really. The SCI building was less than ten miles away; we should have blinked out of the restroom and blinked into Shani Chayyaputra's private rooms without more than a split-second glimpse of the in-between. Instead we were poised here, static, gazing at an unmoving display of lights.

Reflexively I opened my hand and poured more stars into the transformation. I could "see" Ingrid and Colton doing the same thing; they were shadowy, insubstantial figures to my sight here, but their stars were twisting funnels of moving lights.

Then, with a bump, we were back on the tiled floor of the restroom in the Student Union. The transition was anything but gentle. I sat down on the floor, hard. Annelise grabbed Colton's arm and, instead of steadying herself, made him lose his balance so that the two of them hit the tiles a moment after me. Ingrid was the only one of us who kept her feet and her dignity.

Naturally. It *would* be Ingrid, wouldn't it?

"What happened?" Annelise demanded as soon as she scrambled to her feet.

I got up a little more slowly. I'd whacked my tailbone on those tiles. "Remind you of anything?" I asked Ingrid.

She nodded, more slowly still. "That time when we were..." She swallowed hard and went on. "In... 1957. And we couldn't jump back to our own time."

Colton nodded. "Like that, only different. That was a kind of... *squishy* resistance. This felt more like bouncing off something hard and being knocked back to our starting place."

Mr. M. raised his head a few inches. "It would appear that the Master of Ravens has learned something from the Center for Applied Topology."

"What?"

"Is it not obvious? Just as you have hardened the shields around your office and your homes so that no unauthorized person can teleport into them, so has he hardened the shields on his apartment inside the building."

"Oh." He'd learned from us, dammit. I hadn't considered that possibility. "What can we do about that?"

"Short of sending someone to enter the apartment by normal physical means and remove the protections, nothing. And even then, he would have to find the tokens. Chayyaputra may well have disguised them."

"That would be a suicide mission," said Colton.

"Yes, very likely." Mr. M. didn't seem fazed by the notion. But then, given that Meadow had never gotten around to equipping his snake body with retractable hands, he could be pretty sure that he wouldn't be the one sent on the mission.

There was a hammering on the door and several soprano voices demanded to know if we were through yet.

"Repairs," Colton shouted. "There's been a sewage backup."

"Eeew!" The girls moved on, presumably to use a different restroom; the building had several, and if we'd been thinking clearly we would have assembled in a less accessible one. Oh well, too late now.

"The lobby," Ingrid said, "we'll have to go in that way after all. We'll need Jimmy to spot for us."

She turned sideways and disappeared. A moment later she stepped out of the air and back down onto the tiles, holding Jimmy's hand.

"We need you to picture the lobby of SCI," she told him.

"Yes, but what—"

"Just do it, okay?"

Ingrid and I took Jimmy's hands, and Colton wrapped an arm around Annelise. We were an untidy, scruffy group, trailing a stepladder and aquarium equipment, some of it not very securely held; I hoped everything would make it through the in-between all right.

There were no problems of that sort; no such luck. None of us, and nothing that we held, passed through that hard, reflective barrier. The only thing that was better about this attempt was that I had my knees bent and was balanced on the balls of my feet, half expecting the vigorous bounce-back. So I didn't fall on my butt this time.

Progress.

Of a sort.

"He's got the *whole building* shielded!" Ingrid exclaimed.

And now I was getting dizzy. I checked my colleagues. Ingrid and Colton also looked kind of pale and a bit wavery, as though they weren't completely here. I was familiar with the sensations attacking me; although we could now feed stars into a visualization slowly enough to make short jumps relatively simple, at the beginning of our teleportation adventures any jump of more than a mile would send a topologist to the floor with low-blood-sugar shakes. We were a lot stronger now – strong enough that we hadn't thought it necessary to sugar-load for a mere ten-mile jump powered by three topologists – but all three of us had poured a lot of our energy into the two attempts to get through Shani Chayyaputra's shields. (A lot of stars, too, but the good thing about taking a finite number of objects out of an infinite set is, we still had as many stars left as we'd begun with.)

"Food," Colton said.

We hauled the stepladder and other equipment into the cafeteria across from the restroom, gave Annelise and Jimmy some money, and sent them off to buy whatever high-calorie food they could find. While we waited for them to return, Ingrid tore open a sugar packet and dropped the contents into her mouth.

"Ick," said Colton. "How can you do that?"

"Like this," Ingrid said, repeating the treatment with another sugar packet. "Emergency sugar." She began to look somewhat less like an ice sculpture of herself. She might be extremely fair, but her hair and face did normally have *some* color. You had to see the energy-drained version of her to recognize what was missing. "You know what? This isn't a trap after all. You try to lure people into a trap, not to lock them out."

I took a packet out of the stack of condiments. So did Colton. She was right; I felt significantly less transparent and more three-dimensional after swallowing it.

"Doesn't do a lot for me," Colton said glumly.

Ingrid looked at the empty packet in his hands. "Of course not. You're eating Splenda, you idiot!"

"It must be some other kind of trap," I said, grabbing another sugar packet.

"What's Splenda?"

"A low-calorie sugar substitute that does absolutely nothing for your blood sugar."

"You couldn't have warned me?"

"I thought you could read!"

Okay, we were irritable as well as shaky. Fortunately, our non-mathematical colleagues came back with actual food before we could descend farther into childish squabbling. We grabbed utensils and fell on the plates of food with only a slight attempt to avoid resembling a pack of harpies. When we'd inhaled all the hamburgers, milk shakes, and slices of pie on the table, I sat back feeling slightly bloated but very much here. I was even willing to answer my phone when it rang – checking first, of course, to make sure the caller wasn't Lensky. I wasn't sufficiently recovered to face him quite yet.

What I had to face turned out to be much worse.

"Sally," purred a low, velvety voice that I recognized instantly. "We have *so* much to talk about, don't you think?"

I sat up straighter and waved at the others to hush them. "I don't talk with people who harm my friends."

"Oh, there's no need to take that tone with me," Chayyaputra said, sounding amused. "Nothing irreversible has happened to your friend yet. Nor need it happen, if you act intelligently."

"And your definition of *acting intelligently*?" I cupped a hand over my free ear to muffle the echoes of conversation and clattering dishes in the room. I didn't want to miss anything here.

"Giving me what I want would be intelligent. I do not have much use for your friend. The poor fish. I will be happy to return him to your colleagues."

"Just like that?" I didn't believe it.

"There will, of course, be a price to pay."

That I could well believe.

"The pictures on Miss Ginny's cell phone were extremely interesting."

Blast! I hadn't even noticed her taking pictures.

"You and your friend Lensky had quite an amusing time in Wimberley, did you not? You must have laughed to think what a fool you had made of me. Now it will be my turn to laugh. Surrender yourself and Lensky, and I will give your friend back."

"That's not a very good deal," I said. My throat had suddenly gone dry. "Why should we give you two for one?"

"Because you have no bargaining power?"

"It's not a matter of bargaining," I said, "it's a matter of what's available. I can't deliver Lensky; he is too paranoid for me to trick him into this. If you want a trade, you can have me for Ben. Nobody else needs to be involved."

We talked for some time more, but I wouldn't be moved from my position that I had no power over Lensky. Eventually, and somewhat reluctantly, he agreed to take me alone in exchange for Ben. We spent some more time haggling over the details of the exchange before everything was agreed.

I hung up and was immediately mobbed by my friends.

"Was that Chayyaputra?"

"What was that about Lensky?"

"What kind of a trade did you agree on?"

I thought that last had been perfectly clear from my half of the conversation. "Straight up. One for one. Me for Ben."

"You can't do that, Thalia," Colton said.

Annelise's lower lip trembled, but she said, "No. Ben would never forgive me if I let you sacrifice yourself for him."

"Who said anything about sacrificing?" I asked. "Obviously, I'm going to cheat." Unless, of course, I failed and got turned into a fish.

"How?"

"Let me explain. Quickly – we don't have much time. For starters, we're meeting at Mayfield Park in one hour."

Ingrid groaned. "Remember the last time? He can bring all the grackles he wants to a place like that."

"I'm counting on you and Mr. M. to keep the grackles too busy to interfere. Now that Meadow's given him customized flash-bangs as well as lasers, it should be a piece of cake. Mr. M., are you loaded for grackle?"

"Of course!" Mr. M. said indignantly. "How could I act as your armed guard if I did not bear arms? But I will not leave you to face this so-called 'god' alone, Daughter of Stars."

"Mr. M., you have to. Look, here's how it's going to work…"

I went over the details of my plan. There weren't many; there were too many contingencies and we had no time to prepare for every possibility. If things went as I hoped, we would be able to retrieve Ben without giving Chayyaputra anything in return. If they didn't – well, we'd just have to think on our feet, wouldn't we? And in the worst possible case, I would surrender to Chayyaputra in return for Ben's freedom. I didn't mention that part because we didn't have time for an argument, and anyway I hoped desperately that it wouldn't come to that. I did not want to spend the rest of my life as a fish, let alone a fish in Shani Chayyaputra's custody. Even the prospect of getting out of the wedding was not enough to make that particular outcome attractive.

Annelise's part in the plan was to go back to the Center for Applied Topology and keep Lensky too busy to wonder where everybody else had gone. Her talent for nonstop conversation would doubtless be stretched to its limit, but I had faith in her. She wouldn't even have to lie to him – as long as she didn't let him get a word in edgewise to ask any questions. After putting the fish-rescuing equipment back in his car – all but the bolt cutters, which

Ingrid would keep – Jimmy would join Annelise and add what he could to the distract-Lensky project. If necessary, he promised, he would tell Lensky all about the advantages of statically-typed programming languages.

I felt sorry for Lensky. But even being told all about statically… statistically… whatever Jimmy said… was better than what would happen to him if Shani Chayyaputra got hold of him. I thought.

Colton, Ingrid, and Mr. M. would come to the park with me but separately from me, all hidden by camouflage. I needed to have my own, separately controlled camouflage going.

Now that we'd refueled, teleporting to Mayfield Park would be easy. And thanks to Prakash's work on using two topological applications at once, we could arrive already camouflaged instead of just stepping out of the air and upsetting any possible witnesses. In fact, my plan depended on the other three being unnoticeable to Chayyaputra himself.

All four of us had been there recently enough to form a good mental picture of the area around the same lily pond where we'd met the Master of Ravens, almost one year ago, for a similar exchange. That time it had been an exchange of data for hostages. Almost nothing had gone as planned, but we got Lensky's niece back and the Master didn't get the data he'd wanted, so I considered that venture to have been a success. I could only hope that this would work out as well.

Once at the park, I left Colton, Ingrid and Mr. M. in their own camouflage at the far end of the pond. The plan, such as it was, depended on my being able to drop my own camouflage while they stayed concealed.

Last time we'd been here, it had been a Sunday afternoon and the park had been full of visitors. This had made things extremely complicated both for us – we're not supposed to do any applied topology where outsiders can see it – and also for Lensky, who had some trouble getting a clear shot at the Master of Ravens. It would have been much easier for him on this warm weekday afternoon. Our only potential witnesses were a couple of college kids dressed in full hiking gear, complete with sunshades and extra water bottles. And they were just setting off to explore the trails that went off down the hill from the old house. I thought they wouldn't have noticed us even if we'd stepped out of the air into full visibility, instead of manifesting as slight blurs of our backgrounds.

I missed Lensky, but he couldn't be here this time. He couldn't even know this was happening until it was all over. I spared a thought for Annelise, hoping that her inventiveness wouldn't desert her under Lensky's piercing blue stare. He was in as much danger from Chayyaputra as I was, and he didn't have any paranormal abilities he could use to protect himself.

A peacock waddled up to me and let loose a deafening screech, after which it looked up at me just as though it could see right through my camouflage. I looked back where Colton and Ingrid should have been standing with Mr. M. Nothing was visible but a slight shimmer of light where their camouflage projected an image of whatever was behind them. But two peahens were prancing in and out of the borders of their camouflage. They looked very odd indeed, with their heads disappearing and reappearing and their tails flipping in and out of sight. And their nodding heads, when I could see them, seemed to be looking precisely where Colton's and Ingrid's faces would be.

Peacocks could see through Ben's camouflage algorithm? Who knew? I just hoped grackles were not similarly gifted, or I was screwed. We really hadn't given enough thought to the effect of an open covers visualization on different kinds of optic nerves, had we? Another detail for further research – assuming I lived to return to my real work.

We were a few minutes early, and I didn't see Chayyaputra yet. Careful to keep my camouflage up, I took slow deep breaths and tried to absorb the peace of the gardens. Actual palm trees – not that common in Austin – towered above us; the pond at my feet was bright with pink and yellow water lilies raising colorful bursts of petals above the flat green leaves. Where the water lily pads didn't cover the surface of the water, I could see red and golden koi moving lazily among the lilies and other plants. If I could keep my mind off the giant water moccasin we'd encountered last year, this place was a sub-tropical paradise.

Well. The water moccasin and the Master of Ravens. At least the original Paradise had had only one serpent.

There was a disturbance of the air behind me. I turned sharply and saw two separate blurs of camouflage where there had been only one. The smaller blur faded and resolved into Prakash Bhatia. "Thalia, where are you?" he called in a low voice. "You need to know—"

I dropped my own camouflage. "What, Prakash?"

"Lensky knows."

I glanced at my watch. He'd gotten the truth out of Annelise in less than fifteen minutes! "Is he coming here?"

"Yes, but he is driving only. I came to warn you... and also so that he could not ask me to teleport him."

Idiot! There'd been nothing to stop him from pretending to agree and then teleporting to some other place where he could strand Lensky in safety until this was over. "Listen, Prakash. I need you to wait in the parking lot. When Lensky gets here, grab him and teleport both of you out of here."

"What? Why are you wishing this? Where should I be taking him?"

"Oh.... Never mind, I'll get Colton to do it."

Last winter Colton had saved all our lives by taking a bomb that was about to explode, teleporting back to his home in the Panhandle and dropping the bomb on some tumble-down buildings that his father had always meant to demolish. If he left Lensky at the family farm now, there was no way Brad would be able to get back from the Panhandle in time to interfere with us. And he would be *safe*; Chayyaputra would never guess where to look for him.

I turned and talked to the blur where Colton had to be and explained what I needed. He dropped camouflage; Prakash joined Ingrid and she raised shields and camouflage over both of them. Prakash might be a bit of a jerk, but he was an outstanding mathematician; it was thanks to his research earlier this semester that we'd learned how to do two applications simultaneously. It was possible he'd be useful here.

Colton ambled back towards the car park, not even bothering to use camouflage. Why should he? He'd never been face to face with the Master of Ravens and he could easily pass for a normal visitor wandering around the park.

With my mind freed of that worry, I was able to give Chayyaputra my full attention when he blinked into existence about twenty feet away, accompanied by his usual annoyance of grackles. The birds dispersed and settled on nearby bushes, allowing me to see that he was carrying a bucket – and not an empty one, judging by the way he held it.

Ben! I dropped camouflage and let Chayyaputra see me.

13. A destructive force of nature

"*Dear* 'Sally,'" Chayyaputra said with an oily, very fake smile. "Are you ready to come to me? A man and his promised bride should be close, should we not?"

A little trickle of sweat ran down my back; May was coming in unnecessarily warm. It was *not* a chill going down my spine. "Put the bucket down and back off," I said. "I want to be sure you aren't cheating us."

Chayyaputra did as I asked, though he didn't give me much space; he only took three steps back. I moved forward, cautiously, and drew my invisible shield close to my body so as not to betray its existence.

So far so good; there was a pink fish in the bucket, swimming as best it could under the handicap of a heavy metal tag clamped to its back fin. But we should have brought Jimmy! None of the rest of us had any idea whether or not this fish looked like the ones that he and Ben had freed. All I knew was that Jimmy said the fish had been tortured with an iron tag, like this one, and that removing the tag was all that was necessary to allow them to resume their human shape.

"We'll have to verify that you've actually produced Ben, of course," I said, talking briskly and trying to pretend this had been part of the deal all along. It damn well *should* have been part of the deal. I'd been thinking so hard about keeping Lensky safe that I hadn't given enough thought to verification. "I'll just get the bolt cutters…" Which would be a neat trick in itself, given that Ingrid was holding them and that I didn't want the Master of Ravens to know of her presence. If I needed backup, best that it was a surprise to him, right?

Chayyaputra moved right back up to the bucket, polished shoes crunching on the lightly graveled pathway, so close that I could smell his lilac-scented hair oil. "That was not part of the agreement. I have brought your friend; you must come with me."

"How do I know that's Ben and not something you randomly pulled out of your aquarium?"

"You will see soon enough. But I'm not fool enough to free your friend before you yield yourself to me."

I shook my head. "Nuh-uh. Verification first, or no deal."

"You will just have to take it on faith!" The rings on Chayyaputra's outflung hand flashed in the sunlight, and his gesture loosed a three-pronged spear of blue fire that crackled harmlessly against my shield.

"What? What is this? You dare try to cheat *me!*" he shouted. He waved again to summon his grackles. They fluttered and clawed against the shield but could not reach me.

"You… *fool,*" Chayyaputra said. "I brought what you demanded, and you could have had him safe if you had not tried to cheat me. Now see if you can find your friend before the larger fish eat him!" He kicked the bucket; it fell on its side right at the edge of the pool. Water and a smallish pink fish poured out of the bucket and into the murky pond. My last sight of Ben – if that was Ben – was of his salmon-pink tail flicking him beneath a lily pad.

"And now I'll have *you!*" He swept his arm through the air again and then again, bringing fresh waves of grackles to surround my shield. Maintaining the shield became more difficult than I'd anticipated under the simultaneous attack of so many beaks and claws. I couldn't do anything for Ben now; I could barely protect myself. I opened my hand and tried to funnel even more stars into the algorithm that defined the shield, but it was a fool's errand: as I knew perfectly well, the constant flow of stars couldn't be increased beyond my ability to guide and control them.

The park seemed to be in deep shadow now. An effect of the dueling magics, or did the place itself react poorly to our flailing attempts at control? In the corners of my eyes I could just see streaks of bright light beyond the grackles, driving some of them away. A moment later there were loud noises on either side of my shield, accompanied by flashes of blinding light, and more of the grackles fled. Mr. M.? I made the mistake of glancing behind me, and in that moment of distraction I lost my visualization of the shield manifold and a grackle clawed my face. As the trident of blue fire lanced towards me again I threw myself to one side and hit the ground awkwardly. A sharp pain lanced through my ankle, but I didn't have time to nurse it. I brought up camouflage, scrambled to my feet, and ran.

But just running wasn't good enough; he could track me easily by the moving blur. And I really didn't want to keep running on that ankle. I reached into the dark place at the back of my head where I do math problems and visualized the construct Ingrid had used for flight. Move the planes closer, closer… there! In six-dimensional space I danced between the glowing planes whose energy supported me and shifted with me. In three-dimensional space I was flying, rising above where Chayyaputra would think to look for me.

But I was no longer shielded, merely camouflaged – we still can't handle three applications at once – and the black birds were swooping all around me. The air was thick with black wings and sharp claws and beaks, and the grackles' raucous cries drowned out all other sounds. Oh, *hell*. Like peacocks, grackles were unaffected by camouflage's masking of me with images of the background. And that had been my *second* bad miscalculation; the first had been thinking that my applications of topology were enough to hold off a god and the creatures who served him as long as necessary.

Flapping wings and pecking beaks and scratching claws all assailed me at once, and I couldn't maintain the image of planes intersecting in six-space. The air around me chilled to freezing and I felt myself on the verge of free fall. It would be a long way down now, much too long. I tried to swoop down to earth before I lost my visualization of the flight construct, but I was still too far above ground when gravity seized me. I landed awkwardly on my right knee and elbow. The knee had banged into a rock; the elbow was only skinned. Probably. I didn't really have time to assess the injuries.

A hand gripped my wrist, pulling me upwards, and I smelled Chayyaputra's sickly-sweet lilac-scented hair oil again. Who'd have guessed that a god would have bad taste? He probably had who knew how many worshippers willing to give him garlands of fresh flowers, and here he chose an artificial "lilac" scent that had never seen the outside of a chemistry lab.

The grackles were forming around us. As soon as we were totally surrounded, he would try to force me back to his building. I screamed, *"Brouwer!"* and the familiar keyword called up our own teleportation algorithm in my mind automatically, faster than I could have built it from scratch. I pictured the far side of the pond and said *"Brouwer"* again as the flapping black wings closed in all around me.

Absolutely nothing happened.

I wasn't on the far side of the pond. But I wasn't in Chayyaputra's office either. Nor in his aquarium. My feet – and my butt — were still planted solidly on the yellowish dirt and scattered gravel of that path in Mayfield Park.

With my topology counterbalancing his magic, we were reduced to a physical struggle. I kicked out, landed a foot on his shin more by luck than planning, but didn't do much damage. I should have worn boots. He hauled me upright and I tried unsuccessfully to butt him in the face with my head. I wasn't tall enough, and I didn't have the strength to break his grip. Could I try what Annelise's self-defense instructor had taught her, beginning with a hard palm to the nose?

I never found out, because right then a fist came through the black wings that surrounded us and landed on the side of Chayyaputra's head, rocking it to the right. The grackles squawked and a number of them fluttered upward, allowing normal light and sounds to reach me again. Chayyaputra dropped me and Lensky put another fist into his ribs, then hit the god's chin so hard I was surprised his neck didn't snap. Chayyaputra sank to his knees, waved one arm feebly and was covered in grackles.

A moment later neither the grackles nor their master were there.

And once again, a man's hand dragged me to my feet.

"We," said Lensky, "have some talking to do."

Breathing hard, I looked around our little corner of the park. Ingrid and

Mr. M. were visible, but a six-foot blurred image of wavery palm tree trunks beside them suggested that somebody else was still camouflaged. On the far side of that blur Prakash was frozen in place, looking as he'd recently donated way too much blood. As for Colton, he was making a doomed attempt to hide behind the others. He would have done better to use camouflage; he was so large that bits of him stuck out behind Prakash and Ingrid.

"First I have to – have to find out—"

I limped towards Ingrid.

"Ben is all right," she said quickly. "He swam right toward us and let me pick him up to cut the tag off."

Figured. Even in fish form, Ben's intelligence shone.

And I guessed he wasn't a fish any longer. That wave of cold I'd felt hadn't had anything to do with my flight application failing; it must have been Ben, drawing energy out of the surroundings to rebuild his mass. He was probably inside that blurred image of tree trunks.

Prakash was staring at his shoes. He looked mortified. "I was not fighting for you, Thalia. Even the *snake* was fighting in its way, but *I* could not move – against – the *god*."

I suspected that Prakash, primed from childhood to see Shani as a literal god, had experienced the avatar differently from us. Later I learned that was true. Where we Americans had seen only a rather short man with oily hair, Prakash had seen a many-armed black figure draped in gold and mounted on a giant black bird. Where I had seen an insubstantial crackle of blue fire, he had seen the god stabbing at me with an actual three-pointed blade.

I didn't have time to question him now, though. "It's all right," I said awkwardly. "I mean – we all do what we can, isn't it?" He had this annoying ability to make me start talking like him. "I'd never have survived if you hadn't figured out how we could hold two applications of topology at the same time; think about that, why don't you?"

I turned to glare at Colton. "As for *you* – what part of 'keep Lensky out of this' did you not understand?"

"By the time he got out of his car you were already in trouble," Colton said. "I couldn't think of anything but running back here to help you. I was too rattled to teleport, and it wasn't like it was that far. But he got to you way ahead of me. I've never *seen* anybody move that fast."

"Shall we go home now?" Ingrid asked. "Ben's getting cold."

Oh. Right. Jimmy had said something about people's clothes not transforming with them, hadn't he? Behind that six-foot blur there was probably a naked, dripping-wet Ben. Again! This would be the second time in less than a year that an adventure had ended with Ben soaking wet and missing some or all of his clothes. I wondered if he had an unsuspected affinity for water.

"Right, let's go. Shani might come back." Being inside our own shielded space suddenly seemed *very* attractive.

Ingrid and the tall blur beside her blinked out of sight.

"See you back at the office?" Colton asked me.

"No." That was Lensky, and he sounded royally pissed off. "Thalia and I want some privacy."

He should speak for himself. *I* would have been happy to put off this conversation until he'd had time to calm down a bit.

"And we're not going by magic carpet, either. I," he said pointedly, "had to drive here. And now I'm going to drive back. Thalia, if you'd be so good as to accompany me?"

It was a challenge, not a request. His blue eyes sparkled with something that was almost certainly not love, and the vein at his temple was jumping again. He handed me into the car with a care that might have been confused with courtesy—unless, as I did, you felt the tension in his body. I slid in, buckled my seat belt, and stared straight ahead as he walked around the car and sat behind the wheel.

He managed to clash the gears coming out onto 35th. That's not easy to do with a modern car.

"I can explain," I said into the icy silence that followed.

"Can you, now? This should be interesting. How many times have you promised me to stop throwing yourself into danger?" His fingers drummed on the steering wheel.

"Yes, but—"

"This time was different?" he interrupted. "How many times have you said that?"

"Well, it was. It wouldn't make sense for you to go up against the Master of Ravens. I have ways to defend myself against magical attacks—"

"And yet, you needed a bit of crude physical help at the end, didn't you? And it was just blind luck that I got there in time to slug the s.o.b., wasn't it?" He stopped at a red light and slewed round to face me. "This is the kind of thing we should face as a team, Thalia. I should have been with you from the beginning."

An impatient honking behind us; the light was green. Lensky stomped on the gas and we lurched forward, then he braked so hard I was flung against the seat belt. That pedestrian was really perfectly safe; he didn't have to give us the finger when he reached the curb.

"I'm not going to argue while you're driving like a maniac," I said.

"Fine! We'll finish this at home!"

"Fine!" I folded my arms, suppressing a slight wince. The scrape along my elbow where I'd made that emergency two-point landing was beginning to hurt, now that the terror and the adrenaline were wearing off.

The rest of the drive was finished in a silence so oppressive that I felt as if a storm was going to burst over me out of the cloudless May sky.

Not necessarily inaccurate, that. My internal barometer was predicting cloudy with a chance of tornados.

I didn't want to tell him why I'd had to leave him out of the loop on this latest debacle, and he probably wouldn't have accepted my reasoning anyway. I figured I'd just keep my head down and let him yell at me until he got tired of yelling — same strategy I used with my family. Only Lensky, the rat, tunneled under all my defenses, first by terrifying me and then by being nice to me.

It started in the living room. On the short way from the parking space to his condo I had concentrated, with mixed results, on not limping. By the time we got inside my knee was complaining fiercely. So was my ankle. But I didn't want to sit down because that would have facilitated his looming over me. That – the looming, I mean — was bad enough when we were both on our feet.

I sat anyway, and before I was ready. When Lensky sank onto his deep, squashy sofa I stayed on my feet, opting for speed and mobility in case I needed to throw things. But he reached up, put an arm around me, and pulled me down beside him. It was almost impossible to move away... and after just a few moments I thought, why bother? Being close enough to feel his body against mine was already diverting my thoughts from the epic fight we hadn't quite had in the car. With any luck, he was feeling the same way. Maybe we could go directly to cuddling without passing through the battle zone. I kissed the side of his neck, nibbled gently on his shoulder, wondered if it was too soon to try and get his shirt off.

"Thalia. Talk to me."

"Mmm?"

He put his hands on my waist and scooted me a couple of inches away from him. "You have to stop rushing off by yourself to save the world. We're supposed to be getting married in a few weeks, and you're still treating me like the retarded child who can't understand adult business. If having paranormal abilities makes you feel that superior to me, maybe..." He sighed deeply and ran a hand through his hair. "I don't know. Maybe we should call the whole thing off."

I felt very cold. Sure, I was dreading the circus of the wedding; what sane person wouldn't? But it would be bearable because on the far side of all the foofaraw of dresses and cakes and invitations and place settings there would be Brad. Loving me. Forever.

Now, with just a few words, he'd shown me a bleak alternative: Brad. Walking out of my life. Forever.

Because there was no way we could go back to what we'd had, that fragile balance of love and sex and words unspoken and (on my part, anyway) refusal to think about the future. Not now. Too many of those words had been spoken.

"Brad, I *love* you. And I don't feel superior to you. Like you said, we're a team. You can do some things I can't and I can do some things you can't and we should definitely work together."

"And yet, you keep doing things like this. First you went off to Wimberley by yourself—"

"I had to be there by Sunday night!" I interrupted him. "Before Jimmy got that crazy idea of having me impersonate Chayyaputra's nonexistent fiancée, I was going in there as a temporary waitress hired to help Margo out for just that week. We couldn't wait for you to get back; it would have looked too suspicious if I turned up there in mid-week. And I'd have lost valuable snooping time."

"*I* joined you in mid-week."

"Yes, and look how that went! Webster was immediately suspicious of you."

"Only," Lensky said, "because he associated me with you, thinking the two strangers had to be connected. The man's a raging paranoiac."

"Oh, I don't know. Is it paranoia if people really are spying on you?"

That would have made a nice philosophical distraction. Sadly, Lensky didn't take the bait. "And what about today? What exactly was so secret about this rescue trip that you couldn't share it with me?"

I thought of an analogy that might get it across to him. "You told me once not to get in the way when people were shooting, that I'd be a distraction you couldn't afford. Remember?"

"Oh, I remember telling you that. And I'm struggling to remember when you ever actually respected that request."

"There haven't been a lot of bullets flying around lately," I said. "How can I demonstrate compliance with your request if you don't provide any people to shoot at me?"

He was shaking his head slowly. "Thalia, how do you manage to twist things around like that? Now it's *my* fault you haven't been shot?"

"That's not exactly what I meant... My point is that it's the same thing when I'm trying to ward off actual magic with applied topology. You can't help, and you're a distraction I can't afford."

"Because that kind of battle never gets physical," he said with heavy sarcasm. He inspected his knuckles and blew on them. "I'm no more at risk than any other non-magical staff member, and I'm a hell of a lot more useful in a fight than Jimmy or Annelise."

"Or Meadow?" I wasn't even going to mention Annelise's Krav Maga training; I was pretty sure that Mossad instruction or not, Lensky could take her with one hand tied behind his back.

Lensky laughed. "Meadow? With or without flash-bangs and sonic weapons? Okay, I'm not entirely sure about her. That is a formidable young woman." He looked at me and his eyes softened. "In your own way… you're pretty formidable too." He bent his head and drew me close for a long kiss that made my head swim. I put my arms around his neck and returned it. He demonstrated his newly acquired interest in one-handed bra unfastening. We might have made it into the bedroom without any more discussion if I hadn't squeaked when his other hand brushed against my sore elbow.

"What's the matter?"

"Skinned my elbow in the park. It's not important."

"Show me."

"It's nothing really, just a little graze…"

"*Show me.*"

I couldn't see much of it myself, but Lensky sucked in his breath when he saw the back of my elbow in the light. "Love, that's *bad*. Why didn't you tell me? Want me to take you to the emergency room to get it taken care of?"

"It's not that bad!" I squinted. Okay, what I could see of it looked worse than I'd expected. "Just help me wash it and put something over my arm so I don't get blood on the furniture."

"Yes, of course that's all that matters to me, protecting the furniture."

"Well, I already burnt a hole in your bedroom carpet back in January. I don't want you to start thinking of me as a destructive force of nature."

"Oh, you're a force of nature, all right," he breathed into my hair.

"So, no ER?"

"Only if you tell me honestly about all your injuries. Because when we came in you weren't walking like the only problem was a skinned elbow."

"Oh, my jeans protected the rest of me pretty well."

But he had them off me, and my T-shirt too. Instead of proceeding to the kind of shenanigans that usually followed disrobing, he checked me all over for bumps and sprains and bruises. I yelped when his fingers dug into my right knee, and again when he flexed my ankle.

He picked me up and carried me to the bed, setting me down very gently. "That knee is going to be the size of a cantaloupe if we don't get some ice on it," he said, leaving me and going to the kitchen. He offered me the classic remedy, a bag of frozen peas for my knee, and then he crushed ice cubes in a zip lock bag for the ankle. Then he rinsed the dirt and grit out of the raw patch on my elbow, very gently, while I clutched the frozen peas and tried to think about something else. He wrapped some gauze around my arm, eased me into a comfortable position on the bed, and said, "Stay there and keep those ice packs on. I'll be back in a few minutes."

I actually started to fall asleep. The whole right side of me hurt, and the attention given the knee had only encouraged it to start up a nasty throbbing, but I was so tired. I probably needed to eat after applying all that topology in the park, but finding food seemed like more effort than it was worth. *Breathing* seemed like too much effort; good thing that function ran on automatic...

I startled awake at the sound of his key in the door. He'd come back with cold packs, more gauze, and antibiotic in a spray can. "Just washing that skinned place hurt you so much," he said, "and all I had here was a tube of antibiotic ointment. I didn't want to hurt you again by rubbing it on."

The antibiotic spray was cool and only stung slightly on my raw flesh. After that he produced another spray bottle that covered the scrape with some kind of thin, flexible film. I picked up the bottle when he set it down. "Wound dressing spray for *cats, dogs, and parrots?*"

"You're not big enough to need the one for horses."

"Oh, in that case it makes perfect sense."

The frozen peas were getting mushy by now and the plastic bag of ice chips was mostly ice water, and leaking at that. Lensky took them away. "Once the cold packs freeze, we'll do another ice treatment. For now, you should take a couple of aspirin and rest."

"It doesn't hurt that much." Maybe it did, actually, but I didn't like what a big deal this was getting to be.

Ignoring me, Lensky shook a couple of white pills out of a bottle and handed me a glass of water. "Just take them and quit arguing, okay? It'll help reduce the inflammation."

"You're sure it's just aspirin, nothing else?" A few months earlier — right after the scorched carpet incident, actually, in which I'd been burned as well as the rug — he'd slipped me a Tylenol with codeine. I don't like opiates; they make me too stupid to do applied topology. Tonight, with no idea where the Master of Ravens had gone or what his next move would be, I really didn't want to be that helpless.

This was straight aspirin, and it did mute the throbbing in my knee. The improvised ice packs had also helped.

But what helped most of all was Lensky, lying down beside me and curving one arm over my midriff. Warm and solid and steady.

I fell asleep while wondering how to explain that this time he actually had been more at risk than anyone else. He wasn't going to be pleased when he learned about the bargain I'd made. But I had to warn him. I had to make him understand the danger he was in.

14. The jewel in the forehead of the idol

Austin, Friday

When I woke up, sunlight was pouring through the windows, and I seemed to be wearing one of Lensky's T-shirts. It made a more than adequate nightgown.

"We forgot to do the ice packs again." I stretched. Despite that, I was feeling much better.

Lensky looked amused. "No, we didn't. I put them on you at midnight."

"And I slept through that?"

He grinned. "Not exactly. First you complained about being cold – that's why you're wearing one of my shirts now. Then you demanded something sweet, so I brought you that pint of horrible mixed flavors ice cream you put in the freezer last week."

"The maple crunch praline caramel fudge? How much of it did I eat?"

"All of it."

Now that was sad. Not only had I consumed an entire pint of maple crunch praline caramel fudge ice cream without being wide awake enough to enjoy it, but now we were down to Lensky's choices – plain chocolate or plainer vanilla – until I went shopping again.

"After that you said, 'Mmurfl,' and then, 'Homeomorphism,' and buried yourself in the pillows. I don't know whether that counts as being awake. How's the knee?"

I gave it an experimental flex. "Much better. Hardly hurts at all. See, I told you it wasn't that bad."

"That's good," he said, "because I've been having interesting thoughts while waiting for you to wake up, and I wouldn't want to hurt your knee by being too enthusiastic."

That sounded promising.

Unfortunately, he went on to say, "But we've got to settle this other thing first."

I had been kind of hoping we could brush it under the carpet and get on with his 'interesting thoughts.' But his intense blue stare caught and pinned me, and I couldn't look away. "Thalia... I hate it when you lie to me."

"I didn't! I didn't say anything at all to you about Mayfield Park!"

"Asking Annelise to do it for you amounts to the same thing!"

"Considering we hired her to lie our way out of trouble, I'm seriously disappointed in Annelise. She should have been able to detain you much longer."

"And I," Lensky said, "am seriously disappointed in you."

Time to come clean. "Brad, just give me a minute to explain... I had a very good reason to keep you out of this. Chayyaputra saw pictures of us on Ginny's phone, and now he is going after the two of us specifically, rather than the Center in general. You need to be very, very careful. In fact, I'd really like it if you'd stay inside shielded areas until this is settled."

"You expect me to cower under your magical shields while you go out and risk yourself against him?"

"I have some ways to protect myself that you don't."

"All the same. Throwing you to Chayyaputra while I hide behind you... Not going to happen, Thalia. And what happened yesterday proves that it won't work. Your magical protections weren't good enough to save you. And even though I don't have paranormal abilities, Chayyaputra didn't harm me."

"Not this time."

"That sounds as if you're going to have exactly the same attitude next time the Master of Ravens threatens us. That's not acceptable, Thalia. I want you to promise me that you won't go off on your own against him."

I saw a way to retrieve something out of the situation. "I will promise that... if *you* will promise *me* to stay inside shielded areas until this is resolved."

"Unless we – *we*, Thalia – need to leave those areas in order to deal with an emergency. In which case, you stay with me, understand?"

Probably as good an offer as I was going to get. At least I wouldn't have to worry about Lensky when he wasn't with me; he'd be in the office or the condo, both seriously shielded against strangers teleporting in. "Deal."

He wanted to seal our agreement with a kiss. Fine by me. Come to think of it, there hadn't been nearly enough cuddling and kissing in the last twenty-four hours. I felt I was *due*. And as that kiss developed into considerably more than a token of our deal, I eschewed thinking altogether in favor of feeling and doing.

When we finally got to the office everybody else was there already, and worse, they'd eaten all the doughnuts. I glowered at Will, who was waving the end of a sour cream cruller while having what seemed to be an intense conversation with Colton. "He doesn't even work here," I muttered under my breath.

Annelise caught that. "Give him a break, Thalia. He's lost his best friend, and now he doesn't even have a job."

"He can't go back to work for Logan?"

Jimmy and Ingrid joined us. "Logan is even more depressed than he was before we found Will," Jimmy said. "He blames himself for Eli's death and he says he's not going to set up anybody else as a target. In any case," he added, "I'm not sure it would be possible to resurrect Protect Your Privacy. Logan made a lot of bad business decisions on the way down."

I guessed we were going to be stuck with Will until he found his feet. He did seem to be bonding with Colton over, of all things, movies. They were hashing over all the historical errors in *Dunkirk* and *Darkest Hour*. "Take that speech of Churchill's that supposedly got so much applause in Parliament," Will said, waving the last two inches of his cruller. "The 'fight them on the beaches' speech. In actual fact, he didn't get that kind of applause in the House until later."

"Two weeks later? His 'finest hour' speech after France surrendered?" Colton suggested tentatively.

"Not even then," Will said in triumph. "The House didn't stand up and cheer for him until July, when he reported that the British navy had sunk the French fleet."

"They're very detail-oriented, aren't they?" I commented to Ingrid.

"Will's an R programmer," Ingrid said. "I think being detail-oriented is a necessary though not sufficient condition. And remember when Colton wouldn't stop going on about the exact details of the 1954 Buick Skylark?"

I shuddered. "I do indeed. That seems to have been the thing that most impressed him about time travel. I think we're lucky he never figured out how to bring one of those cars back to our time."

"I think even a mint-condition Buick Skylark wouldn't tempt him into time traveling again. That experience certainly put me off it. Permanently."

"Yes, they would have seen Spitfires, but not with the Merlin engines – those were new!" Will was almost shouting.

"I thought their current obsession wasn't as boring as vintage cars. I may have been wrong." Ingrid's lips twitched as she listened to the discussion, which had now moved on to whether there had been enough Spitfires in the sky before Dunkirk for one of the characters in the movie to have recognized them. Or was it the Spitfire *engines* they were arguing about, the Merlins or Arthurs or whatever? Hard to tell. Especially if you found the topic as monumentally boring as Ingrid and I did.

"How's Ben?"

"In his office working on something, thank God. He bent my ear about the experience of being a fish for way too long; then he stopped, snapped his fingers, said 'That reminds me of something,' and went off to commune with his whiteboard."

"I guess he's okay, then."

"Unless the fish fixation means that he's not recovered from the shock. How was he last night, Annelise?"

"Definitely not in a state of shock," she said with a reminiscent – and reassuring – grin. "Trust me, he re-transformed with all his faculties intact."

I was about ready for some alone time in my office to strengthen my six-dimensional flight visualization, which clearly wasn't as strong as it should be. But I would have liked a doughnut to take back there with me. I had, after all, had an energetic morning even before teleporting Lensky and me from the safety of his condo to the safety of the office.

While I was still lingering wistfully over the empty doughnut tray in the break room, our wandering intern came up the stairs with a little old man in a white tunic over baggy white pants. When Prakash saw me, he looked away for a moment, then squared his shoulders and met my eyes. For once he didn't look snotty and superior.

"Are you going to introduce us to your friend?" Annelise asked.

Jimmy cleared his throat. "I believe we've met. This would be Pandit Navin... um..."

"Navinchandra Balakrishnan," the old guy said. "You may be addressing me as 'Panditji,' easier for Americans, isn't it?"

"I went to Hindu Temple first thing this morning," Prakash said, "asking for help and protection of colleagues here from Shani *dev*. Panditji offered to come back with me to explain true situation to us all."

"I am in debt to Center for Applied Topology for my return to this form," the Pandit said, "and hoping that truth of our Hindu gods will be helpful in dealing with impostor Shani."

I'd been dubious about the usefulness of a lecture on Hindu theology, but the mention of Shani as an impostor certainly grabbed my attention. I followed Prakash and his companion into the break room, as did almost everybody else. Ingrid stepped through the wall to the private side for Ben.

We actually had people standing around the walls. When Dr. Verrick first established the Center, I'd thought that a room with eight whole chairs was more than we would ever need for meetings. Now that room overflowed.

Even Meadow showed up, though in her role as engineering support for Mr. M.'s prosthetic body she had little connection to the Shani problem. Mr. M. himself, of course, was riding in my belt loops. He mentioned that people often came into the *coffee* room to get *coffee* and I shushed him. A singing, flying turtle-snake mage hopped up on caffeine was the last thing this meeting needed.

Last to enter was Lensky. He gave me a friendly nod and closed the break room door so that he could lean against it.

Panditji turned out to be a font of information, some of which might actually be useful. His main point was that, theologically speaking, the man we knew as the Master of Ravens was *not* the god Shani; he was, if anything, a flawed copy of the real god, having taken on only the dark aspect of the god Shani.

"What should we call him, then?" Jimmy asked.

Panditji directed a spate of Hindi towards Prakash, who responded in kind. After a few moments' agitated debate, Prakash said, "He suggests you refer to him as Shani *avatar* rather than Shani *dev*."

The pandit burst into Hindi again. This time Prakash said hardly anything; he just nodded and patted the air until the little man ran out of steam.

"Panditji says that even calling him avatar of Shani is theologically improper, because true avatar would represent god in all aspects. However, he understands that Americans are being confused by details of theology, so you may use 'Shani *avatar*' to refer to him if you like."

"Mighty generous of him," muttered Colton, beside me.

I too felt let down. It seemed that this meeting was likely to degenerate into a theoretical discussion of the more esoteric aspects of Hindu theology. Maybe it was time to try redirecting the Pandit.

"Panditji, what are Shani *avatar*'s weaknesses? How can we defend ourselves against him?" For instance, how could we avoid being turned into fish?

This question unleashed a torrent of miscellaneous information, mostly translated by Prakash because the little pandit was too excited to stick with English. To placate Shani *dev*, it seemed, we should wear black clothing, especially on Saturdays, and make offerings of oil and black sesame to him; we should wear blue sapphires and some kind of bead called *rudraksha*. Shani's metal was iron and his jewel was the sapphire. His weapons were the trident and the bow and arrow...

"Prakash. I don't think Panditji quite gets the idea. Look, if Shani *avatar* is such a flawed version of the true god, how much help can it be to get on the good side of Shani *dev*?"

Prakash translated the question to the pandit, who sagged in on himself as if some vital bits of his bone structure had suddenly collapsed.

Maybe we should get more specific. "Panditji. How was Shani *avatar* able to turn you into a fish? And is there any way to stop him doing that to people?"

The pandit managed to shrug, shake his head, and nod all at the same time. "This avatar should not have so much power, unless…" He switched back to Hindi and addressed Prakash very earnestly, tapping him repeatedly with his index finger.

"He can only have become so strong if he was possessing authentic property of the god," Prakash translated.

Jimmy groaned. "Oh, no. Tell me we're not trapped in a story about stealing the giant jewel from the forehead of the idol."

"Since he has so much power to hurt and wound ordinary human beings," Prakash went on, ignoring Jimmy's plaint, "he may have stolen one of the weapons of Shani."

The bow and the trident. An image of blue fire flickered in the back of my head. Shani's hand had crackled with fire aimed at me; then I'd thrown myself sideways as it stabbed again. And why was I suddenly having flashbacks to the battle with Shani yesterday?

Because he had flung that blue fire at me.

Blue fire in the shape of a three-headed spear.

Aka a trident.

"Panditji, is this weapon real?" No, that was the wrong way to put it; clearly a lot of things we'd classify as supernatural were perfectly real to Panditji. "I mean, can you touch it? Does it weigh anything? Does he have to pick it up physically to attack with it?"

More back-and-forth in Hindi, culminating in a consensus between Prakash and the pandit that once in possession of the weapon, Shani *avatar* could invoke it without having it actually in his hand – but that there had to be, somewhere, an actual physical weapon taken from a shrine of Shani *dev*.

And Shani *avatar* would probably keep that object close to him and guard it carefully.

Colton, Ben and Ingrid exchanged so many meaningful glances that a blind man would have realized this information meant more to them than to the rest of us. But in a rare display of caution – or maybe sadism – they refused to say anything until our friendly pandit left with Prakash, having told us a *lot* more about Hindu theology than we really cared to know.

"Come on, guys," I burst out as soon as only the other research fellows were left in the break room. Well, them and Lensky, who was leaning on the wall and not contributing anything. "What were you not saying in front of the priest guy?"

"It was more what we weren't saying in front of Prakash," Ingrid said.

I stared. "He's kind of a jerk, but surely you don't think he's gone over to the dark side?"

"No, but remember how he froze yesterday when you were in trouble?"

"I didn't actually see it. Being otherwise occupied at the time."

"Well – it was bad. I think he'd be more of a liability than an asset on this next job."

"Which is?"

Ben took the lead. "We may have seen the weapon."

"It was hanging right there on the wall," Ingrid mourned, "and I wrote it off as a piece of kitsch for tourists!"

They described it to me and it certainly sounded like what the pandit had been talking about. Trident. Made of iron, Shani's metal. Studded with what they'd taken for blue glass, but probably were actual sapphires. And definitely kept close to Shani himself.

"So all we need to do," Colton summed up glumly, "is to get into Shani's apartment in the SCI building, which is now permanently shielded against us, and get out again with the trident."

"We'll think of something," I said with more confidence than I felt.

For the first time in this meeting, Lensky dropped his imitation of a statue leaning against a wall.

"That," he said, "is what I'm afraid of. You – all four of you – have a track record of overlooking little problems like the chances of injury and death when you 'think of something.' I want you to promise that you'll consult with me *before* launching into some dangerously hairbrained scheme."

"Does that mean," I asked, "we can go ahead without consultation if our scheme *isn't* dangerously hairbrained?"

His reaction to that bright idea was, literally, unprintable.

15. The experience of being a fish

Eventually we went back to our separate offices on the far side of the wall. Brainstorming about how to get into SCI hadn't produced any good ideas; maybe we'd do better if we reverted to our normal style, sitting alone and sketching constructs that might do what we wanted.

At last, that's what Colton, Ingrid and I were doing. As we were to discover, Ben was taking his powerful but impractical brain in a somewhat different direction.

"Mr. M.," I said, "do you have any idea how to break a permanent shield?"

"Certainly. It is not a complicated task. As I have already explained to you, all that is needed is for someone to enter the space that is being shielded and remove the mage tokens on the perimeter of the shield. If I wished to remove the protection over these offices, for instance, I would erase the diagrams and axioms written on the outer walls. In the case of the Master of Ravens, I suspect the shield is maintained with the aid of grackle feathers, so you would look for those first."

Okay, his answers were consistent if unhelpful: he'd told us the same thing in the restroom. Somebody would have to get into the building and wander around unquestioned. Great! If we'd been able to do that, we could have just taken the trident without even bothering about Chayyaputra's shield.

That brought another question to mind.

"If someone is physically inside another mage's area, I mean a space that he had shielded against them, can they teleport to a place outside the shield?"

Mr. M. hummed for a while and clicked his scales softly. "I cannot answer that," he said at last. "Much depends on the way in which the shield was constructed. In the case of these offices, yes, a miscreant who had gained entry by non-magical means could then teleport himself away; the permanent shield you are using is simply an extension of the algorithm for your personal shields, which were designed to prevent attack from outside. The only way to discover whether Shani's magic works in the same way is to test it."

So, unless we could do something to disable his shield over the building, someone would not only have to sneak in and steal the trident, they might have to get away without teleporting. *Great.*

I wandered out to the public side to see if Annelise had happened to replenish the doughnut supply. She hadn't. I wanted to gripe about that, but in an excess of tact I merely complained to her that I couldn't think of any way to get into the SCI building unchallenged.

"Ben will think of something," she said with the serene faith of someone who isn't expected to solve the problem herself, and went back to her crossword puzzle. I understand some people find them soothing.

"Thalia, where are you? I've thought of something!" Ben called from his office on the other side of the wall.

Annelise and I looked at each other and sputtered.

"The man does have a sense of timing," I allowed.

I started to Möbius myself back to the private side, but I bumped into Ben coming the other way and we both came out into the public room. "This is good," he said cheerfully, "I can show you and Annelise at the same time." He glanced at some symbols jotted on his shirt cuff.

"I *wish* you wouldn't write on your good shirts," Annelise said plaintively. She'd invested time and effort in teaching him to order the tailored Italian shirts that actually fit his lanky build; it must have been painful to see him attacking the cuffs with a ball-point pen. However, I felt the two of them could work on that problem in their personal time.

"If you've figured out how to get through Shani's shields," I said, "let's get

Ingrid and Colton, and you can tell us all at the same time."

"Oh, that's not it," Ben said. "This is *much* more interesting. If it works."

"Ah, what happens if it doesn't work?" Ben's topological ideas were always interesting but sometimes also catastrophic. Witness the time he set fire to Allandale House while trying to create light. "Like starting fires with Riemann surfaces," I reminded him. "Or sealing yourself in an impenetrable shield that blocked every way of communicating with you from outside. Or—"

Ben pushed his shock of light brown hair out of his eyes so that I could get the full benefit of his wounded-doe expression. "Riemann fire has turned out to be quite useful," he defended himself. "And the silly-putty shield was just a stage in development on the way to making useful shields. Anyway, I've completely thought this one through. Theoretically it's perfectly sound. I just haven't actually done it yet, and I thought you'd appreciate the fact that I'm collecting witnesses before I demonstrate it."

I threw my hands up. "Demonstrate at will. Just don't take too long, okay? *Some* of us are trying to solve *real* problems here!" And making zero progress, which is probably why I was so irritable with him.

Ben took off his glasses and carefully placed them on Annelise's desk. "Don't want to break them," he said, as though that was a complete explanation. Or any kind of explanation at all, come to think of it.

His eyes went vague and his lips started moving. I couldn't hear what he was saying so softly; everybody who worked at the Center had a desk fan to complement the ineffective, retro-fitted air conditioning, and on a day like this the hum of the combined fans drowned out quiet conversation. I wondered what he was visualizing, and whether it would be useful, decorative, or disastrous.

Then a curtain of fire roared up between us, startling me into taking several steps back.

The fire alarms went off and completely drowned out Annelise, whose lips were moving now.

The automatic sprinklers started shooting out jets of water. One of them squirted directly into my right eye. When I dodged, a second one tried to soak my hair.

And Colton came barreling through the wall with a green-painted cylinder labeled, "This is Not a Fire Extinguisher." (The trustees feel that the chemicals in fire extinguishers would be harmful to the fabric of the building. Since we feel that a conflagration would be even more harmful, Colton honored their restriction in his own way.)

He put out the fire with one long swooping spray from the non-fire-extinguisher. The alarms stopped and the sprinkler system turned itself off. Everything was okay again, with the minor exceptions that we were all slightly damp and that Ben had disappeared.

I couldn't even make out the slight blur that gave away use of our camouflage algorithm to people who knew what to look for.

His clothes were crumpled on the floor, and they seemed to be twitching slightly; but whatever was under them wasn't nearly large enough to be Ben. With a sense of foreboding I picked up his discarded shirt. Maybe the jottings on his shirt cuff would give us a clue—oh, no. No. We weren't going to have time to work this out mathematically; there was a fish flopping under the shirt.

How long could it live out of water? Did Ben have the sense to transform himself back into an air-breathing form immediately?

It didn't seem so.

"Thalia! Fill the sink in the bathroom!" Annelise grabbed the fish and I ran to follow her instructions.

The sink was only a little over halfway full when she came in with her hands full of writhing fish, but after she put it into the sink the water rose almost to the top. The fish stopped struggling and I could see something moving rhythmically along its side; fins or gills or something like that. Ben would know... oh. Right. We couldn't exactly ask him now, could we? And this fish didn't have a tag that we could remove, so how were we going to turn Ben back into himself? I scowled at the bulgy-eyed, scaled critter in the sink. "You'd better remember how to reverse the transformation, or I'll tell Dr. Verrick what you've been up to."

Dr. Verrick had been first our topology professor, and then our director after he created the Center for Applied Topology as a refuge for those few of

146

his students who had a talent for making topological theorems do things they were never designed for. We learned later that he too had that talent, and had lived through some long and lonely years thinking that he was the only mathematician who was, as he put it, cursed with the supernatural. The discovery of four more applied topologists in his own classrooms had given him a new lease on life.

He wasn't very active these days; he wasn't as young as he used to be, and the last year's alarums and excursions had taken a lot out of him. But his tongue was as sharp as ever, and yes, being stuck in fish form probably wasn't nearly as frightening to Ben as the prospect of a formal reprimand from the Director. Of the two options, I know that I'd take the involuntary-swimming one every time.

I shivered. The bathroom seemed to be getting actually *cold*, which was way beyond the capabilities of our retrofitted air conditioning system. There was even a film of ice around the edge of the sink... and...

The fish seemed to be getting bigger.

And pinker.

Water spilled over the edge and froze as icicles, framing the sink with a delicate frieze of ice for just a moment; then the sink pulled out of the wall under Ben's weight and he skidded over the edge himself. He had, quite obviously, brought nothing with him. But I should have anticipated that, seeing he'd left that little pile of garments on the floor outside the bathroom.

I averted my eyes. "I'll, um, I'll just get your clothes."

It appeared that the entire staff of the Center had gathered in the central room while Annelise and I were dunking the fish. With Lensky front and center. They started questioning me before I'd even picked up all of Ben's discarded clothing.

"What the (triple-barreled obscenity) just happened?" demanded Meadow.

"What burned?" Ingrid asked.

"What kind of fire was that?" Colton asked, "Look, the floor isn't even scorched. So what *did* it burn?"

I made a sloppy stack out of Ben's clothes. "It was Ben's idea," I said, "I'll let him tell you all about it."

"Where *is* Ben?"

I jerked my head towards the bathroom.

Lensky hadn't joined the chorus of questioners. He just stood there with his arms folded and one foot tapping in a style that I, personally, found ominous. Now he said, very calmly, "Ben is in the bathroom?"

"Yes, and I need to get these to him. He's cold and wet."

"The whole office is cold," Jimmy said. "Did he figure out how to fix our air conditioning with topology?"

"Ah, not exactly."

"Your friend Ben is in the bathroom," Lensky repeated. "You were with him. And his clothes are out here?" Lensky's always had kind of a *thing* about Ben and me, though I'd thought he was getting over it. Right now he did not seem to be completely cured of that particular bit of paranoia.

"Annelise is in there too," I said quickly before anybody else could take a prurient interest in these little details. I opened the bathroom door a crack and shoved Ben's clothes into Annelise's waiting hands.

"I'm not sure whether that makes it better or worse," Lensky said after I abandoned Ben to figure out for himself how to get dressed in a closet-sized room full of plumbing fixtures. "Would you object to my asking Ben to restrain his amorous impulses in the office?"

I rolled my eyes. He knew perfectly well we hadn't been staging an orgy in the tiny third-floor bathroom. "Don't be stupid. I don't think it would be physically possible to have a threesome in there."

Jimmy, Colton, and Will all got the same distant expression, as if they were trying to picture the possibilities.

"You two are too tall," Will said to Jimmy and Colton.

"You're probably not flexible enough," Colton told him.

"Thalia's small *and* flexible."

"Harper does yoga. If she came back…"

"We could run some tests…"

"We could *not*," I snapped. "That's not the kind of research we do here." I turned to Lensky. "And FYI, it's Ben's *experimental* impulses that need restraining."

Ben finally came out of the bathroom, Annelise behind him. His clothes looked even more disheveled than usual, and he was dripping on the floor.

"I can hardly wait to hear what concatenation of circumstances led to your becoming both wet and inadequately dressed – *again*," Lensky said to him.

To be fair, I'd thought about that when we were in Mayfield Park. And this episode made *three* times in less than a year. I could hardly blame Lensky for wondering if there was more than coincidence involved. For a perfect gentleman who had never, ever hit on a girl who wasn't already interested in him, Ben did seem to have a lot of trouble keeping his pants on.

Ben blinked at him myopically. "Where are my glasses?"

Annelise picked them up from her desk and handed them to him. He slipped them on and blinked at us again through the smeared lenses. "Ah, that's better. I can't *think* when I can't see."

"Does that mean that if I ask Lensky to take charge of your glasses, you won't get yourself into trouble again?"

Ben ignored me in a way that implied he was above responding to my childish taunts. "It's because I've been a fish quite recently, I think," he began.

"Yes! Two minutes ago! What were you *thinking*?" Annelise's cheeks were pink.

Ben waved a placating hand (fin?) in her direction. "Not that. I mean the first time. Chayyaputra actually did me a big favor, giving me the experience of being a fish. It was just a matter of defining a function that would map me onto a fish, and I felt sure that could be done topologically. And it worked! See, I defined a continuous mapping with an energy-shedding property to account for the difference in mass, and I made sure it was reversible before I applied it. I just, just had a little trouble *remembering* the reverse mapping when I couldn't breathe."

Colton grumbled, although quietly, that Ben's turning himself into a fish didn't do anything to solve our current problem. "It might," Ben said. "You know how the fire came out of nowhere when I transformed? I've just had another idea…"

Ingrid, Colton and I simultaneously told him *not* to have any more ideas, we'd already had enough crises for one day. "What we want now," Ingrid said, "is a nice quiet session with you and a whiteboard, to see exactly how you did this."

"I'm not sure you will be able to replicate it," Ben warned. "I'm the only one here who really knows how it feels to be a fish."

"Just show us the mathematics," Ingrid said.

"I knew this girl in high school who was remarkably like a fish," Colton said. "A cold one."

All right, it was a bit of a distraction from the problem of stealing the god's trident. But I was as eager as the others to find out the topological basis of shapeshifting, and I rationalized that sometimes it was good to take a little break from an apparently intractable problem. Perhaps my subconscious would come up with a solution to the trident problem if I pretended to be thinking of something else.

Sadly, a nice quiet afternoon with Ben and a whiteboard was not in my immediate future. He claimed he had to talk to Lensky about something first, and while we were waiting for him Mom called. Had I forgotten that we were to meet at Beth's Bridal Salon for me to try on wedding dresses? Well yes, I had. My life *had* been rather full recently. What with posing as a god's fiancée, rescuing Ben from his first sojourn as a fish, fighting with Lensky, and rescuing Ben from his *second* sojourn as a fish, I felt I could be excused for forgetting minor details.

Mom, of course, did not consider the Wedding Dress Selection Trip a minor detail. For her it was probably one of the high points of the pre-wedding: looking at her daughter in a series of sumptuous gowns.

I don't do sumptuous, you know? I'm too short, and not exactly graceful. T-shirts and cutoffs are more my style.

But for once Lensky aligned himself with Mom. "If you're really going to go through with this, you will have to have a suitable dress." He quirked one eyebrow at me and I sighed. Was I really going to have to be stifled, poked, pinned, extinguished under mountains of lace and white silk, just to placate my mother and convince Lensky I was still committed to marrying him? I accepted that I couldn't get married in my treasured Ramones shirt and my favorite cut-offs, but I'd been hoping to negotiate some kind of middle ground between that and Death in White Satin. Couldn't I get married in my little black dress, the one I used for obligatory Moore Foundation parties?

It seemed that was not an option. Lensky even told me to take his car – naturally I'd never before set foot in this Bridal Salon place, so I couldn't teleport myself there. And, as he pointed out, he would have to stay at the office anyway until I came back to teleport both of us home. Abiding, he said, by our agreement.

I still haven't figured out how a deal I'd set up to protect Lensky got turned into me getting stuck with doing yet more bride stuff. He's twisty like that.

So while my colleagues were presumably getting an introduction to a fantastic new application of topology, I was stuck in South Austin, being pinned into white satin and trying not to look at my reflection in the triple mirror that some sadist had built into one end of the salon.

"This was the first dress I asked Beth to reserve for you," Mom announced happily. "As soon as I saw it I said, 'Thalia!'"

How strange. I would have said, "*Merde!*" Or possibly "*Merde alors!*" I'd have to ask Aunt Alesia which was appropriate.

The top half wasn't so bad, apart from being designed to show off curves I don't have. But from my waist downwards the ruched satin broke out into an extravaganza of frills and giant, three-dimensional, cabbage-sized fabric roses decorated with iridescent glass beads. I looked as if I was standing in a giant meringue – one that was fixing to rise up and consume me. I looked at Beth of the Bridal Salon, but she was smiling and clasping her hands together as though ravished with delight.

"I don't think…" I started.

"This is one of my premier creations," Beth said, "and perfect for a lovely young girl like you."

"Ah… it's very unusual," I said, "but I don't think it's quite *me*."

"Oh? What do you dislike about it?"

For starters, I wasn't lovely or all that young, but that was far from being the only problem with this disaster. "I, ah, I'm sure it would look wonderful on somebody a little taller." A blatant lie. Even Ingrid, almost six feet tall and crowned with yards of silver-blond hair, couldn't have carried off the Monster Mutant White Rose Exhibit. And Beth had to admit, when I pointed it out, that I was somewhat overwhelmed by fabric roses the size of my head. The only person who thought I looked good in it was Mom, and she's prejudiced in my favor.

That dress disappeared, not nearly quickly enough, and Beth lifted the next dress over my head. The basis of this one was a simple shift of silk gauze, and apart from being nearly transparent it would have been okay had Beth only left it at that. Unfortunately, her fix for the transparency of silk gauze had been too much of a good thing. Layer after layer of white silk gauze wafted over my head, each a little shorter than the previous one. Some of them snagged on my shoulders and elbows on the way down.

I looked as if I'd failed to fight my way out of a mosquito net.

"Of course," Beth said faintly, "you'll look taller when your hair is styled."

That was news to me. But it was true that short black hair straightened and swept up with plenty of gel looked, well, out of place with dresses like this. *I* looked out of place.

"She's letting her hair grow out for the wedding," Mom said.

"I am?"

"You can't wear *stefana* on top of those... those *spikes*." Stefana are traditional Greek wedding "crowns," nowadays usually just wreaths of white porcelain flowers with pearls and crystals, and they're an essential part of the ceremony. For both bride and groom. I hadn't yet broken it to Lensky that he was going to be spending some time in church wearing a wreath of artificial flowers. A sparkly one. "Her hair is naturally curly," Mom told Beth, "just like mine. It'll be beautiful with a white satin ribbon threaded through the curls."

"How long until the wedding?"

"Six weeks."

"Hmm. Well. I hope it grows fast."

"It will have to."

After dissing my hair, they went back to smothering me under dresses that were in general too full, too flouncy, and much too white. I lost track of time and become a machine programmed to raise and lower my arms on command. I began planning to duck under the crinoline supporting the Scarlett O'Hara model and crawl out of the shop. I mentally sold Lensky's car for two tickets to a Caribbean isle without Internet or phones. Or extradition. And once I began thinking about what we could do in the luxury hotel that had magically appeared on this dream island, the fantasy carried me past innumerable dresses – well, *I* wasn't enumerating them, anyway – in most of which I looked like a small sallow blemish on the billowy white creations. Blinding white silk and olive skin just don't work together, at least not on me.

Even Mom began to droop a little as the afternoon wore on. But she was absolutely determined that I would be married in a proper wedding dress if it killed her, and Beth said that today was the absolute deadline for picking a dress that would have to be altered to fit in a mere six weeks.

Eventually I climbed out of a giant white pom-pom and begged for mercy. "No more, please!"

"I don't know that I *have* any more," Beth announced.

An hour earlier I would have been delighted to hear this; it was my ticket out of the salon. Now I was too tired and dispirited to throw my clothes on and escape. I sagged down on a chair in my bra and panties and avoided Mom's eye. It didn't seem fair that I should feel guilty for failing to live up to her fantasies, but I did anyway.

Even my underwear was inappropriate for the kind of dresses Beth had been bringing out; she'd made numerous comments about how much better they'd look if I were wearing proper foundation garments.

"Don't just sit there like that," Beth said, "you'll catch your death!"

True, the combination of sweaty bare skin and laboring air conditioning was kind of uncomfortable. So when she tossed me a loose ivory satin robe and told me to pull it over my head while she searched the stock room for something else that *might* be satisfactory, I complied.

The deep off-white satin of the robe was actually much more to my taste than the starkly white confections I'd been climbing in and out of all afternoon. Creamy, ivory, almost golden in the shadows of the folds… I looked down, idly pleating the fabric with my fingers and cataloguing the subtle color changes, until I heard Mom draw in her breath.

"Thalia," she said. "Thalia!"

"Yes?" I supposed I was going to have to pick the least obnoxious of the dresses I'd tried on. I searched my memory; surely there'd been at least one that I didn't hate?

"Thalia, stand up. No, over here." She urged me into the spot before the mirrors again. "Look at you! You're glowing!"

She was right. The rich color of the ivory silk complemented my skin instead of fighting with it. And there weren't any puffs, sashes, cleverly cut jackets or monster cabbage roses to get in the way and complicate my life. "Too bad I can't just wear this," I said idly.

"You can!"

"I can?" The sleeves of the robe fell to my fingertips, the "empire" waist was somewhere around my actual waist, and six inches of fabric puddled on the floor at my feet.

"Alterations," Mom said. She took a handful of fabric at the back of the robe and pulled it up and away from my body until the front almost looked as if it fit.

It *was* possible. The square neckline and Empire waist made me look as if I had actual curves, and the heavy, soft, creamy fabric fell to the floor in folds that glowed golden in the shadows.

I could get married in something that wasn't hideously embarrassing, something I actually liked. "Mom! I love it! But will Beth sell it to us? Without, you know, fussying it up?"

"For what the alterations on this are going to cost," Mom said, "she'd sell me the rug on the fitting-room floor."

16. Bombers' moon

I'm going to assume that you have no idea how much measuring and marking and pinning has to be done, *after* you've picked out a wedding dress, to make sure the alterations are right. I do, now, and I've got the pinpricks to prove it. Let's just say that it was dark by the time we got out of Beth's Bridal Salon, and Mom and I were both starving. I talked her into the daring plan of getting something to eat at a restaurant and leaving Dad to fend for himself, but that didn't work out quite as well as I'd hoped. We'd just been served when Ingrid called me.

At first I thought it was somebody else using her phone, because like Meadow, Ingrid doesn't do hysteria. Even when she thought she was trapped in 1957, the only way she betrayed that she was rattled was that she actually hugged Jimmy when he and I showed up to retrieve her. I knew the experience had gone deep for her, because she was still leery of teleporting for fear of another accidental time-slip, but she never talked about her fears.

Ever.

So when she called me only to babble incoherently about terror and time travel and disaster and Lensky, I knew it had to be bad.

"Didn't Brad wait for me at the office?" I interrupted. It *was* rather late, but it wasn't like him to be impatient. And he'd *promised* not to go home on his own. Hadn't he? And in any case, I had his car.

"He did," Ingrid said, "that's the trouble."

"Well, is he okay?"

"I – don't know! Thalia, you have to come back right away!"

"On my way."

I scooped our dinners into to-go boxes, paid, and dropped Mom off at her car in approximately the time it would have taken me to reject just one poufy wedding dress, and even that took too long. Then I broke a few minor traffic laws getting back to the office, second-guessing myself at every red light. Should I just have teleported? But what if we needed a car? Oh, help. Ingrid had her car, why hadn't I thought of that?

I was on the freeway, terrifying a few idiots who hogged the fast lane only to drive the exact speed limit, when I did think of that, and it was a bit late to do anything about it then. I couldn't exactly start teleporting at seventy-five miles an hour. We'd never been good at matching speeds when teleporting; even an emergency jump from one place to another frequently ended with somebody losing their balance. I'd probably smear myself across the office like raspberry jam if I tried to teleport there from the freeway.

Oh, yes, and it's generally considered poor traffic manners to abandon a speeding car, right?

I parked at the first piece of bare curb I saw after exiting the freeway. From that spot in West Austin I teleported directly to Ingrid's office on the private side of the third floor.

She was huddled in the chair behind her desk, shaking uncontrollably.

"Ingrid!"

She had never been fond of being touched, but I went around the desk and put my arms around her anyway. "Are you all right? What happened?"

She took a great shuddering gasp and sat up straight, brushing me off. "Oh, *I'm* all right," she said. "I'm fine. At least until you kill me."

"For?"

"For losing Lensky."

"You're not his guardian," I said absently. *"What happened?"*

"It was the Master of Ravens."

I was already terrified for Lensky; now a cold sweat prickled all over my body. "Ingrid. *Is Lensky…*"

I couldn't say it. I couldn't even make myself go and look in his office. The room darkened. I thought my mind must be shutting down.

"Not dead. I don't think. But lost… Oh, Thalia, you'll never find him!"

Ha! My brain came humming back to life. And now I had purpose as well as life. 'Dead' was the only thing I couldn't fix. 'Lost' I could and would deal with, but the first step was to get Ingrid calmed down enough to tell me exactly what had happened.

"Where's everybody else?"

"They went out to Hole in the Wall for burgers and beer and commiseration. Lensky said he had to stay here until you got back, and I wanted to work out some consequences of Ben's transformation theory, so it was just us two when *he* came. And I was back here on the private side."

"He? The Master of Ravens? Shani Chayyaputra?"

Ingrid nodded, tried and failed to gulp down a sob, buried her face in her hands.

But the offices were shielded; how could he have gotten in here? Maybe Jimmy could get some sense out of her. I stepped back and called his number.

When he answered, I could hear the noise of a band behind him. Evidently Hole in the Wall was having a '70's nostalgia special this week, because the band was doing the instrumentals for "L.A. Woman." And the creaky, croaky voice belting out the lyrics sounded like Mr. M.

Must be a hell of a party.

"Jimmy. Can you sober up, grab Mr. M., and come back here?"

"What, all of us?"

"Whoever's still there."

"That would be all of us. Except you… and Ingrid… and… Lensky."

He was speaking with the exaggerated care of somebody who suspected that last drink had been one too many. "I don't care who else comes, but hurry. *Ingrid needs you.*"

Moments later, Ingrid's office was full of happy topologists and staff members. Or – no, not happy exactly. But definitely sloshed.

I chewed my fingernails while Jimmy hugged Ingrid and patted her back and said soothing nonsense to her.

"What occasioned the drunken orgy?" I asked Ben, who was quietly hiccupping beside me. "Celebration?"

"More like licking our wounds. Things... didn't go so well this afternoon."

"What things?"

"Later." Because Ingrid had given one last forlorn sniff and was finally ready to tell her story.

"After we all got back—"

"Back from where?"

"SCI," Ben answered. "Remember me telling you I'd had another idea? I thought of an absolutely *brilliant* way to get into the building without teleporting."

"Except," Meadow said, "it didn't work."

"We *almost* pulled it off," Ben defended himself.

"It was a good plan," Will said. "I helped him work it out. And Lensky okayed it. Well, the general idea, anyway. It's possible we should have thought a little more about the details."

"He *did?*"

"Yeah, that's why he was so pleased when your mother insisted you had to go try on wedding dresses. So that you wouldn't be involved. Because, see, it wasn't totally *safe...*"

These two geniuses had decided that setting the inside of the SCI building on fire would force the fire brigade to break down the doors, after which they would simply walk into the building instead of trying to break the anti-teleporting shield.

"That part worked just fine," Ben insisted. "I manipulated Riemann surfaces to start a bunch of little fires all over the first floor, and Colton and Ingrid used the same algorithm to set Shani's bedroom on fire. We didn't need to be inside the building for any of that, and he hadn't thought of shielding against remote applications of topology."

"But you didn't get the trident?"

"It was confusing," Ben said. "Firemen all over the place, water spraying everywhere..."

It hadn't occurred to the geniuses that firemen were not likely to allow a handful of civilians to stroll into a burning building, and they'd been – reading between the lines – reprehensibly sloppy about keeping camouflage up. Nor had it occurred to them that the offices might be empty at night, but the Master of Ravens would almost certainly still be there. It was, after all, where he lived.

There were doubtless innumerable embarrassing details that Ben and Will were glossing over, but right now I didn't care; all I wanted was to know what had happened to Lensky. And that was Ingrid's part of the story.

The Mathematical Mafia and the Center support staff had returned to Allandale House tired, wet, scorched in places, and humiliated by their failure. They had – almost unanimously – decided to go across the Drag to bury their sorrows in beer and live music rather than listen to Lensky's corrosive analysis of their mistakes. Ingrid was the only one of them who had felt that a nice quiet hour with topological theory would be more soothing than liquor and noise, and she hadn't been eager to talk with Lensky either. She'd buried herself in her office on the private side with her reference books. She successfully lost herself in the ramifications of transformational mappings until she noticed raised voices out in the main office.

The internal walls on the third floor were, to say the least, flimsy. When voices were raised, they were audible all over the floor. Once she registered the fact of shouting and started to listen, Ingrid could hear everything that was being said.

The first thing she learned was that the Master of Ravens was in the office, and he was furious.

"How did he get in?" I'd thought Lensky was safe in this shielded place. "Did somebody erase the tokens on our walls?"

"*We* walked into the SCI building – before the firemen threw us out again," Ben said. "Maybe he did something similar. Teleported himself to the stairs and just walked up and in without using magic. We usually leave the door at the top of the stairs open, and anyway the lock's busted." He flushed and looked away from me. We were both remembering just who had disassembled that lock while researching how to open locks topologically.

"I knew that," I admitted. We'd all known it, we just hadn't considered the implications. Nobody expected the Master of Ravens to walk in on his own two feet. For a bunch of supposedly high-powered intellects, we had been remarkably stupid, hadn't we? *And Lensky paid the price.* Whatever it had been.

"So Brad and Chayyaputra were yelling at each other," I prompted Ingrid.

"He was angry," she said again. "About us setting his building on fire. He thought it had been your idea, Thalia, and he said some things about you that… well, Lensky got angry too. I think he tried to hit Chayyaputra again, only he was on guard this time and his grackles protected him. Then Chayyaputra said he was going to teach *you* a lesson by disposing of Lensky."

"You said he wasn't dead!"

"He isn't. I don't think. Chayyaputra said that would be too easy for him. And you. He said he was going to transport Lensky through space and time to a place where you'd never find him."

I closed my eyes for a moment, fighting off despair. Where was Brad now? Maybe I'd been too confident about dealing with 'lost.'

"Then he said a bunch of stuff that didn't make any sense. The grackles were keeping Lensky from reaching him, I think. He was having fun taunting Lensky about what he was going to do, too much fun to just do it right away. But then – then everything went quiet. And I called you." Ingrid's eyes were rimmed with red. "Thalia, I am as bad as Prakash. I didn't even try to help. I *froze* as soon as Chayyaputra said that about sending Lensky out of his own time."

A very small part of my mind, the part that wasn't focused on staying quiet and repressing my own urge to wail with grief and fear, reminded me that Ingrid's experience of being trapped in the wrong time had left her so nervous that she wouldn't even teleport if she could avoid it. Eventually, I supposed, I would not hate her.

For now, I didn't much care how guilty I made her feel. I needed to know every word Chayyaputra had said, to comb through them for any possible clue. "Go back over it again. Don't leave anything out."

"I told you," said Ingrid, "it didn't make any *sense.*"

"I don't care, tell me anyway!" There had to be a clue somewhere, there *had* to be. Because… I did not know what I was going to do, if there wasn't.

Once I had teleported to Lensky when I didn't know where he was. But we'd been in the same town – and the same time – then. Now when I reached out mentally to him, I felt nothing. A blank emptiness. Distance, or years, or the evil work of Chayyaputra: something was hiding him from me.

If I was to find him, it would have to be by old-fashioned detective work, the way Jimmy and I had once located Ingrid and Colton in the Britfield of 1957. Lensky might not be able to teleport himself back here, but he was easily as bright as Ingrid or Colton when it came to sending messages to the future. There *would* be clues. There might be some even now, in what Chayyaputra had said.

"Ingrid. *Concentrate.*"

She closed her eyes. "I don't remember – ohh…. Yes… He said that since we'd brought fire and flood on his building, he was going to give Lensky a first-hand experience of fire and flood under a bombers' moon."

Will stirred. "A bombers' moon? You're sure those were his words?"

"I told you it didn't make any sense."

"What else did he say?" Will's eyes were blazing now. What was he seeing that I had missed?

"Oh, then he talked about chess, of all things."

"What exactly did he say about chess?"

"That Lensky was a pawn who was going to meet a rook. And then he went back to his nasty, gloating threats. He said that if Lensky was very unlucky, he would live through the night without being burnt or blown up or buried, and then he would have a long, long time to think about Thalia grieving and searching for him."

"Burnt, blown up, buried," Will repeated slowly. I wished he wouldn't. I was already seeing nightmare images of what could have happened to Brad. "And he specifically mentioned a rook? You're sure about that?"

"Oh!" Colton exclaimed. "*Bombers' moon.*"

I snapped my head around to look at Colton. "That phrase means something to you two?"

161

"England," Will said, "the Blitz."

That wasn't quite enough to clarify it for me.

"When the moon was full and the skies were clear," Will amplified, "that was what the English called it – a bombers' moon, meaning the German planes could see to bomb London."

"So... you think somewhere in London? During the war? Those five years?" A long period, but it was a lot more checkable than all the millennia of human history. Or the *future*... I had no idea what I'd do if Chayyaputra had possessed the power to transport Brad into the future, so I decided not to think about it.

"Oh, the Blitz only lasted about nine months," Colton said, "and there wasn't a clear sky every time the moon was full."

Better and better. From uncounted millennia, to five years, to nine months.

"But Chayyaputra said," Will put in, "that if Lensky survived that one night, he would have a long time to live and grieve. The rest of his life. So he can't have been sent where he would be in danger day after day. I'm thinking – the last night of bombing. May 10. It was a terrible night, possibly the worst night of the Blitz. And there was a bombers' moon that night."

I began to feel a tiny, tiny sliver of hope. It was almost painful. Was it possible that they had figured out the city *and* the day? If I could take myself back to London on that date, might I be able to teleport across the city to wherever Brad was? Would it be much harder than finding him in Austin had been, that one time I teleported to his presence rather than to a known location? All right, London was bigger. But I knew him so much better, now, than I had then.

It still bothered me that we were leaning so much on a single reference. No, that wasn't right. 'Bombers' moon,' and 'burnt, blown up, buried.' My heart gave a painful squeeze. I had to stop that. Think of it as a reference, not a prediction. A puzzle piece. "So I need to put myself in London on May 10 of – what year?" During the second world war, was all I knew.

"1941," Will said, "but I think we can narrow it down more than that. One of the parts of London that suffered most on that night was the Elephant and Castle district." He seemed disappointed by my lack of response. "Don't you get it? Elephant and Castle – Rook! Think what the chess piece looks like."

I couldn't picture it.

"Nowadays it's just a tower," Will said, "but it used to be an *elephant* with a tower on its back. That was the sign for the Elephant and Castle pub. See, that's the rook Chayyaputra meant! That district took the worst of the bombing on May 10."

Three reference points. I'd have liked more, but you go with the data you have. If this wasn't enough, I could come back and start the slow grind of searching contemporary publications for the clues that Brad would surely have left me, as soon as he had a chance.

But I didn't think that would be necessary. I guess some of Will's absolute certainty must have rubbed off on me. "You can use the pub like a beacon," he said, "but you'd better get there right at the beginning of the bombing. And whatever you do, don't go inside."

"Why not?" Okay, so it was a bar, so what? I've been in bars; I'm twenty-four, not sixteen.

"Because it burned down that night, and I'm not sure exactly when or what happened. You don't want it getting hit by a high explosive bomb while you're inside, do you? So don't *be* inside."

17. Falling stars

London, May 10, 1941

The first thing he noticed was the noise. The city was dark, but from somewhere came an uneven, whining drone that might have been caused by some poorly maintained machine in a factory. Except that it seemed to be moving towards him, getting louder and louder. He stuck his hands in his pockets and shivered. This place – wherever it might be—was *cold*. As his eyes adjusted, he realized that it was not as dark as he'd thought; a full moon turned the city street before him into a pattern of sharp, crisp lights and shadows. And maybe it wasn't that late, either. There were still people on the street.

A wailing siren overrode the distant noise. The few people who were out on this dark street glanced up at the sky, then ran. On the far side of a star-shaped intersection he saw the outline of a low, squarish brick building without windows. Most of the people headed for that. Others seemed to disappear as if the street had swallowed them up. He began to understand how after a man pushed past him. "If you're not using this doorway, mate, get out of the way!" Lensky turned and saw the deep, arched entrance to some kind of shop behind him.

"Get to a shelter, you idiots!" somebody else shouted as he ran past.

Lensky backed up into the doorway where the first man was huddled. There was plenty of room for them both. He wanted to ask what they were hiding from, but clearly everybody else knew. He didn't want to be marked as a stranger or a madman in this place – wherever and whenever it might be. He kept his mouth shut and watched and listened.

The high-pitched, irregular sound of engines was much louder now.

Suddenly the night bloomed with hundreds of white, flickering lights. They came down over the city like cascades of diamonds, like clusters of falling stars. Was this what Thalia saw when she talked about her magic-enhancing stars? And if so, why was he seeing them now?

He didn't think they could be the same as the invisible stars that Thalia claimed to carry in a pocket and hold in the palm of her hand. These stars were much larger than that, and they were falling directly overhead and all around him. They whistled as they came down, then clattered upon landing like a bunch of empty tin cans. As he watched and shivered, he saw two blue-white flames spring up, one on a window ledge and the other on a house roof.

He could see clearly now: more flares were dropping, hundreds of them, bathing the street in a white glare that eclipsed the moon. He stared at the weirdly beautiful scene, trying to pick up some clue as to where he was. *And when*. But he wasn't ready to think about that part yet.

What he could make out in the strange, cold light looked like an ordinary city street of office buildings with small shops occupying the ground floors. The building style was somewhat old-fashioned, not much like the blank facades of glass and granite in a modern city. And he might not even be in America: the signs were in English, but what American city had so many separate little shops? He could see signs for a greengrocer's, a tailor's and a tobacco shop among more normal-looking stores. All the windows were smaller than he was used to seeing. The lettering of the signs, like the style of the buildings, was curiously ornate.

His gaze stopped, arrested by a black empty square that didn't reflect the light like the other shop windows. Oh – there was no glass in the window. A sign tacked to the door read, "More open than usual." Open even when closed, eh? And what kind of a city was it where nobody looted the unprotected shop?

The tin-can clattering noise sounded again, louder and closer, and a sizzle of bluish-white flame sprang up across the street. Two more of the mysterious stars came down almost immediately afterwards, just a few doors farther down the street.

"Come on!" his companion in the doorway shouted. He ran across the street, shoulders hunched, and began kicking and stamping at the flame. "What you waiting for, think the bloody wardens can put them all out?"

Lensky awoke from his near-trance into a reality in which the flickering white lights were not beautiful stars, but nasty little things trying to incinerate whatever they touched. He ran down to the two new fires. One was on the pavement; he stamped on it. The other one had landed in a flower box which he wrenched free and threw upside down onto the pavement, so that the dirt could smother that flame. But even while he was working on those two, more fires started up and down the street. Then he heard a new noise: a faint whistling that grew and grew into a deafening shriek, then into a roar that ended abruptly. He looked up just in time to see the wall of the nearest house shudder and bulge out in a way that solid bricks should never have been able to do, swaying as though they were no more than a heavy curtain.

A body slammed into his back, taking him down into the gutter. "*Cover your head*, you bloody fool!"

Lensky wrapped his arms around his head as the sound of falling bricks and timbers overrode all the other noises around him. Something struck his shoulder as he waited to be buried in the rubble.

After a long, tense moment the sounds of the collapsing building ceased. He hadn't been buried under it after all. He hadn't even been seriously bruised.

The man who'd pushed him into the gutter hadn't been so lucky. A jagged piece of timber had gone through his back. His neck was twisted, the eyes open and staring.

Lensky's head felt thick and confused. What should he do? Oh – close those eyes. That was what you did for people when they were dead. But as he got to his knees, all thought of the dead was driven out of his mind by the sound of whimpering. It seemed to come from under the remains of the collapsed building.

"Oh, please, someone, help me!" The whimpering turned to quiet, gasping sobs. By the light of the still-falling incendiaries he could see that a large beam had fallen at an angle in the pile. It was almost buried under bricks and dust and broken timbers, but there was a space beneath it where somebody might have survived. He couldn't reach it now: there were more bricks and debris blocking the way to that space.

He began throwing bricks aside, trying to get to whoever was trapped. It was harder after he got rid of the bricks and had to deal with the pile of dust and sand and small stuff at the edge of the beam. He scooped it out with his bare hands, frantic with the fear that whoever was under the beam was being suffocated by stuff like this even as he worked. "It's all right, you're going to be all right," he said over and over as he scooped and tossed. It seemed to take forever just to clear that small heap. Was that a rag he saw under the beam? If only he had a flashlight – No, not a rag; part of a woman's dress. He reached one arm under the beam, groping for the woman, and caught hold of something – a shoulder, he thought. When he gripped it and tried to haul the woman out, he heard her thin high scream over all the other noises that filled the air.

"Are you hurt?" he shouted into the narrow space. "Trapped?"

"No – no, it doesn't matter. Pull me out. I won't scream."

He pulled, felt her body shifting, dragged her towards him.

The mass of rubble above them also shifted. He wondered if he would be able to get her out before it moved again and buried them both. With one more desperate heave he got her mostly out from under the beam, but when he tried to pick her up she clung to something underneath there.

"Let go of that, whatever it is!" he shouted at her.

"I can't! It's our Ellie! I'll not go without her!"

Lensky felt a warning tremor in the beam that sheltered them. "*Let go*. I'll get her," he promised, and lifted the young woman in his arms. Her back was wet. No – her back was *raw*, laid open on one side from shoulder to hip. He tried to imagine what kind of courage had prevented her from crying out while he dragged that open wound across broken stones. Couldn't.

There were two more people behind him now, quietly and efficiently moving the bricks and other debris that he'd tossed out of his way without thinking. He passed the injured woman to them and plunged back under the beam. Almost immediately he found what she must have been holding on to: a small, cold hand. He pulled, hoping to get the kid out of the rubble quickly, and the hand came loose in his.

It was cold as ice against his fingers.

***

Someone was washing his face, pouring water over his eyes. They didn't seem to want to open, but slowly he became aware of a warm yellow light that was quite unlike the devilish blue-white of the falling stars.

"With us again? That's good!" said the woman holding the bowl of water. She dabbed at his face again with a damp rag.

"What happened? Where am I?" Too late he remembered that he shouldn't betray his ignorance. Fortunately, the woman took his question as natural under the circumstances. Less fortunately, the answer left him clueless as before.

"Reporting Post 12, Newington Butts, Elephant and Castle."

Something about a rook stirred in his memory.

"I'm Mrs. Dabney," she introduced herself. "I'm a WVS volunteer. One of the wardens found you wandering around outside. You were a terrible mess; we thought at first you were wounded, but it seems to be just your hands. Bombed out, were you?"

"I remember digging through rubble."

That seemed to be the right answer.

"Do you remember anything else?"

Yes, but he didn't want to remember it. "Was – was I with anybody?"

"No, but..."

"But what?"

"I'm so, so sorry," Mrs. Dabney said. "You were alone, but you were carrying a child's hand. Your daughter?"

"No. A neighbor's child." So to speak. "She, ah, the mother was badly injured—"

"They'll have taken her off to hospital, then."

They were sitting at a small table with some playing cards on its top and an opened metal box partially covering the cards; it looked as though Mrs. Dabney had tried to push the players' hands of cards aside to make room for her first aid kit. Such as it was. He glanced at the contents of the box and read the hand-printed labels. Gauze, Vaseline and boracic acid powder appeared to be the mainstays of the kit. No clotting bandages, no wound spray, no antibiotics… It was remarkably primitive.

He looked around the small, cluttered room, continuing to take stock. In two corners of the room there were buckets full of sand; a third corner housed an odd assortment of tools – a shovel, a hacksaw, two crowbars. There was something like an old-fashioned bicycle pump leaning on a bucket of water.

"Salvation Army!" called a clear young voice from just outside the room. "Penny for a cup of tea and a bun."

Lensky shoved one hand into his pocket, then remembered that any small change he might have would be modern American coins. He strongly suspected they wouldn't be accepted here. He shook his head at Mrs. Dabney's questioning look.

"Is that Pammie?" she called. "Thought I knew your voice. Look, Pammie, this man's been bombed out of his house with nothing but the clothes he was wearing – and they're a disaster themselves, because he immediately started digging to rescue his neighbors. How about a free cup of tea for him?"

"All right, Virginia," the girl said, "just this once, but don't go telling anybody." She ducked under the low doorway, hands full. "Here, you'll be needing these," she said, handing Lensky a mass of dark knitted stuff that turned out to be a pair of gloves and a watch cap. "There's no charge for the hat and gloves; they're donated. And here's your tea. I'll collect the mug on my next round." She set a cracked mug of brownish liquid on the table, with two small rounded pieces of bread.

"Do you have any sugar for the tea? He's recovering from shock."

Pammie shook her head with regret. "I'm sorry, we ran out of sugar half an hour ago. *Everybody* is shocky."

"Oh, well," Mrs. Dabney sighed, "I never use my ration anyway." She rummaged in a black handbag and pulled out a small round box, dumped the contents in Lensky's tea and stirred briskly.

"There you go, drink up, you need it," she encouraged him.

As the Salvation Army girl left, three men trudged into the room. All were wearing broad-brimmed metal hats, dark blue uniforms almost covered by yellowish dust, and grim expressions.

"The shelter?"

"Bloody sandwich shelters," one of the men said. "Blast sucked out the walls and the concrete roof crushed everybody inside. Nothing we could do, nor the heavy rescue squad neither. They'd have been better off on the street than hiding in one of those jerry-built death traps." He gave Mrs. Dabney a stern look. "If you get caught outside, Mrs. D., mind you make for the basement under the Sally Army post. That's proper pre-war building, that was. It won't collapse on you."

"I heard," put in another man, "as they run out of cement when they quick-built all them brick shelters and just kept putting them up with nothing but lime mortar."

"Nonsense!" said Mrs. Dabney. "Mr. Churchill would never have allowed such shoddy work."

"Churchill," Lensky croaked through a throat gone suddenly dry. He realized that he'd been kidding himself when he thought he had adjusted to being whisked into a different time. Everything he'd noticed so far had been ambiguous, but this…

"Old Winnie wasn't PM then, it was that tosser Chamberlain."

Winnie… Winston. Churchill.

The Master of Ravens had somehow moved him, not only across an ocean, but across eighty years, or close to that. Nearly half a century before he'd been *born*… and into the middle of a war. Lensky looked down at the mug of tea which he'd been using to warm his hands, and gulped it.

"So you got bombed out?" The elderly man who'd spoken first looked at him. "Waiting to be called up, are you?"

Suddenly Lensky realized that he was the only able-bodied young man he'd seen since awakening to this nightmare. Two of the wardens had white hair, and the third limped on an artificial foot.

"No – I'm American," he said.

"Ah! A war correspondent. You'll be sick of war and ready to head for home now, I'll be bound."

Home. "You have no idea," Lensky said. "But I… can't leave just now." America wasn't in the war yet? So this must be before December 1941.

"He's a hero!" Mrs. Dabney put in. "Bombed out in that first strike tonight, and what does he do but crawl out of the rubble and dig like a maniac to rescue his neighbors."

"Eh? Well, if that's your notion of fun, Yank, stick around. We'll likely have more for you to do before the night's over. If—"

A whistling scream drowned out whatever the warden had meant to say next. All three of the wardens and Mrs. Dabney threw themselves to the floor; so, tardily, did Lensky. He felt the floor recoiling and springing back, punching him in the stomach, and almost lost the sugary tea he'd just drunk. A roar succeeded the shrill noise of the approaching bomb.

"That'll have taken out some of Walworth Road," said one of the wardens as the noise died away.

"Sounded farther north than that to me," said another one, scrambling to his feet. "New Kent Road?"

"Come on, mate!" The man with the artificial foot gave Lensky a hand up. "Wherever it was—we can use your help! Bloody rescue squad never shows up in time to be any bloody use."

They left the post, already running. People in the street pointed the way to where the new bomb had hit.

18. The death of a city

London, May 10, 1941

I stepped from the black space and glowing lines of the in-between into a tapestry of fire.

I was facing a narrow, tall, ornate building with a painted statue overhead, and the statue was – yes – an elephant with a tower on its back. For the first time I allowed myself to believe that Will's analysis had been correct and that I would find Lensky somewhere around here.

But I was late; clearly the bombing had already started. On either side of the building the streets were going up in flames. The fire was almost beautiful if you didn't think about what it meant: a shimmering light and color show of pinks, yellows, oranges and reds. Halfway down the left-hand street a single building flared up in blue and green fire. I wondered what chemicals had been stored there to color the flames.

I wondered if they were explosive.

And I wondered if I could compose myself enough to reach out for Lensky, to teleport across London if necessary. I'd hoped that he would be right here, at the building Will had called, "Lensky's rook." It did look as if I'd come out of the in-between at the same place I'd started, give or take seventy or eighty years. The queer, old-fashioned buildings were completely different from the last ones I'd seen in our own time, but I was still standing at a six-armed intersection. There couldn't be so many of those in London, could there?

Furthermore, the Elephant and Castle pub had been my target. But Lensky was nowhere to be seen – and I *would* have seen him; the fires made the streets as bright as day. Perhaps I'd come through too early after all, to a time just before Shani Chayyaputra tried to maroon him here? Or perhaps some of Will's reasoning was wrong? Or – I would *not* think of this – all the reasoning was wrong, and Lensky was in some other place, in some other century.

I'd taken several agonizing days to prep for this journey. Ben kept telling me, "Take as long as you need, it's time travel! You can go back to 1941 today or next week or next month!" Intellectually I knew he was right. But every hour I waited felt like an hour in which I was abandoning Lensky. I hadn't flown to London until the night of May 9 – our time – and I'd been at the Elephant and Castle intersection in modern London on the morning of May 10. And now I was still in May 10, only it was night, and it was 1941.

Everybody in the Center had helped to prep me. I was wearing a vintage dress located by Ingrid and a shapeless black coat belonging to Meadow, and a scarf tied under my chin concealed my unfashionably short hair. I'd attracted some curious glances in modern London, but evidently I didn't look strange enough to cause any excitement in the vibrant diversity of a modern city.

London of this time was less diverse, and women paid more attention to the dictates of fashion, so blending in was correspondingly more important. Where I couldn't or wouldn't match the styles of 1941, we'd gone to some length to find a workaround. For instance, women of this era carried purses, but I hadn't wanted to have to keep track of one. Being without a purse wasn't enough to make me conspicuous, but substituting a fanny pack was unthinkable. Annelise – who actually knows which end of a needle to thread, putting her way ahead of the female mathematical community – had stitched unobtrusive side pockets into the seams of my dress to hold tissues, burn gel, sugar cubes, a handful of stars, and all the antique English coins Jimmy had been able to scrounge from local collectors and dealers. The really important stuff was stitched and pinned into the front of the dress. The only flagrantly non-period aspect of my appearance was the heavy silver belt I wore, with its ornate buckle.

Mr. M. had flatly refused to allow me to go back to the Blitz without him. And now I was very glad of his company. Will and Colton had drilled me on recent history and on the hour-by-hour history of this particular night, but they hadn't prepared me for the feelings – the terror and the urgency that filled the streets of London tonight. A city cringing under a rain of death and fire! I realized how lucky we were in America; not only had I never experienced anything like this, but I'd blithely assumed that I would go my entire life without such an experience.

I saw an old man covered in dust stumbling towards me out of a burning street. "Where is my house, where is my house?" he cried over and over.

A woman cringed in a doorway next to the Elephant and Castle pub, sobbing breathlessly.

Someone farther away was screaming.

I hadn't expected the noises either: the roar of fires, the continuous tinkling clatter as if somebody were repeatedly dropping a tray of silverware, the uneven drone of airplanes overhead, the recurring thud of heavy guns firing, a shrill whistling in the air.

The whistling grew louder. It turned into a deafening roar and ended with a crash that knocked me down.

I was slow getting to my feet, still shaky from the long teleport across the years and disoriented by the blast. Some men in funny-looking, broad-brimmed metal hats came running out of a building to my left. One of them stopped dead in front of me, swore in Polish and hauled me upright.

This one wasn't wearing the metal hat, only a dark knitted cap that covered most of his blond hair. His sport coat was torn, and his pants were a disaster: ripped, stained in places with something dark, and covered with yellowish dust.

"We have to stop meeting like this," he said. "I can't be expected to pick you off the ground in every century of human history."

"Brad!" I threw myself on him and hugged him. Under the layers of dust and grit he was warm and solid as ever. The cold fear deep inside me melted. In that moment all I wanted was to stand there forever, holding him close and feeling his strong, steady heart beating against mine. "You're hurt?"

"No, just dirty."

"Well, you can wash up when we get back." I began building the picture in my mind: the modern Elephant and Castle intersection, with the dawn of a new day in 2018 just breaking.

"Kiss your girl and come on, Yank!" one of the tin-hat men called.

He took my shoulders and held me away from him. "I can't go yet, Thalia. They need me here."

I opened my mouth to tell him that he was an insufferable egotist. Need him? Nonsense! This war had already been fought quite competently without his help! But he talked over my objections. "Go to a shelter. No, not *that* one." He waved at a sign saying "AIR RAID SHELTER" in front of a squat brick building, then pointed across the intersection and down a different street. "Those brick things aren't safe. See the Salvation Army post? Get into their basement and wait there for me. I'll be back." He crushed me to him for a quick and totally unsatisfactory kiss, flavored with dust and grit.

And then he ran after the tin-hat brigade.

'Safe' wasn't a word I'd have used for any part of this fiery nightmare. I started towards the street he'd pointed at.

Away from a screaming that suddenly raised to an agonized wail. It sounded like somebody burning to death.

It probably *was* somebody burning to death.

"It's that way," Mr. M. said helpfully, and he didn't mean the Salvation Army post.

When I turned in the direction he'd indicated, I saw men holding fire hoses and pointing them at a tall house that was going up in flames. Even as I watched, the spray of water from the hoses shrank to a stream, to a trickle, to nothing.

The front of the house collapsed on itself, briefly revealing the interior in cross-section – walls, rooms, furniture, all bright with licking tongues of fire – and a man in one of the ground-floor rooms, lying awkwardly face-down across the floor under something. The flames blazed up around him and he screamed again. It was the worst sound I'd ever heard.

His hair was literally on fire.

"Mr. M! I need the strongest personal shield we've ever raised! Help me do the shield, feed your stars into it." My own stars were streaming from my hand into a sphere just outside the shield, building camouflage all around me. It's not nice to confuse outsiders by letting them see our topology applications, and besides, somebody might have tried to stop me.

I probably looked like a pattern of moving flames as I picked my way into the burning house; that was what everything around me looked like. The firemen certainly didn't seem to notice anything. But then, they were busy calling for help: Send more pumps! Fix the bloody hose! What the (expletive) happened to the (obscenity) water pressure?

They were beginning to sound like Meadow Melendez.

I dropped camouflage once I was inside the building, because I was afraid the trapped man wouldn't respond well to a disembodied voice. From here it was obvious how he'd been caught: a sofa had fallen through the ceiling, landing squarely across the backs of his thighs. I had to drop my shield in order to grip the thing and heave it up. Heat flared around me, instantaneously drying my mouth and throat. "I can't hold this up for long," I croaked, "pull your legs up!"

As soon as he did that I dropped the sofa, grabbed him and raised both shield and camouflage around us both. I tried to pull him to his feet. "Can you walk? I need you to walk." I could teleport us if necessary, but I'd have to drop camouflage; we still couldn't manage three applications simultaneously, and the shield was absolutely necessary. With his wobbly cooperation I got him vertical, but he was unsteady on his feet. I put his arm over my shoulders. It was a good thing that Londoners of this era, the ones in slum districts like this one anyway, were not very tall.

"I can walk," he half-whispered. "Can't see though."

"Don't worry about it, I can do that part." His voice sounded very rough. Had the fire injured his throat, or was it just irritated from the clouds of ash and dust?

Getting out was trickier than getting in; the floor was covered with burning debris and I had to guide him to sidle along a narrow plank that provided the only smooth path to the street. I could sense the fires raging at my shield, consuming the additional stars Mr. M. was sending into it.

Once outside, I dropped both shield and camouflage, momentarily exhausted. One of the firemen exclaimed, "Where the bloody hell did you come from?"

I waved a hand back at the burning house.

"I can't believe it. I *don't* believe it. I never saw you in there, lady – and nobody could have walked through that fire!"

"You must not be very observant," I said. "Didn't you notice when there was a gap in the flames? That's when we took our chance to get out of the building. I guess you were too busy complaining about the water pressure."

His mouth opened and then closed again. "All right. I'm insane. I'll deal with that later. Just go to a shelter, Miss. Please!" He pointed at the brick building that Lensky had warned me against.

"He's badly burned." I waved at the man's face, which was so horribly blistered that he hardly looked human. "Can you—"

"First aid at the wardens' post." He pointed at the building the tin hats – and Lensky – had come from.

I had to steer my man over there; his eyes were covered with blisters. I hoped he was not permanently blind. After handing him over to a very proper English lady in a very dusty uniform, I actually did set off for the Salvation Army post.

But I never got there. Blue-white stars kept falling from the sky and turning into fires on the ground. There were always more fires springing up all around us, and more people trapped by them. I popped sugar cubes to counter the drain of doing so much applied topology, and kept on collecting people from burning buildings. I quickly discovered that my first trip had been comparatively simple. Most of the time there was no path by which to reach the trapped people. They were on landings above collapsed stairs, or screaming out a third-floor window of a house whose first and second floors were already ablaze beyond even my ability to shield, or cornered behind the burning rubble of a shattered building. I had to start teleporting myself in and the fire victims out. Some of them realized they hadn't been moved in just the usual way and got hysterical about that, but I quit worrying about it when

I realized that their cries were just blending in with the general confusion of the night.

Without Mr. M. I'd never have been able to do it; as I said, we still can't do three applications at once. I left shielding entirely up to him while I teleported under camouflage. Even with his help, I was exhausted before I finished. And slightly scorched in places where the fires had been too much for the shield. Well, when we got back I'd match the rest of the Center staff that way, wouldn't I?

A Salvation Army volunteer shouted something about tea and buns for a penny. I felt in one of my pockets and offered her the first coin I found.

"I can't change a florin! That's too much, luv, haven't you a penny?"

I was definitely not well enough briefed for a friendly discussion about the values of various coins.

"Ah, use the change for people who haven't got a penny?"

"Oh," the girl exclaimed when she heard my accent, "you're Canadian, that's why you don't know our money."

It seemed slightly surreal to be chatting about coins and Canadians while bombs were still thundering down out of the sky, but I would be whatever she wanted me to be if it would get me out of this conversation. I nodded, fished two sugar cubes out of a pocket, dropped them into the lukewarm tea and drained the mug.

Overhead a small plane swooped, making a sound like a buzz saw. I flinched.

"'Sall right, luv, that's one of ours!" The Salvation Army girl pumped her fist in the air. "That's right, get him, get him!" she shouted as the plane's machine guns rattled.

"What's he shooting at?" The small plane was far below the heavy bombers still droning through the sky.

"Bloody parachute bomb – *Yes!* Another bugger gone!" she cheered as an explosion in front of the plane filled the air with veins of golden light.

"Pammie, dear. Language!" It was the very proper lady who'd taken charge of my burn victim.

Pammie turned red at the reproof, but then a shrill whistling sound overhead distracted both of them. It became louder, became a tortured scream, and Pammie and the first aid lady threw themselves down into the gutter. "High explosive, get down, get down!" she shouted at me.

The screaming of the bomb was very close now, and it turned into a roar like a train trying to fit itself into a too-small tunnel.

Leutnant Richard Lehmann had been expecting to die ever since the forecaster announced, "The latitude north of London has no more astronomical darkness." A year ago these bright clear nights had been welcome, but now the English had learned to fight back. To their fighter planes, his wing of Heinkels would be sitting ducks. His one hope was to get in and get out as fast as possible. His was the first bomber group to follow the "Fire Raisers," the task force whose job was to light up the London targets with chandelier flares and incendiaries. It might just be that the unwary English would fail to get their night fighters in the air before he had dropped his load of incendiaries and high explosive bombs and swung away for the return flight.

They had been nearly two hundred miles away, still over France, when he first saw the shifting red skyline that marked London on this night. The Fire Raisers had done their task well – perhaps too well. Between fires and moon, Lehmann felt as exposed as if he were flying in broad daylight.

Now they were over the Channel, with only a little over half an hour to wait until they were in position to drop their bombs. In the moonlight, at four thousand meters, the water looked like a luminous sheet of green glass. His navigator, Fischer, spoke. "The ground speed is 264 kilometers per hour. We shall be over London in exactly thirty-five minutes and ten seconds. You had better climb to five thousand meters. I will tell you when to start losing height again." He fell silent again and the irregular whine of the desynchronized engines filled Lehmann's ears.

As they approached London the pilot caught his breath, awed. The Thames was a serpent of copper light, winding through glowing streets with buildings outlined in fire. White searchlights stabbed up through the darkness. He thought, "They cannot withstand this. No people could. I am watching the death of a city." On Fischer's cues, he took the Heinkel down to three thousand meters. The English searchlights were useless; the entire bomber had a thick coating of black soot that made it virtually invisible from that distance, a black plane against a black sky. He thought the English fighter planes had not yet taken off. With luck, they would not be in the air until after he was over his target. That would be at 12:30, just an hour and a half after the raid began.

The six-armed intersection of Elephant and Castle stood out like a burning star. "Bomb doors open," Fischer reported over the intercom... "Bomb gone." Lehmann felt lighter. They had only to find one more target for the second 500-lb bomb and they would be nearly free to get out of this; the incendiaries weren't so important, they could be dropped anywhere.

19. An order is an order

London and France, May 11, 1941

"That one was nearer home!" the chief warden bawled over the deafening blend of noises that filled the air. The Heavy Rescue Squad had beaten the wardens to the wreckage of Walton's Stores on the New Kent Road. Not that there'd been much for them, or anyone, to do at this bomb site; no one was supposed to have been in these buildings. The standard procedure was to call for silence and listen for any cries for help even if they thought the buildings had been unoccupied, but there was no silence to be had in the Elephant and Castle district this night. They waved goodbye to the Heavy Rescue Squad and headed back towards Reporting Post 12.

This high explosive bomb had indeed landed close to home. It had made a direct hit on the Salvation Army post, passing through the building and all three floors to explode in the basement. One entire side of the basement had been opened up by the bomb crater.

"Look down there," a fireman, giggling in a shockingly high voice, told one of his mates. "Nothing to rescue. They've all been bombed into the bloody wall!"

The "safe" shelter where he'd sent Thalia to wait for him.

Lensky raced to the edge of the bomb crater and threw himself flat. Moonlight and flickering tongues of fire illuminated the far wall of the basement, and there he saw human shapes imprinted on the wall, the only remains of the bodies that had been there when the bomb exploded.

Where he'd sent Thalia to wait for him. Where he'd sent Thalia…

The young fireman was still giggling hysterically. Lensky leapt up and grabbed his throat. "Think it's funny, do you, *mate*? Think it's *funny*?" In that moment of black despair, it seemed as though there would be some relief in smashing that laughing face and throwing the man into the crater where Thalia had died.

"'Ere, Yank, we're all on the same side!" The warden's voice was an irrelevant buzzing, no more important than the shrill whistling of descending shrapnel or the thunder of anti-aircraft guns.

"Brad! Stop! *Lensky*!" Hands on his arm, interfering with his one remaining goal. "Stop it stop it stop it!" a woman screamed in his ear, and amidst the crackling of fires and the drone of the bombers he recognized that voice.

He released the fireman and sat down, hard, against the shattered remnants of a wall. "*Thalia?*"

"Me. Are you going to cut it out now? You really mustn't go around strangling firemen, you know. It's not done here."

The sharp edge in her voice was the sweetest music he'd ever heard.

"I told you to wait for me – there." He indicated the bomb crater.

"See, sometimes it's a good thing that I don't always do exactly what you say."

He reached upwards and pulled her down into his arms; such a small woman, fine-boned, but not fragile. Not, thank God, fragile at all. "And what have you been up to?"

"Helped a few people get out of burning buildings."

"*What?*"

"I raised a shield first, stupid."

"The rest of the Mathematical Mafia had shields when they set fire to the SCI building, and they still got scorched."

"Yes, well, they didn't have nice heavy coats. Or a little help from a mage." She pushed the skirts of the coat aside and the turtle-snake thing poked its ugly little beak out of a coil of silver scales. "The only problem is…"

He cradled her in his arms and rested his cheek on the scarf that covered her hair. "If you're here, and alive, there isn't any problem."

"The thing is… I'm not exactly sure I can take us back to our own time right now."

"Not to mention crossing an ocean."

"No, we don't have to do that topologically. I flew to London. I only had to teleport from Heathrow to this intersection. And, of course, seventy-seven years back. This place looks completely different in our time, did you know?"

"I'm not surprised. From the looks of things, this whole neighborhood will be a smoldering ruin by morning. I expect it had to be totally rebuilt."

"Anyway, about getting home: I've got two reservations for a flight back, one in your name. *And,*" she said triumphantly, "I've got our passports and some emergency cash and a credit card, all sewn inside my dress thanks to Annelise. That girl is a fountainhead of practical skills. But the time travel bit is trickier. Teleporting back all these years pretty well drained me. And as for getting us back – well, I've been doing a lot more teleporting since I got here. And much of it with passengers, which makes it harder. I've been munching sugar cubes, but even so I'm not feeling very strong right now."

"Then rest. There's no hurry." Except, could he find a safe place for her to rest in this madhouse?

He remembered something about teleportation. Topologists expended much more energy taking passengers than teleporting themselves alone, didn't they? She'd just hinted as much. "Why don't you go back on your own. You can rest, eat, take your time. Then come back for me when you're ready?" The thought of being left alone here again chilled him. But letting her stay in this maelstrom of death and fire was even worse.

"At this point, I'm too wiped out to go back, even if it's just me," Thalia announced. But her fingers brushed one cheek as she spoke. That was one of her tells, the hand raised to her face.

"You're lying, aren't you?"

"I'm not going anywhere without you."

"Okay, at least that's honest. Unacceptable, but honest."

"And you can't make me."

That was, regrettably, perfectly true. He shifted position a little, resting his back against the wall. "Oh, well. I don't hear any more bombers. Probably we'll get the All Clear soon."

He felt her renewed tension. "No?" he asked.

"The All Clear won't come until after five in the morning. Will made me study accounts of this night before I jumped," she explained.

"Oh."

"But the problems in this area will be mostly fires, not bombs. At least we can see the fires."

But she'd spoken too soon, or Will hadn't taught her as much as she thought. When the second wave of bombers hit, the light of the fires also showed them the sticks of bombs falling. Where the bombers crossed the moon, they could see them moving through the sky in rows, dropping their bombs simultaneously. Lensky's new friends in the wardens' post were out again in disregard of the danger, telling the Heavy Rescue Squad where people were likely to be trapped, shifting debris where the job did not require the Rescue Squad's special skills. And he could not just sit and watch them.

But where could he possibly leave Thalia while he helped the wardens? Two shelters, a new above-ground brick one and the basement under the Salvation Army post, had already been destroyed. If she was in the remaining brick shelter, she would be at risk of being smashed under its cement roof like the people in the first one.

There was no safe place here. Not in 1941.

"For the love of God, Thalia, go back to our own time!"

She remained obstinately three-dimensional and opaque, and no darkness shimmered around her. Damned stubborn woman!

"Well, at least shelter in a doorway, can't you? Mr. M., keep a shield up around the two of you," he snapped, and dashed to join the wardens without waiting to see if the turtle-mage obeyed his command.

As soon as he'd dropped his second bomb in the Elephant and Castle area, Lehmann released his incendiaries and headed south towards the coast.

"Well, we lived through that," he thought.

184

But to Krause, his wireless operator, he said, "Tell base, 'Mission completed.'"

No one spoke as the Heinkel drove steadily through the night. Lehmann did not relax until he saw the lights of the airfield. "Prepare for landing." He thought that he felt a reduction of tension coming from the entire crew. Their part was over now, and they'd come back safely.

Lehmann made a perfect landing and taxied back to the mechanics. As he climbed from the plane, they were already climbing over the plane, testing every part. Waiting on the landing strip were the armorers, ready to refill the Heinkel's bomb bays with another load of death and fire, but that was no longer Lehmann's concern. A second crew would be responsible for the next sortie.

The frosty grass crunched under Lehmann's feet as he walked towards the office, and he shivered. He was wearing his summer flying uniform rather than the fleece-lined winter jackets worn by the rest of his crew. These would give them a better chance of survival if they were shot down over the sea, but Lehmann preferred the mobility of his summer kit so that he could turn and move freely in the cockpit. He might as well see if he could find one of the warm jackets after his report; there would be no more flying for him tonight.

But as he finished his report, the duty officer said, "Get back to your plane with your crew, check that it's refueled and loaded, and take off again."

Lehmann couldn't believe what he'd heard. Did the high command care so little about the lives of their aircrews that they would force them to take these insane risks twice? "Sir, there must be some mistake. It's practically suicide to fly over England in this weather." And he desperately wanted someone else to take on that suicide mission. He'd done his part.

But the duty officer did not look flustered; only sad. "This order comes from the Field Marshal personally. Due to the large number of missions planned, all crews are to fly two sorties. And tonight of all nights, an order is an order. Tonight we shall finally break the Englanders' will."

"Yes, sir." What else was there to say?

His crew had gone to the mess hall; he was the first one back to the plane. With a sense of unreality, he signed the bomb manifest and gave it back to the head armorer. Soon afterwards the navigator Fischer and his mechanic Scholz joined him, followed by the gunner, Unteroffizier Anschiess. The eighteen-year-old

185

gunner, the youngest of his crew, waited in vain for Lehmann's usual joke about living up to his name (Anschiessen – "to shoot.") But Lehmann was too preoccupied to make a joke about anything.

The wireless operator, Krause, was not with them. Lehmann felt a jolt of hope. He could not be expected to take off without a wireless operator. "Is Krause coming?"

"Yes, Herr Leutnant," answered the ever-correct Fischer. "The Oberfeldwebel will be here soon."

Fifteen minutes later – barely in time for their scheduled takeoff – Krause climbed into the plane, full of excuses. Lehmann thought that Krause was probably as reluctant to make this second sortie as he himself was, and tried to stifle the unpatriotic wish that the man had had the guts to desert. Lehmann's hope was replaced by despair. As the signal for takeoff was illuminated, he thought, "We are all dead men." And as the plane droned on through the night, he felt the cold that he had been able to ignore previously.

20. Lampposts wilting like flowers

London, May 11, 1941

The head warden handed the spade to Brannigan and leaned against the one wall the bombs had left standing. His shoulders obscured the graffiti proclaiming, "London can take it!" Maybe London could, but he wasn't so sure about himself; digging out survivors was heavy work for a man in his sixties.

"Well, there's one thing to be thankful for, lads," he joked. "That block of offices that just went down? My dentist had an office there, and I had an appointment tomorrow. Guess I won't have to go after all."

"I like office buildings, and them empty at night," Brannigan said. "No survivors to dig out."

And by all indications, there were none here. He knew the families that had lived in this next bombed-out building. Two of them sheltered in the Tube every night, and the third one had decamped to relatives in Kent. Might as well enjoy this break; there would be a new disaster soon enough.

"I like survivors," young Finch said cheerfully. He had sat down on a pile of bricks to take off his artificial foot and readjust the stump sock. "They appreciate us," he said while smoothing the sock. "Makes a nice change. 'Oh, it's Warden this, and Warden that, and Warden, you're a flop,'" he half-sang the music-hall parody, "'But it's Thank you, Mr. Warden, when the bombs begin to drop.'"

"And thank the volunteers too," said the head warden with a glance at Lensky. "For an American, he digs like – like –"

"Like an Irishman," said 'Paddy' Brannigan, taking off his tin hat to wipe his forehead. "Say, Yank, when are the rest of your people going to get into this war? If they don't look sharp, me and the rest of my gallant crew are going to kill off all the Jerries before the Americans get a look-in."

"Right, Grandpa, after we clean up this place you're going to volunteer to fly Beaufighters, is it?" Finch jeered.

Lensky wondered if he would change history by telling them, jinx the future of the war. Surely not. It wasn't as if they'd have reason to believe him, after all.

"I am absolutely certain," he said slowly, "that America will be in the war before the end of the year. Next year you will not be fighting alone." Now that he'd learned they were in May of 1941, it didn't take a historian to know that much. December 7, 1941 was, as FDR had predicted, a date that had lived in infamy.

By 3 a.m. the fires were so much worse that the Rescue Squad and the wardens could hardly get to bomb sites. It started when a burning building fell square across one of the streets feeding into the Elephant and Castle intersection. Buildings on both sides went up in flames and the fires chased themselves down the street towards the intersection while exhausted firemen dragged their hoses to this latest crisis.

In this inferno of flames Lensky was no longer cold, but the watch cap and gloves helped to protect his head and hands from the cascades of red sparks that floated through the air. He felt a sudden surge of heat along his side, and slapped at the place where his shirt had caught fire. Then without pausing he slapped Brannigan on the back where a spark was smoldering ominously on his blue serge uniform.

The most important job now was that of the firemen, and after the water lines burst they could only work sporadically as one reserve source of water after another was used up. The nearest, a tank of 5,000 gallons by Spurgeon's Tabernacle, had gone dry in five minutes. Pumps were sent to the Manor Place Baths on Walworth Road, where the emergency supply of 125,000 gallons gave the superintendent a breathing space. He used that space to send a hose truck to the Thames at London Bridge, but the hose laying was a desperately slow task. He also sent pumps to the third nearest site, the basement of the Old Surrey Music Hall, whose 200,000 gallons might preserve the Elephant and Castle district until they could draw water directly from the Thames.

Within an hour the Manor Place Baths had gone dry. Half an hour later, the Old Surrey Music Hall sustained a direct hit, killing seventeen firemen. At the Elephant and Castle intersection, minutes later, the jets of water disappeared as if they had been sucked back into the hoses. All the firemen could do now was clear away wooden structures in the hope of keeping the fires from spreading.

When Lensky looked away down the inferno that had been Newington Causeway, he saw lampposts wilting like dying flowers and flames gusting so wildly that they seemed to join across the street to make a curtain of fire. The paint on nearby cars ran down like water.

When the hoses laid to the Thames were connected the firemen had a little water again, but for every fire they brought under control half a dozen more sprang up. And now the fires had had time to take hold. Sometimes there was nothing to do but spray directly into the fire, and that was not much use. Jets of water vaporized instantly where they met the flames. And even the Thames was not inexhaustible; after two hours of feeding innumerable emergency lines going to all parts of London, it became so low that the hoses choked on the mud at the bottom of the river.

Before that last crisis Lensky had returned to the doorway of the Elephant and Castle pub, determined to make Thalia listen to reason and get out of this disaster – if she hadn't left already.

She hadn't.

Of course she hadn't.

And she wasn't even staying under cover, though he could hope she was shielded. She had found a bucket of sand to help her fight incipient fires at the base of the pub, stamping them out where she could, covering them with sand where she couldn't. When the bucket was empty she looked up, wiped her forehead, and saw Lensky.

At least she had the decency to *look* guilty. But what she said was, "There are more buckets of sand in the wardens' post."

There was a point where you just had to accept the hopelessness of arguing with a woman. Lensky fetched the buckets and joined Thalia in her self-imposed task of saving the pub. At least this building wasn't on fire yet; there was a small possibility that they could do some good here.

"Because I have a sentimental attachment to this building," Thalia panted in answer to his unasked question. "It was my beacon to you."

When the sand was used up, they joined the people running after water trucks with buckets. When water spilled over the edges of the trucks, they scooped it from the gutters and ran back to the Elephant and Castle.

This time, as the blazing skyline of London drew closer, Lehmann felt no triumph in the sight. He still felt that he was watching the total destruction of a city; but he also felt that he was approaching his own death.

"Don't let me die in fire," he prayed. It was the nightmare of all flyers. One pilot that Lehmann knew carried a pistol in the cockpit, saying that he would shoot himself before he burned. Logically, Lehmann understood that he was in more danger of burning from an air attack than from a target he would be over for less than fifteen minutes. But he had a superstitious feeling that London itself was reaching tongues of fire for him, was seeking revenge for the damage he and his fellows had inflicted.

When both his HE bombs had been dropped without incident, Lehmann swung the plane round for his return to base. He felt safer now, even thought he might return alive.

He did not notice the night fighter behind him. Neither did Anschiess or Krause, though both had been told to keep a sharp lookout.

Lehmann's first indication of disaster was a clattering sound and a tongue of flame from the starboard engine. The enemy fighter moved level with him and there was a second burst of fire that shattered the windscreen and most of the instrument panel. As cold air rushed into the cockpit Lehmann cut out the starboard engine and called to his crew over the intercom. Amazingly, Fischer, Scholz, and Krause were still alive, though Fischer was wounded. There was no reply from young Anschiess, who would have been in the rear turret.

He had three crewmen still living. Could he keep the Heinkel airborne long enough to land them safely? Not likely; even if he found a landing place, even if the shattered plane responded, he would have to land by guesswork now that the instrument panel was gone.

The Heinkel lurched to starboard and the stick jerked in Lehmann's hands. At least they were over the quiet countryside now, not over burning London. He knew his duty: to keep the aircraft flying, if possible, long enough to reach the Channel. With only one engine the plane would not likely last long enough for them to be picked up by German rescuers, but at least the English would not have the plane.

He did not think the Heinkel would last even that long.

From the corner of his eye he saw a sudden flame somewhere astern. From the way the Heinkel was shaking he knew they were losing height. It was a toss-up whether they burned in the air or crashed on the ground.

"Bail out," he instructed his crew. He would take the Heinkel as far as he could by himself.

"But, Herr Leutnant, you will need—" Krause began.

"It is an order," Lehmann interrupted harshly.

Within minutes the three living crewmen had jumped into the darkness of the English countryside in the blackout.

The flames astern grew; Lehmann could feel their heat behind him. The plane shook him with its violent shudders. He tugged on the stick, trying to keep the Heinkel up long enough to reach the Channel. He had no control; the plane had begun spinning dizzily.

But despite the spinning, he could see the Channel beneath him now. At this low altitude, it looked not like a smooth sheet of glass, but more like crumpled foil. As the flames roared into the cockpit, Lehmann went through the escape hatch and yanked at the ripcord of his parachute.

"At least I did not burn," he had time to think on the way down.

The water of the Channel was very cold.

But soon he was beyond feeling the chill, or anything else.

21. "London can take it!"

London, May 11, 1941
London and Austin, May 11 and 12, 2018

Before dawn, although the fires still raged, the urgency of fighting them was over. There would be no more water until the Thames rose again. Here and there, leaning against walls, sitting on heaps of rubble, exhausted firemen sat with heads cradled in their hands.

Lensky and I, having won a tiny battle in the midst of an overwhelming disaster, were sitting on the ground slumped against what we had come to think of as our pub. The Elephant and Castle pub stood alone and unburnt in a sea of burnt-out buildings, although the gaily painted statue on the roof was gray with ashes. Across the intersection, the turreted Rockingham Arms and the coliseum-like Alfred's Head also stood in defiance of the destruction that had visited the area. Perhaps there was a special guardian angel for pubs.

Columns of smoke rolled across the sky like clouds, reddened by the flames below them. Fire and reflected fire gleamed from the windows of buildings, where windows remained. The air was hot from the fires, and thick with ashes and dust. But the thundering waves of bombers had stopped.

In a side street, in total disregard of licensing hours, a smaller pub had opened. "Drink it while it lasts," the owner said, drawing beer as fast as possible for the thirsty firemen. Reflected firelight shone on the pub's sign: "The World's End."

Beer… Alcohol had calories; would it help me to recover and teleport out of here? I considered the idea languidly and rejected it. As tired as I was, it would probably just put me to sleep. Anyway, it had been several hours since I'd depleted my mental energy by applying too much topology. An aching back, sore shoulders and slightly scorched hands wouldn't interfere with a fresh effort. I felt fairly sure that with Mr. M.'s help I would be able to bring the three of us forward into our own time.

Fairly sure.

There could be no harm in waiting a little longer. The bombing was over now, and soon we ought to hear the all-clear signal. I found that not only was I dubious about my own teleporting strength, I was also strangely reluctant to leave the ruined streets where we'd lived through this night with the people of London. The people who could not and would not give up, no matter what Hitler threw at them. The people who – although they didn't know it yet – had just withstood the final fury of the Blitz.

Beside me, Lensky's head dropped and he startled back into wakefulness. "It's crazy," he said, "but I kind of hate to abandon them now."

Hours ago I'd called him an egomaniac for thinking his single-handed efforts could make a difference in the middle of a world war. Now I had a different perspective. Perhaps what you accomplished didn't matter; the important thing was that you had tried. All the same – "I know. But this isn't our war. If we try to stay longer, with no contemporary papers and nobody to vouch for us, we'll probably get interned as potential enemy spies. Besides – if there's any good time to leave, this is it. The Blitz ends with this night. London won't be attacked directly again until the V-1's and V-2's start landing."

"When does that start?"

"I don't remember. Last year of the war? Year before? Will and Colton would know." I hadn't taken time, during this night of bombs and fires, to tell him how I'd found him and how much we both owed to Will's detective work. Now I told him how Ingrid had heard and repeated Chayyaputra's taunting, and how Will had used his expertise in history and the puzzle-solving talents of a programmer to connect those veiled threats with this particular time and place.

Lensky took a deep breath – and expelled it in a series of rasping coughs. The air was still full of burning sparks, and it stank of leaking gas and burnt rubber and wood ash and other things I did not want to think about. I needed to get Lensky back to where a modern doctor could check his lungs.

"Mr. M.? Can you help me one more time?"

"Naturally I can. I am not one to give way to my fatigue after such minor exertions."

He hadn't been one to drag buckets of sand and water, either, or to stamp on stray embers. Well; travel with a turtle mage, put up with a turtle mage's arrogance. I put my arm around Lensky's waist and he draped one arm over my shoulders, holding me so tightly it almost hurt.

Drifting smoke and embers obscured visibility, and in any case I was too tired to worry about upsetting outsiders. Anybody who had come through this night with sanity intact was surely steady enough to deal with a little thing like us disappearing before their eyes. I thought about the modern intersection, and about the dawn of the day after I'd arrived in London.

"*Brouwer,*" I said to help me call up the necessary image, and at the same time I opened my free hand and let stars stream into the transition.

***

You probably have no idea how difficult it can be for two filthy, exhausted people to traverse London from Southwark to Heathrow Airport and then to check in for an international flight. Without baggage – which might have made us seem slightly more respectable – and without the opportunity to do more than rinse off the worst of the dust in a bathroom sink. Oh, sorry, a *cloakroom* or *lavatory* sink. Although why they call it a cloakroom I cannot imagine, since it seems to have nothing to do with cloaks. A pity, that; I could have used one to cover my dress. The Blitz had done enough damage, and the dress wasn't improved by my pulling it over my head in a cloakroom cubicle and picking out the stitching that held our papers and money.

As I did with the process of fitting a wedding dress, I shall spare you the details of our return. I only wish I could have been spared them. Suffice it to say that after far too many hours of shuffling forward in lines, showing passports and boarding passes, being questioned by various security types, being stuffed into airplanes, shuffling off airplanes, and standing in line to repeat the whole series, we found ourselves in Austin-Bergstrom International Airport. I was so tired by then that we had to take a cab to the condo; I couldn't have teleported as much as a sugar packet.

Once we got inside, Mr. M. promptly slithered into the shadows with a slight crunching sound. He had been loudly unhappy about having grit in his scales and now all he wanted was to be left alone with some oil and paper towels.

I knew just how he felt. I had grit in places even more intimate.

Lensky and I stripped down in the kitchen and threw our clothes into a black plastic garbage bag before sharing an extremely long shower and falling onto the bed. With my last shreds of consciousness I managed to telephone the office and tell Annelise that everything had worked out okay, we were back and basically unharmed, and we would get together with everybody for a debriefing when we were good and ready.

Eventually, and much too soon, I registered that someone in the room was singing "There'll be Bluebirds Over the White Cliffs of Dover." Croaking, rather.

"I thought you were into classic rock now."

Mr. M. raised up his front twelve inches and preened. He was now *very* shiny. "I am, but I have been inspired by our recent experiences. Although," he said meditatively, "'Light My Fire' might be appropriate."

"Stick with the bluebirds," I suggested, and threw an arm over my eyes in an attempt to get back to sleep.

I may have succeeded, because the next time I became aware of the world, Lensky was standing over me with a cup of coffee while Mr. M. zoomed around his shoulders, trying to dip his beak into it. "When did that turtle-snake of yours learn to fly?"

I sat up and took the coffee. "We've all been able to do it for months now. Ingrid's algorithm, remember? I suppose it was inevitable that he'd figure it out too."

"I," said Mr. M., "do not use such petty mortal things as *algorithms*."

"Just for that," I told him, "you're not getting any of my coffee. Not. One. Drop." He would have had to be extremely fast in any case. I drained the cup and handed it back to Lensky for a refill. I looked at him, bleary-eyed. "How come *you* are so disgustingly energetic and cheerful?"

"I treat my body right and keep it in good condition," he said, "unlike certain people whose idea of exercise is repeatedly hoisting a coffee cup. You should start jogging with me."

"I have too much respect for my knees to do that. *I* think you're recovering faster because you didn't have to do any of the heavy lifting. Teleporting, I mean."

"There is that," he admitted.

It appeared to be morning again, so in the fullness of time – that is, after I'd had another shower to remove the remaining grit from my hair – we went out to breakfast. I was relieved to find that somebody had retrieved Lensky's car from where I'd abandoned it and put it in his parking space here. There might never be any need to discuss that part of the emergency with him.

Huevos rancheros with a sufficient quantity of authoritative hot sauce always make it easier for me to face whatever is coming next. Too, I had suffered some long-term draining in 1941 from repeatedly applying topology to the very limits of my ability. I mopped up my eggs with tortillas and biscuits alternately. "I'm going to need a lot of food for the next few days," I warned Lensky.

"So what is new about that? Feeding you is already one of my major budget items. Are you planning to eat *all* the tortillas?"

"Yes." I moved the basket of tortillas over to my side of the table, just in case Lensky thought he was getting some of them.

"I suppose," I said after finishing off everything but the salt and pepper shakers, "I suppose we ought to be worrying about the Master of Ravens." I looked wistfully at the small puddle of egg yolks remaining on my plate. They were too liquid to scoop up with my fork. "Are there any more tortillas?"

"No."

"Biscuits?"

"No. And I called in to the Center while you were still snoring luxuriously."

"I do not snore!"

"Okay, you don't snore. You just snuffle. Like a little pig. It's actually kind of lovable. Ingrid told me that SCI is closed. That fire your impetuous friends started seems to have done more damage than they realized at the time. The grackles are acting normal and the Pandit says Shani has probably gone back to India. For the time being."

"Did you tell her that we would come in after breakfast?" I shoved my fork through the puddle of egg yolk, but couldn't pick up enough to make it worthwhile.

"I did. Shall we go?" He dropped some money on the table and stood up.

"What's the sudden hurry?"

"I want to get you out of here before you embarrass yourself and me by licking the plate."

Our colleagues were about evenly divided between relief that the rescue mission had succeeded and concern that the things we had done in the past might have changed history. I thought that worry was silly.

"Obviously we haven't changed history, we're back here and everything's the same."

"There could be long-term effects we don't know about yet," Will fretted.

"The same could be said of Ingrid and Colton's little excursion to Britfield in 1957," I pointed out. "That didn't change anything and I betcha this didn't change anything either. I think history is a lot more robust than you think it is."

"You saved the Elephant and Castle pub," Will said. "That's a *big* change."

"Maybe someone else would have done it if we hadn't happened to be there."

Will shook his head. "It's *known* that it burned down that night. Look, there's a picture of the wreckage in this book." He set a heavy coffee-table book down on Annelise's desk and flipped through the pages, looking for the picture he remembered. Suddenly he stopped flipping.

"Did you find it?"

"In – in a manner of speaking," he said in a hollow voice. "Look here."

The full-page, black-and-white photograph clearly showed an intact, if slightly charred, Elephant and Castle standing between two devastated streets.

"See, even the book says it survived. You're just confused. You were probably thinking of some other building; a lot of places really were bombed flat or burned down."

Will shook his head and wandered off to talk with Meadow Melendez. He spent a lot of time with her over the next few days. He said that he suddenly found engineering and physics very soothing; something about the same input producing the same results every time.

EPILOGUE

The next six weeks were relatively peaceful. Once we were out of crisis mode, we were able to put together what I'd picked up at the retreat with the data Jimmy had lifted from the SCI computers, and the outlines of Chayyaputra's scam became clear. Alec had bragged of his boss's amazing ability to figure out which of several new businesses would succeed. What Chayyaputra had actually done was to identify start-ups whose only competition was other local businesses, and then put the competition out of work by code-hacking and removal of key people. He himself had done the removal part. I strongly suspected Yung-Su Park of involvement in the hacking, but had no evidence.

As for his victims, Renata Rivera had revived her cyber security company after her unplanned six weeks' absence; Jimmy's friend Logan hadn't done so well. The other companies he'd destroyed were long gone.

We talked about how to stop similar attacks from SCI, but for the moment there were none. It turned out that the fire had indeed done more damage than we realized; the building was nearly gutted. Shani Chayyaputra did not return to town, and a brief online notice in *Whirred* confirmed that SCI had closed its doors permanently. The nice young people I'd met at the retreat would be looking for new jobs. I felt some sympathy for those who, like Ginny and Alec, really hadn't known anything. Maybe they'd be more cautious next time they got a job offer that was too good to be true.

I didn't dare hope that the Master of Ravens was gone for good, but I was grateful not to have to deal with him immediately.

I had a wedding to survive.

Actually, I wouldn't have bet on my even surviving the wedding preparations. There were more than enough tricky incidents to get through.

There was, for instance, the moment when Lensky opened his mail and discovered that the City of Austin wanted him to pay six hundred and fifty dollars for abandoning his car beside a fire hydrant, even though Colton had moved the car before the city tow truck got there. Okay, that wasn't, strictly speaking, part of the wedding preparation, but for a few minutes while he was throwing his weight around and shouting I was afraid my little oversight about parking might derail the whole project. Fortunately, once he'd let off enough steam he decided it was funny that I hadn't even noticed the fire hydrant and lovable that I'd ditched the car there because I was rushing to find out what had happened to him.

Another mini-crisis, more serious, occurred when my aunt Berenice from New Jersey told Lensky's twelve-year-old niece Linda that she couldn't be a flower girl in the wedding because she wasn't a member of our church. That was completely untrue and poisonous nonsense besides, but at least I didn't have to deal with it all by myself. My mom and Linda's mother tackled Berenice together and reduced her to a tearful refusal to act as my *Koumbara* during the wedding. My only contribution was remembering *not* to say that I hadn't asked her anyway and that I certainly didn't want somebody as nasty as Berenice standing behind me at all, let alone close enough to exchange the wedding crowns on our heads. I'd already asked Aunt Alesia to be our *Koumbara*, which – unlike most other roles – did require the participant to be a member of our church. I mean, even *Lensky* didn't have to be Greek Orthodox; he'd been baptized as a Catholic, which our church considered acceptable for a spouse. In a kind of marginal, strictly limited way, of course. Let's not even discuss what they think of the various Protestant heresies.

We got through that and a dozen other crises and finally, on a golden evening in June, Lensky and I stood in the vestibule of St. Elias to exchange rings. Technically this was the betrothal ceremony, although in modern times the wedding ceremony usually proceeded about ten seconds later, so the separation no longer made a lot of sense. The only slight awkwardness here happened because nobody had mentioned to him that we wear our wedding rings on the *right* hand. He said afterwards that between that and our making the sign of the cross backward, getting married felt like trying to drive in England: everything happened on the wrong side. (He's wrong, of course – we do things properly, it's the Catholics who get it backwards – but the man is absolutely unreasonable on some subjects.)

After the exchange of rings, the actual wedding ceremony went into high gear, with incense, singing, lighted candles for us to carry to the altar, and all the other trimmings. At least, so I am told, and there's photographic evidence to support the story. I myself was in a state of paralyzed terror in which most of my perceptions were shut down, with only occasional brief flashes of clarity. I do remember when the priest placed the wedding crowns on our heads, because I was impressed at Lensky's staying so calm about having to wear a wreath of pearls and white porcelain roses.

I'm told that Aunt Alesia switched the crowns on our heads three times, but you couldn't prove it by me. As for the reading from the Gospels, it was probably the same passage read at every Orthodox wedding ever, but this time it was just white noise to me; I didn't take in a word. Then suddenly there was a cup of wine in front of me; I must have missed the blessing the priest said over it. We each took three sips and I did not spill any, though my hands were shaking. When it was time for the triple procession around the altar while everybody sang the final hymns I felt absolutely certain that I would trip over my own skirts, but somehow I didn't.

And at the end, after the wedding crowns had been put away for us to keep, after the final blessings had been said and all the hymns sung, there was Brad. Holding me in his arms. And between us there was surely enough love to last forever.

Continue reading for a first look at the next Applied Topology book,
A Smokeless Flame.

At first sight, the room was grey, dingy, and unspeakably depressing. On a second look, it was worse. There were no windows, and a metal plate bolted over the small barred opening in the door prevented any possibility of getting a glimpse outside of the room, even the sight of what was probably an equally dim and dingy corridor. The plate and bolts were on the outside of the door, which would have prevented most people from trying to loosen them. I didn't bother because I had little hope that the view on the other side of the door was any better.

The air hissing through the ceiling vent was cold and smelled stale. This was the end of a long hot Texas July, a time when I am normally pro-air conditioning, but from where I was now – lying on a clammy cement floor – the coolness was decidedly unwelcome.

Since I was already lying on my back and staring at the ceiling when I came to, I spent some time contemplating the ceiling air vent. It was about the size of half a sheet of typewriter paper. Even I wouldn't be able to fit through that opening, and Colton would have had to be fed through in pieces. I lay quietly and considered our other options. Besides the one that they were probably expecting, that is.

Whoever "they" were.

Colton had been working on a topological application that would demolish abandoned, ramshackle outbuildings for his father and other farmers, but I didn't know how much control he had; he had taken his experiments out to a field of prickly pears off Highway 183, where there was plenty of room for error. In any case, I wasn't sure it would be a good idea to use his application on the door of a cell that had no other outlet for the resulting blast. Then, too, Ben and Ingrid and I weren't up to date on that project. Colton would have had to blow out his own cell door, then find each of us – and that was assuming we were all in the same building – and free us individually. Before any of the nice people who'd locked us up noticed any unusual goings-on.

Fortunately, as researchers at the Center for Applied Topology we had one very obvious way of departing the scene. I just wasn't sure it was time for us to use it yet. The way we'd been treated so far suggested that our captors had some serious misapprehensions about the limits on our abilities. It might not be wise to give them any more data than we absolutely had to.

I'd been the last of the four of us to be captured. It had happened when I was leaving the office – this evening? Yesterday? After being drugged twice and having lost my watch, I wasn't at all clear on the passage of time. I remembered making a gesture towards cleaning my desk – well, okay, piling the papers in neat stacks. The office had been very quiet, but I hadn't thought much of that. Mathematicians aren't very noisy, and it was late enough that our receptionist and the rest of the support staff had probably gone home. It had been quite a while since lunch; I thought I'd just check out the break room, in case there were any leftover doughnuts to help fuel my trip home. But when I walked the Möbius strip through the blank wall between the research division and the public side of the Center, there had been no one in the outer office but two strange men, and the double doorway to the stairs was wide open. We really need to replace that lock one of these days.

One of the men grabbed me while the other slapped my arm with something sharp. Oh, hell. I've been sedated like that before. I don't like it. I had just enough time to think *Dammit, not again* before I fell into darkness – not the clear darkness of the in-between, shot through with intersecting lines and spiraling shapes of brilliant color, but a cloudy and stifling darkness that suffocated thought.

When I came to, there was something around my wrists and my arms ached from being forced into a strained position. I was in a dark place that roared and vibrated alternately; if it hadn't been for the pain, I wouldn't have been absolutely sure I *was* conscious and not having a nightmare. A couple of tugs convinced me that I wouldn't be able to free my hands by any normal techniques. It was probably safer, just for the moment, to pretend I had no other options. I sat still and tried to feel out the darkness around me.

After a few minutes I could sense other people. No, nothing paranormal about that; there were subtle shifts in the not-quite-total darkness, movements of the air from someone's breathing, other tiny cues that we don't normally rely on.

"Thalia?"

It was Ben's voice, barely audible over the noise around us.

"Ben! Are you all right?"

"Sssh. Yes. All three of us are okay."

"Who else?"

"Colton and Ingrid."

So, not Lensky. Of course not. He hadn't even been in town.

"Mr. M.?"

"Haven't seen him. You've been out the hell of a long time. What did they do to you?"

"Drugged, I think." That made me aware that my mouth was dry and my head was pounding; not things I really wanted to focus my attention on. Well, maybe they were; it was better than thinking about the strain on my arms and shoulders or the nauseating bouncing of the vehicle we seemed to be in. "You?"

"Same, except it wore off faster."

I tried to focus. It wasn't easy. "Well, I'm smaller than the rest of you. If they gave everybody a dose geared to people Colton's size, I'm surprised I'm not dead. What happened to you guys?"

Ben, Colton and Ingrid had stories almost identical to mine, except that Ben and Ingrid had been snatched when they left the building. Colton, like me, had been caught on his way to check out the doughnut tray. They had no idea what had happened to the support staff, and that was worrying them too. Ingrid, who was supposed to be marrying our computer expert Jimmy in six weeks, was being very carefully *not* hysterical in a very controlled tone of voice. As she said, we had to get ourselves out of this before we could do anything to help the others, so there was no point thinking about them right now.

Her voice hardly even quavered when she said it, so we all emulated her stiff upper lip. Unfortunately, that didn't help us come up with any creative ideas.

We were, we thought, in the back of a windowless van that was on a highway. Probably not I-35, we didn't hear that many trucks and semis blaring to right and left of us.

We couldn't use our best escape option while cuffed to rails that seemed to have been bolted to the inside of the van. Colton tried to pull the rail on his side loose, but he couldn't get enough leverage on it. And even if we had been able to get loose, I didn't really want to try teleporting out of a speeding van. Too much chance of winding up smeared across our destination point.

"We could try the way you got out of Balan's trap in January?" Ben suggested tentatively.

"Umm. That was rope I burned, that time." And it hadn't been a pleasant experience; my hands and wrists got burned too. This time could be even worse, because it felt like I was confined by plastic zip ties now. "I don't specially want to melt plastic onto my skin. Anyway, I didn't have to generate all the heat by myself; the carpet caught fire quite well. I don't think there's anything in here that we can burn." Not to mention that while Riemann fire might free our hands, it wouldn't solve the problem of teleporting while moving at high speed.

"Nothing we can reach, anyway," Colton said grimly, "and maybe it's not such a good idea to demonstrate the Riemann technique to them if they don't already know about it."

And there was something I should have thought about earlier. "They could have this van bugged. Was that why you were practically whispering, Ben?"

There was a brief pause, then he said, "Yes. I thought we'd better not talk about anything they don't need to know."

That pretty much restricted us to disjointed trivialities for the rest of the journey. I guessed that during the long silences my colleagues were doing the same thing I was: mentally running through the things we might be able to do to escape, or failing that, to give our attackers some grief.

One very small bright spot did occur to me. "Colton, did they carry *you* down both flights of stairs?" Our offices were on the third floor of a Victorian mansion with no elevators.

"Probably. Although having been out cold at the time, I don't really know. Why?"

"I'm just hoping they have permanent back injuries from trying to bench-press somebody your size." Colton was an extremely large and athletic young man. He'd played football for his high school and could have gone through college on a football scholarship if he hadn't developed an interest in mathematics and a corresponding distaste for repeated concussions.

After another half hour of being shaken and stirred, I thought of something else. I just wasn't sure how to convey it to the others without conveying the same information to our hypothetical listeners.

"I expect it wouldn't be a good idea for anybody to go to the office just now."

"Well, *duh*, Thalia," Ingrid snapped. "I may not go there ever again. Thanks to the Center I have now been defecated on by grackles, shot at by terrorists, transported back..."

"LA LA LA," I singsonged to drown out what she was about to say. After a minute Colton joined in with his high school fight song and Ben contributed an off-key rendering of "The Eyes of Texas." It's hard to get that one wrong, but Ben is specially talented.

"Very well," Ingrid said when we ran out of breath. "I get the message. All the same, I don't mind telling you that *this* time I am feeling *permanently* fed up with the Center for Applied Topology."

The residual drugs must still be dulling her mind; I couldn't think of any other explanation for her saying "fed up" instead of "disenchanted" or "surfeited." Well, that was another reason not to try anything now, when we desperately needed to be working with perfect clarity. Access to our stars would have come in handy, too. I could sense that mine were in the front righthand pocket of my jeans, like always, but that didn't do me a lot of good right now; no contortion was going to get my fingers and that pocket together. I didn't want to ask the others about theirs. The stars were something our captors wouldn't have noticed, and I really didn't want them to start thinking about invisible stuff we might have. Invisible to them, anyway.

"I understand," I said now to placate Ingrid. "I'm just thinking about the interesting times we've had, the places where we've *all been together*. Remember the giant water moccasin?"

"You mean at—"

This time Ben was the first one to start singing.

"Yes, *there*," I said when he stopped. "I wonder if we'll ever be free to visit that place again. It was… really beautiful… apart from the snake. I bet it's even beautiful *in the dark*." And the water moccasin was dead now. Shot by our worst enemy, actually. One of several miscalculations he'd made.

"Colton wasn't with us then," Ingrid said helpfully.

"But he knows the place I mean, don't you, Colton? It was where we *went fishing* in May."

There was no chance to escape, or even to make trouble, when the van finally stopped; the guys who'd snatched us came in through the back of the van and repeated the drug treatment. When I came to this time, I was on the floor of this dank gray room, looking up at a depressing bluish-tinted light fixture.

On the good side, my hands weren't tied, and there was a chair. After I had contemplated the bejesus out of that air vent in the ceiling, I got up and seated myself. Now, instead of having my whole body in contact with a cold concrete floor, it was just my butt on a cold metal chair. A slight improvement. I was stiff from lying on the cold floor and sore from being bounced around in the back of a van with my wrists cuffed. I did creak slightly on getting up, but I don't think it would have been obvious to any observers. I'd grown up with two older brothers, both on the large side; they'd given me lots of good practice in not wincing when I got hurt. It had often stood me in good stead with Lensky, who tended to overreact when he found out I was even slightly injured.

I had plenty of time to sit on the folding metal chair and contemplate the situation. There wasn't anything to look at that could take my mind off it. There was a bucket in one corner, next to a bottle of water, but I didn't want to think about what that implied. If I had to use that bucket in a room that as likely as not had hidden cameras, the light was damned well going to be off first; I could do that much small object manipulation without making it obvious there was anything paranormal going on. Let them try to get their twisted kicks out of watching my heat signature through night-vision lenses.

The next phase started without warning: the door slammed open with so much force that it hit the wall with a loud *clunk*. If the demonstration of that much kinetic energy was meant to intimidate me, it was working. I hadn't liked being manhandled by my kidnappers, and I liked even less being at close quarters with the man who swung the door shut behind him now. He was big like Colton, though much older: tall, stocky, with thinning brown hair and big meaty hands. I shivered involuntarily. It wasn't just the size of him that frightened me; his eyes were worse. They looked like doorways into a chaotic, gray hell.

"Where are they?" he demanded.

"If you mean my friends, I'd like to know that too!"

"Don't worry about your friends. Worry about yourself."

Oh, I was already doing that.

He prowled around the narrow room. I didn't much like it when he was behind me; I could feel the short hairs on the back of my neck bristling. Too bad. There was only one chair in the room, I was seated in it, and I wasn't going to give up that paper-thin symbol of superiority for anything short of actual violence. I did stick my hands in my jeans pockets. They'd taken everything away from me except the one thing, or properly speaking *set* of things, that I was most likely to need. That wouldn't have been out of generosity, or even carelessness: like most people who can't apply topology the way we do, they wouldn't have been able to see that I had a pocketful of stars. Even Lensky had been known to refer to that collection as a handful of nothing.

If the gray-eyed man got violent with me, though, he just might encounter the effects of those stars and the way they enhanced our other abilities. I thought wistfully of using Ben's trick with Riemann surfaces to ignite his pants, but it wasn't time to show my hand. Yet.

"We've spent enough supporting you jokers," he growled eventually, "it's time you made yourselves useful."

Ah.

That told me a lot. He must be a representative of the secretive three-letter agency that funded the Center for Applied Topology in the hope that our paranormal abilities would eventually develop into useful tools for them. In fact, we'd already been quite useful to them, but I decided not to bring that up. I didn't feel at all secure that the CIA was going to treat us any better than any other bunch of unaccountable bullies. The one thing about our captors' identity that gave me hope was that this was *Lensky's* agency. If anybody could find out what had happened to us and where we were being held, he could. If anybody would storm the gates of a CIA black site to free us, he would. And he'd succeed, too.

"It might help," I suggested mildly, "if you explained what it was you needed our help with." Being polite about asking wouldn't have hurt, either, but it seemed that bridge was already burned.

"I told you. We want you to find them."

"Find who?"

He stopped prowling and glared at me. "You're supposed to have been told."

"Nobody has told me a damned thing."

He raised his hand in a threatening way and I said hurriedly, "Look, it's not in my interest to lie to you about that. You can check up easily enough. I was unconscious when your goons threw me in here and you're the first person who's been here since I regained consciousness."

"Damned incompetents. They really didn't brief you?"

"No. Would you like to tell me what this is about?"

"I… My…" He stopped, glanced up at a corner of the room, and started over. I'd had conversations with Lensky that went wrong in exactly that way. What was this guy not telling me? "The bombing," he said eventually. "Last week. We have reason to believe that the bombers used paranormal means to effect their entrance and exit. You need to find out who they were and where they went."

"And you think I'll be better able to do that from a cell in a mystery location than from the comfort of my own office?" I laughed at the expression on his face. Though it wasn't all that funny, really. "And without the benefit of knowing what you spooks have already figured out about the bombing?"

"Why did you call us spooks?"

"You'd prefer me to say spies? Okay. You spies, then."

"How did you –"

"You did begin this conversation by bitching about funding us," I pointed out. "Do you really think we still haven't figured out where our grant comes from?"

"Your funds are passed anonymously through the Moore Foundation for Mathematics Research."

I shrugged. "That may have been the intention, but placing one of your own case officers in the middle of the Center kind of blew the anonymity bit, don't you think? You know, you're as bad a liar as I am. I do hope, for the sake of our country's security, that your colleagues are a bit better at this spook business."

His face went through two or three contortions before he settled on a sternly commanding expression. "Certain of my colleagues require a demonstration of your capabilities before opening up a classified investigation to you people. You will demonstrate what you can do, then we will decide how we wish to use you."

I had a strong feeling that things should go the other way around. We should decide what use we would allow them to make of us, and then we should demonstrate only those paranormal abilities that would support such use. I had absolutely no inclination to write a blank check for this man with the crazy gray eyes.

"There are a lot of things we can't do alone," I tried. Coming up with a unified strategy against these nuts, for instance. Too bad we'd never developed an application of topology that would enable telepathy. "It would work out better for everybody if you allowed us to get together and work as a group." Better for us, mostly.

"First," he said, "we're going to explore what you *can* do alone."

I shrugged. "Fine, but that doesn't amount to much."

The back of his hand slammed against my cheek without warning. I nearly fell out of the chair. My eyes watered, my face hurt and I *really* wanted to introduce him to the concept of Riemann fire.

"That was a lie. Do not lie to me again; you will regret it. We already have evidence that you, at least, can do quite impressive work on your own," he said. He resumed pacing around my chair; I resumed consciously *not* turning to keep the bastard in sight. He might be making me nervous, but I didn't have to let him see that. "Last fall you removed materials from a locked safe and then teleported yourself and Lensky from San Antonio to Austin."

Okay, that much would have been in Lensky's report. But he wouldn't know – not from official reports, anyway – the full extent of our teleportation range, or the fact that on occasion we had teleported through both space and time. The second wouldn't do him much good anyway. It wasn't like I could teleport myself to the time just before the bombing. Only the years before I was born were open to me, and of those years I'd already made a dent in 1957 and 1941.

As for the range, I felt it was highly desirable that they continue to underestimate us.

"That jump from San Antonio to Austin nearly killed me," I said with feeling. "Didn't Lensky put in his report that I passed out on the floor when we came through in Austin?"

He looked smug. "No, but it doesn't matter. We've already determined from other evidence that you can't teleport as far as a hundred miles, and that you can only go to places you've already seen."

I wondered what other evidence that would be. The second part was true enough, but as for the range – apparently they didn't know about our travels to Britfield, well over three hundred miles from Austin. Or about Colton's impromptu visit to the family farm in the Panhandle.

Good.

"And for your information," he said smugly, "this facility is nearly two hundred miles from Austin. Since you were brought here in a closed van, there's no place you have seen that's close enough for you to teleport yourselves to."

He thought that? Fine, let him think. I could go along with that theory as long as it was convenient for me.

"If there's no place we can teleport to, how are we supposed to demonstrate it?"

"Come with me."

Author's Note

For information about the Blitz, I am indebted to far more histories and memoirs than there is space to mention here. I would like to mention three particularly useful books.

The City that Would Not Die: The Bombing of London May 10-11 1941 (1960), by Richard Collier, was an invaluable account of the last night of the Blitz, with particular attention to the Elephant and Castle district.

The Longest Night (2005), by Gavin Mortimer, revisits that night and adds more recently available material, including additional translations from interviews with German pilots.

Steven Humphrey's *The Elephant and Castle: A History* (2013) gives yet more details of the night of bombing, as well as very useful context on the history of the district before and after the Blitz.

Additionally, I am indebted to my husband for the nit-picky little details that only an obsessive World War II buff would complain about in *Dunkirk* and *Darkest Hour*. Going to the movies with him is always an education.

Also by Margaret Ball:

Applied Topology series:

A Pocketful of Stars
An Opening in the Air
An Annoyance of Grackles

Harmony series:

Insurgents
Awakening
Survivors

Earlier books:

Disappearing Act
Duchess of Aquitaine
Mathemagics
Lost in Translation
No Earthly Sunne
Changeweaver
Flameweaver
The Shadow Gate

www.ingramcontent.com/pod-product-compliance
Lightning Source LLC
Chambersburg PA
CBHW061146170626
46809CB00003B/1002